Hector of the Glens

Hector Thomson

Copyright © 2002 Hector Thomson

All rights reserved by Hector Thomson. No part of this book may be reproduced or used in any manner without written permission from the author Hector Thomson.

ISBN: 9798637891436

DEDICATION

This book is dedicated to William Cameron of Troon and Roddy Morrison of Loch Eynort. You gave me the gift of piping against all the odds. I miss you every day.

Slainte!

Acknowledgements

First of all I would like to thank you the reader for buying and reading this book.

A huge **thank you** to my fiancée Gusty for undergoing the torturous process of proof reading my super pants spelling and grammar and a huge, huge **thank you** to my cousin Andy for proof reading and helping with my website design. Cheers Pugnacious!

Last of all, but by no means least, I would like to thank the rest of my family and friends for their support and encouragement. Slainte to one and all!

CONTENTS

Chapter 1	Pg 1
Chapter 2	Pg 26
Chapter 3	Pg 51
Chapter 4	Pg 76
Chapter 5	Pg 98
Chapter 6	Pg 131
Chapter 7	Pg 161
Chapter 8	Pg 202
Chapter 9	Pg 240
Chapter 10	Pg 275
Chapter 11	Pg 312
Chapter 12	Pg 342
Chapter 13	Pg 364
Chapter 14	Pg 389

CHAPTER 1

I don't know if I was wild because I was beaten, or beaten because I was wild, but I did know one thing. I knew I was meant to do something, I didn't know what, but I just knew it would be something rare and wonderful.

My road to Damascus finally came to me at the age of seven when my parents took me to the Edinburgh Tattoo. The mighty castle gates swung open and the crowd erupted to a sound, a rare and wonderful sound. I was hooked. I just knew I was born to make that sound.

"Mum, Mum, what's that sound?" I asked.

"It's the power of the pipes, Hector."

"I want to play the pipes, Mum - no, no, I really do!"

Mum gave me a gentle smile as she patted my head.

"I know, Hector, I know."

Mum had astutely learned, over the years, that restrained empathy was the best way to quell my ambitious zeal.

"So you'll no be exploring Scotland on a space hopper?" Mum asked.

"No now, Mum, am gonna be a piper!"

Mum nodded with wise agreement.

"Am glad, son, a was always worried about the Ben Nevis descent."

Dad shook his head at Mum in disbelief. He could feel a fresh wave of my unbridled zeal about to rob him of his sanity. Mum clasped Dad's face and kissed his balding brow.

"Would you have him any other way, Dad?"

"Mute would be good," Dad hissed.

But it was too late, for I was smitten. My wee wellied feet stamped with uncontrollable joy to the piper's music and my heartbeat nearly tore the toggles off my duffel coat. I closed my eyes and prayed, 'God, I know I ask for a lot of things, but if you make me a piper in the regiment, I swear I will never ask for anything ever again . . .'

All the way back in the car I pleaded with my parents that this time was different. This time I really knew I was going to be a piper, but my years of enthusiastic attrition had taken their toll.

Dad's patience finally snapped.

"Shut it! Every bloody week it's somethin. I want to be an Eskimo, a want to be a jockey, a need a horse. A horse! We're dirt poor. Where the hell would we get a horse from?"

Mum tried to lighten the situation.

"Fair's fair, Dad, he did settle for a space hopper!"

"Don't you encourage him," said Dad. "I mean it, Hector! One more peep about being a piper and I'll tan yer arse into a base drum!"

Our scowling eyes met in the car mirror: the immovable object meeting the irresistible force. Mum quickly restrained my wellie from kicking the back of Dad's seat.

I tried my best to forget about being a piper, but it was no good. The music had bitten deep into my little Scots heart. In a way I knew Dad was right, and I could understand his anger, but I couldn't help being me. There wasn't a man in the county that would cross my father's temper, but I just knew I had to be a piper, and if that meant having my arse turned into a base drum then so be it.

I scoured the local papers and Yellow Pages, but I couldn't find any adverts for piping tuition. Week after week, month after month my dream tormented me.

My schoolteacher, Mrs Campbell, noted my muted zest for life and voiced her concerns to my mother.

"Mrs MacTavish, I have been a schoolteacher for 32 years and I don't know many seven-year-old boys who can successfully convince me that Bonny Prince Charlie was an Italian syphilitic midget with no more right to command the Jacobite Army than King George III! I would give anything to have my class restored back to mayhem rather than have its orchestrator laid low. If there is anything I can do to help Hector, please name it!"

I shuffled my way out of school towards the bus stop when I heard it! It was faint, but it was there, and it was more wonderful than ever! My wellies went into stag mode, as I helplessly bounded towards the sound. I screeched to a halt outside the church where a young piper was playing the pipes for a newly wed - and still happy - couple.

The young piper was dressed immaculately in his full Highland uniform: he looked magnificent, and he knew it. I waited until he had finished playing and clapped for all I was worth. He did his best to ignore all my attempts at conversation.

"I need to learn, I really do!" I begged.

The boy promptly sparked a fag up and contemptuously blew the smoke into my face.

"What's your name?" he asked.

"They call me Hector!"

"Well, Hector, the man for you lives in Magerton. They call him Fuckin Mental!" The boy grinned. "His real name's Murdock Dunbar, and it takes seven years to learn the great Highland bagpipe - seven, long hard years, Hector."

"I don't mind hard work, what's this man like?"

"O he's good, and he's still one of the best teachers you'll ever find, but he really is mental! I'm not even sure if he teaches now."

"Well, there's only one way to find out," I said, smiling to the boy.

I thanked the boy and trotted off home with new-found hope.

I began my search for Murdock Dunbar in the town of

Magerton during an Ayrshire monsoon in June. Magerton was a wee coastal holiday town about 30 miles south of Glasgow. It was optimistically advertised as 'Scotland's Answer to Acapulco' (this statement was diplomatically withdrawn when Mexico threatened to sue for defamation of character).

For some unknown astrological quirk, the Earth's orbital pattern always managed to deny poor Magerton any contact with the sun. Magerton's Armageddon-like weather conditions made it the mainstay for only the toughest of Glaswegian holidaymakers. Magerton's borough sign had been affectionately altered by its regular clientele to read, 'MAGERTON TWINNED WI' ATLANTIS'.

The battle-hardened holidaymakers would defiantly dig survival holes on Magerton's wild beach. Huddling around their Primus stoves in rain-soaked, sand-ridden pakamacs. Futilely trying to spoon Marvel into their mugs, as they were blasted by force ten gales. Some brave souls would fling the dried milk into their mouths and gulp down the scalding hot tea directly from their Thermoses, mixing the Marvel in a molten-hot swallow.

Young Scot males displayed their Clydeside martial art skills by taking a dip in Magerton's, sex changing cold sea; a feat that no reproducing polar bear would even have considered. To the Glasgow holidaymaker, comfort was for the weak. The true

Glasgow holidaymakers proudly sported their hypothermic, hail-dented skin as a medal of honour (Magerton being the VC of all holiday endeavour).

I sneaked out of my bedroom with my piggy bank money and began the six-mile assault to Magerton. I was only seven and as broad as I was long. I was bedecked in my usual forced apparel of a lovat green jumper, with a wool density that could have repelled any known bullet or laser, a Hunting Stewart kilt, a pair of heavy-duty Dunlop wellies with a wee, brown leather sporran and belt. My whole sartorial elegance was crowned by the most gruesome of haircuts, which my dad administered with hand shears and a pudding bowl. The whole ensemble gave me the appearance of an extra from Agincourt.

My wellies made good progress across country and soon found their way to outside the entrance of Jekyll's Tavern, a known haunt of my intended quarry. I stumbled through the bar doors into a dense fog bank of fag smoke and whisky fumes. I stepped over the dead research beagles and groped my way to the bar. The landlord immediately made me feel at home with his warm familiarity.

"Fuck off!"

I cleared my throat and addressed my less than congenial host.

"Excuse me please, I'm looking for Mr Murdock Dunbar."

"Well, Mr Dunbar," sneered the landlord in an exaggerated Morningside accent, "is that rather endearing gentleman beltin the other not so happy gentleman's head off ma new, copper-topped table."

I marvelled at the mountain of a man who was chastising the man's head for the unpardonable crime of over-watering his whisky.

Murdock Dunbar was a 60 a day, six foot six, hard drinking, womanising, tower of prime Scots beef, as the poor man rebounding off the table would gladly testify.

Mackeesh was giggling as his head went back and forth off the table.

"Alright I admit it!"

Murdock released Mackeesh with a victorious smile. "Did you honestly think I wouldnae recognise an over watered single from a double!"

Mackeesh was still giggling and completely unrepentant. He took pride in his round dodging skills, and to be pitted against the great Murdock Dunbar was the icing on the cake. Murdock sauntered up to the bar.

"Same again, Tam."

The landlord nodded in my direction.

"You've a visitor, Mr Dunbar."

Murdock took one look at me and growled.

"Beat it!"

"I'll b-buy you one, Mr Dunbar," I stammered. "A Grouse and he'll water his own, thank you."

The landlord nodded to Murdock, and Murdock nodded back.

Murdock turned and smiled at me.

"You'll be having one yourself . . .?"

"Hector, Mr Dunbar, that's ma name."

"No! Are you havin a dram?" Murdock thundered.

At the bold age of seven, I puffed my chest out and bellowed deeply.

"Eh, no thanks, Mr Dunbar; I'm driving!"

Murdock let out a loud bray of laughter, which was crowned by harmonious hoots from the rest of the bar.

"No, I insist!" Murdock said, raising a fabulous question mark eyebrow. "Same again, Tam, a large yin."

As I stared at the large unforgiving glass with dreaded revulsion, it seemed to grow and grow, until it had achieved giant cartoon proportions. I took a deep breath and launched it down my throat. I wanted to retch as soon as the whisky hit my mouth, but I was determined to hold it down out of sheer bloody-mindedness. The skin on my face turned every colour of a Dulux paint chart, as every last ounce of breath evaporated from my body. I tried to straighten my face, but I looked like a young boy who had just been French kissed by his hairy-lipped granny.

"What do you reckon?" asked Murdock.

"Aye . . . like silk, Mr Dunbar," I spluttered back, wiping my mouth.

The bar convulsed with empathic cheers. I loved being the centre of attention and didn't mind being the butt of the joke. I smiled at Murdock who looked at me with a wry grin of mischief as he engineered my new impending doom.

"Same again, Tam! Hector and me have got a thirst on."

"No," I pleaded, "I've no got enough!"

"I insist!"

"Dear God, no . . ."

Murdock slammed a mountain of change hard onto the bar. Murdock was enjoying his sport, and he wasn't going to make this easy for me.

The latest glass of whisky seemed to flex itself and taunt me. I could hear the jeers and the money changing hands. I scowled at Murdock and launched the second optic missile down. If the first whisky had been a rough ride this one was Alton Towers in a glass. I had to swallow the whisky twice, just to keep it down.

"Mr Dunbar, I want to play the-"

"Same again, Tam," Murdock cheered.

"No!" I screamed. "I just - I just want to play!" It suddenly went quiet and I began again. "I've run six miles, got soaked and drank your whisky. I want to learn the pipes, Mr Dunbar."

Murdock just shrugged and turned his back on me. "Please, Mr Dunbar, please! I need to learn, I've just got to."

I wheeled around and marched towards the door with anger and tears in my eyes. Murdock's hostile command cut the taut silence.

"The 20th of June, six o'clock, Drymill Cottage. Have a chanter, a Logan's Tutor Book, and don't think I'm promising anything!"

I wanted to hug him and scream my thanks, but

I was cute enough not to. I just nodded my thanks and tried to suppress the biggest Cheshire grin from splitting my face in two.

I didn't feel the cold rain or tire with the miles as I ran homeward into the wind. If anything the whisky spurred my wee wellies on. As my home came into view, my heart leapt into my mouth. The window to my bedroom was closed and the light was on. I had sneaked out with the light off and the window jammed open, on the latch.

I approached the window with the gingered stealth of a Highland wild cat. Luckily the window was only just pulled to. I pulled my body through the window and wondered when the wrath of my father would descend upon me. Instead, a wonderful warm sense of relief came when I noticed a plate of tattie scones and a flask. This wonderful act of thoughtfulness bore all the hallmarks of my mum's endless love.

Mum was the calm caring haven of love that held our wild family together. She bore the world's troubles on her shoulders with a quiet majesty, which could touch even the coldest of cold hearts.

Mum's head eventually popped around my bedroom door.

"Hector, where have you been?"

"Magerton, Mum."

"You're lucky your dad didn't catch you," Mum whispered.

"Mum, Mum, I'm going to be a piper, a real piper, I really am, Mum!"

Mum hugged me into her huge Scots bosom to calm me down.

"Jesus! Have you been drinkin whisky, Hector?"

I nodded my head into her chest and yawned.

"I'm going to be a piper, Mum, I really am."

Mum rocked me off to sleep.

"I know, Hector, I know."

In the morning Mum waited until Dad had gone to work before giving my door a tap. I wandered through in my vest and pants, bursting to give Mum the full details of my latest adventure.

Mum had prepared my breakfast with her usual culinary expertise. It was piping hot and cooked to perfection with four pieces of toast, sweet crispy bacon (about half a pig's worth), fresh tomatoes, mushrooms, scrambled eggs, sausage, black pudding, fruit pudding, a huge bowl of steaming Ready brek, a large jug of fruit juice, some bananas and one of those enormous, blue and white striped sixties mugs, which held about a gallon of hot strong tea.

I sat up at the table and tried to suppress my laughter.

"I'm no that hungry, Mum."

Mum gave me one of her marvellous acceptance nods, as if it was okay. Mum was superb at these - she knew they always cracked me up.

"That's fine, Hector, I've only given you the light Scots-a-nental," Mum teased.

Ironically enough, this really was a light breakfast by Mum's standards. Mum cooked with so much love you could taste it in every single mouthful. Her whole passion and soul went into even the simplest of meals. The result was food that made you eat every last morsel. This was rather unfortunate, as Mum also displayed her love by the quantity of her food. Her overabundant and infinitive portions were widely known as, 'Hazardous Waists'. Mum was completely immune to abuse or any pleas for calorific mercy.

"That's too much, Mum, a cannae eat all that!"

"Hector, there's kids in Africa that would be

glad o that!"

"Mum, Africa couldn't eat all that!"

"Do you want some more, Hector? There's plenty left."

"No! No, bugger off! Mum, I can't eat any more, stop, please stop! No more no, no!"

"It's the best of stuff. Come on you're a growin boy."

"No! I'll leave home if you give me any more, I will, Mum, I mean it!"

"No use leavin on an empty stomach," said Mum, adding another dollop of scrambled egg.

Mum was the unflinching commander of the Scottish SAS (shortbread and scones). She was deadly with shortbread, but her preferred choice of weapon was the scone. This culinary commando could mass-produce an arsenal of beautiful scones from nowhere, tempting even the most ardent of foes into unconditional surrender. It didn't matter where or how you met my mum, you would always leave with at least half a dozen scones.

Mum could resolve any situation with the omnipotent power of the humble Scottish scone. Even the Woman's Institute quaked in fear from this prolific extremist.

I relayed last night's adventure to Mum between mouthfuls of breakfast and slurps of tea. Mum tried her best to confine her outbursts of laughter, as a serious conscientious parent.

"Jesus, Hector, when you do it, you do it, son. You know Dad will kill you if he finds out."

I nodded in slow, resigned agreement. Mum just smiled one of her 'it'll be all right' smiles and ruffled my hair.

My mother is without a doubt the most honest and decent caring person I've ever known, but even Hannibal would have wept with shame at the breadth of her tactical genius. Life had made Mum the most seasoned of all field marshals.

"How long we got, Rob Roy?"

"Until the 20th of June, Mum - gives us two weeks."

Mum paced the kitchen with her field baton (the MacTavish rolling pin) clasped behind her back. Mum suddenly wheeled around with Machiavellian triumph brimming from her face.

"If this is gonna work, you're gonna have to go to hell and back."

Mum paused for diplomatic thought, but realised there wasn't any where I was concerned, so she gave me an unsugared broadside of reality instead.

"Look, you're barred from all school trips after that fiasco with the missile testing range. You're barred from the Boys Brigade for running Mr Tweedy over with a piano from the attic! You're barred from the Scouts for ruining their Comet Watch, when they photographed that damned rocket you let off. Dad views anything you do as a potential source of embarrassment or disaster. Dad's ex SAS, but you scare the shit out of him, Hector! He's a proud man. He hates everybody thinking his son is - Scotland's answer to Baader Meinhof!"

I nodded my understanding.

"So what's the plan, Mum?"

"Well, the first stage is to make Dad want you out of the house at any price and that's really gonna require some hellish martyrdom from you! Jesus, I wouldn't want to be your heed or arse for the world." Mum winced, rubbing her own bum in sympathy. "Are you really sure you want this?"

"I am, Mum, a really am! Anything else?"

Mum wedged a huge fruit scone into my mouth and carried on talking.

"You've got to oppose any suggestion that you want to play the pipes, and you've got to do it convincingly or it will be all for nothing! If Dad thinks you don't want to play the pipes, he'll figure you don't want to play them because you can't get into trouble and that's exactly why he'll insist that you will play the pipes!"

Mum began work on a new batch of scone dough. I loved watching her think. She wiped the flour from her hands.

"You don't start on the pipes straight away?" Mum asked.

"No a don't, Mum. A have to learn the finger work first on a practice chanter."

Mum smiled.

"Your Dad would work a year without rest if it bought you true happiness and gave him peace. How much does a good practice chanter cost?"

"A don't know, Mum, but they're about two foot long, made of wood and look a bit like a whistle with a round bit on the bottom called a sole. Oh, and I'll need a tutor book as well. These scones are really delicious, Mum."

Mum burst out laughing.

"You can lay off with the trowel, Hector, you'll get your chanter - and book."

Stage one of 'Operation Birthday Boy' was now put into operation. I moped around the house and got under Dad's feet, asking him inane questions at the most inopportune times. I received some heavy slaps for my troubles, but I stuck it out as each blow drove me closer towards my dream of becoming a piper.

Twenty-four hours a day, seven days a week I relentlessly gnawed at Dad like a starved leech. Dad would have gleefully dispatched me to the infinite fires of hell if only he could have found a perfectly inhumane way of doing so. I carefully and gradually built up my onslaught, so it would peak just before the day of my birthday.

The morning of my birthday finally arrived. I collected my thoughts and rehearsed the plan, one last time, in my mind. It was imperative that I didn't look overjoyed at my Mum's birthday present or acknowledge Dad's shock.

I was my usual hyper self in the morning, and began by trampolining on Mum and Dad's bed.

"It's me - the pinnacle of your careers. I am the loving son of your loins and today is my birthday!"

"That's it, I'm going to fuckin kill him," Dad snarled, through gritted teeth.

Mum just laughed and punched Dad playfully on the thigh.

"Dad, he's just excited."

"Excited, he's fuckin insane!"

"Father! Less o that, it's the boy's birthday. Hector, have a look under the bed and see if you can see anything."

"Great, Mum, Dad's dirty old pants. They're just what I've always wanted. Oh, wait a minute, here we go - pressies!"

I opened my cards first, giving them the obligatory shake to dislodge any money, completely disregarding the names or sentiment.

Before I go any further I think I should point out that I was never hard done by or stinted on. It's just that Dad didn't think that toys made really good presents.

He once bought me the most impressive Hornby train set you ever did see. It had lots of trains, tunnels, track, points and models. This would have been great, but my Dad banned me from playing with it because it ran on electricity. He was terrified I would electrocute myself or torch the house. Although this would seem rather over-cautious, you will soon discover that the incredible and disastrous have always been close companions of mine.

I ripped my first present open; it was crap Sandalwood talc.

"Thanks, Gran!" I boomed, without looking at the present tag.

Mum and Dad giggled.

"You'll thank me one day, ya ungrateful wee shite!" replied Gran with lightning scorn.

Pressie number two was a large oblong parcel bound with ruthless efficiency - it weighed a ton. I struggled to lift it up and shake it next to my ear.

"Is it socks, Dad?"

Mum was now under the duvet, slapping me and trying not to laugh. It was the usual; there were books on every conceivable academic subject.

"Thanks, Dad, we're just about to start on the Romans at school, and a don't mean Saint Joseph's!"

Pressie number three.

"A junior sewing machine, just like the one I gave you last year, Mairi, except this one's broken," I said, smiling insincerely.

"No need to thank me, dear brother."

My sister Mairi sneered, depositing all the saliva she could muster with a venomous kiss on my cheek.

"Get ma garage keys, boy!" Dad ordered.

Mum stopped him.

"I changed the bike for something a lot less dangerous, don't worry you'll thank me. Here you go, Hector, this is from Dad and me."

I ripped the paper off with the ferocity of a marauding Viking. I masked my joy with puzzled disappointment.

"Christ, Mum, a stinkin recorder!"

The words had barely left my mouth before my Dad's fist resounded off my jaw.

"You show your mother respect, boy!"

The blow sent me reeling from the bed and bounced me off the wall. We were halfway there. It just needed Mum to finish it off. I pulled myself off the floor, giving my best hurt scowl.

"Look, Hector, it's a practice chanter and a tutor book. You're going to learn to play the bagpipes," Mum announced tentatively.

Dad naturally looked quite stunned.

"Is he?"

"It gets him out the house, Dad, keeps him busy, it's Scottish and the guy who teaches it is a pure psycho," Mum answered astutely.

"I'm no going - that guy's off his skull," I pleaded.

"You're going and that's final!" Dad ordered.

We had done it! I was on my way to becoming a piper. I clenched my fist and inadvertently cheered:

"Yes!"

My dad's eyes began to narrow into a piercing scowl, as a cold wave of reality began to sweep across his brow. I grabbed my chanter and scuttled off while the going was good.

Mum had gone all out: the practice chanter was of superb quality and crafted from the finest African blackwood, with a heavy silver sole and ferrule. She'd even got me the Logan's Tutor Book. Mum had scrimped and saved to give me the best start possible.

I was only eight years old and I already knew what I was going to do for the rest of my life, and I just knew I was going to love every second of it.

Dad drove me to school in the pickup and I could feel his stare burning into me. Dad stopped the pickup a bit before the school gates. He lifted my chin up and stared at me with a softened smile.

"If you don't think I can tell when I've been stitched, think again! All I ask is two things. If you are gonna be a piper be a good one. I can't think of a prouder thing I'd wish my son to be. I'll back you all the way. You can practise whatever hour of the day you want, and I mean that! You'll only ever anger me if I don't hear you practising, okay? And Hector! If you try and convince your class that William McGonagle wrote the Bible again, I'll personally tan your arse! Now go on, beat it!"

I walked on air that day. I turned down all fights and congratulated every schoolboy jeer about my kilt, as a wonderful and thoughtful observation. They all thought I was especially nuts that day, but I felt like a king. My wee dream was about to come true, and I just knew my life was about to become one happy long adventure.

As soon as school finished, I shot around to old Amy Stewart's, to find out more about the legend called Murdock. Lots of folk thought old Amy was a witch. Amy helped perpetuate the myth by pretending to cast spells on the truly wicked. People were genuinely petrified of Amy, but to me she was the greatest comedian and storyteller in the world. Amy knew everyone - and everything about them. We were both considered odd - I suppose that's why we became such great friends.

Amy smiled as she stoked her great coal fire.

"Yi no sex, drinkin, fightin, gamblin and womanisin?"

I paused for awhile and then nodded.

"Well, by Christ, Murdock does! He practically invented them. Oh - he's an awfy, awfy, man, but by Christ, Hector - that man can play!"

CHAPTER 2

I worked like a Trojan until I could produce a rough scale on my chanter. I desperately wanted to impress Murdock right from the off.

When the big night finally arrived I jumped into Dad's pickup with Dandy jealously clambering in behind me. Dandy was my insane and completely wild hunting beagle. He did whatever he wanted, whenever he wanted, and I just loved him to death. Dandy was permanently covered in mud and sticky-Willie - and was a true credit to his breed.

The pickup fired its way out of the lodge gates and spluttered its way down our brae. Dandy assumed his usual position, by nuzzling his head out of my window, his floppy beagle ears expertly riding the rushing air like the wings of a great canine plane. As we pulled up outside Murdock's house, Dandy let out a magnificent bay to announce our arrival.

"I'll pick you up outside the chippy at ten. I warn you now! If you break his pipes, play up or pack this in through laziness, I'll flay the skin off your arse.

Here, stick this money in your sporran and don't lose it!" Dad warned.

"Thanks, Dad, a'll no let you down - honest."

I had barely gone three steps before Dad yelled after me.

"Hector! Ya eejit! You've forgotten your book and chanter."

Dad handed me my tutor book and chanter with the look of a beaten man.

"Sorry, Dad, I'm just so excited."

"God help him!" Dad muttered, driving off.

I brushed Dandy's paw prints off my kilt and admired my big, black glossy wellies, which had been especially hosed and polished for the occasion.

I knocked loudly on the large, well-beaten door. The door immediately flew open to reveal the menacing figure of Murdock, in his vest and jeans. His fists were clenched and a wild look of livid anger fizzed from his face.

"Hope you're no another time waster," Murdock growled.

"No, no look!" I cried, showing off my new chanter.

"Did your mum keep the receipt, Hector?"

"I've been workin hard, Mr Dunbar!"

Murdock smiled at my outrage.

"Come on in then. Let's see what you can do."

As I followed Murdock down the hall I admired the treasured oil paintings that lined the smooth, emerald green walls.

"These are great men, Mr Dunbar. This one's Piper Kenneth Mackay at Waterloo and this one's Piper Findlater at the Heights of Darghi."

Murdock gave me a surprised look and a reluctant nod.

"In here, Hector."

As I entered the room my heart froze. Instead of being alone, there were 11 other boys already sitting at Murdock's, great teaching table. Murdock grinned with amusement as he ushered me to my place.

Murdock stared hard at each one of us in turn.

"For the next seven years I will teach one of you to become a piper and over the next few months we'll find out who wants it the most. You will have to win your place here. Have any of you had piping tuition before? Any musical training at all?"

"No–Mis-ter-Dun–bar," we all chorused back with sheep-like classroom rhythm.

Murdock scanned our faces again, his stare becoming more menacing than ever.

"I need total honesty – any at all? It's important . . . All right, let's begin."

I was straining at the leash to show my scale off to Murdock, so when he asked who wanted to go first I took off from my chair like a kilted Harrier jump jet.

"Me! Me, Mr Dunbar, me!"

Before Murdock could say or demonstrate anything I proudly went up the scale. I was just about to go down the scale when my head stung sharply. I looked up and saw the sole of Murdock's chanter hovering above my head.

"First of all, never muffle your chanter on your knee, and if you don't mind, I'll show you what to do and you can copy me. Do you understand?" Murdock stormed.

I nodded, as I rubbed my aching head.

Murdock paused and cunningly asked, "Where did Hector go wrong?"

A tall, skinny rat-faced boy called Roland Stone smirked.

"He played closed and open Cs, Gs and As!"

Murdock unleashed his chanter like a striking cobra onto Roland Stone's head, displaying his full mastery of Chanter Fu.

"How would you know? Unless you had been taught before and I know you have! Get out! Ya lying - sleekit shite!"

The boy picked up his chanter and ran for his life.

"And then there were eleven," Murdock chaffed.

My gloated smirking to the group was quickly subdued by Murdock's, cold damning glare.

"I must have honesty and mutual respect, gentlemen. Three times I asked for honesty and three times he lied to me. Disrespecting someone who has had the heart to teach himself from a tutor book, is the lowest of the low. Pipers lead - and brave men follow. They inspire by daring example. You must learn to forge your character so you are worthy to become a piper. A piper must have heart, gentlemen, above all else - heart!" Murdock nodded. "That's what will make you a piper, nothing else - and nothing less! If you remember only one thing, gentlemen, remember that!"

"Mr Dunbar, how do you know that I've no

been taught before?" I asked.

"Because, my dear wee Hector, you played the book's scale with three finger positions, which are no longer used in piping light music and no one teaches that badly!"

The next boy carefully watched Murdock and proceeded to easily surpass my scale, which had taken me a week to learn. Murdock stared at the boy with satisfaction.

"Keep that up and you'll go all the way, Donny Anderson."

Donny Anderson was a good friend of mine. He usually accompanied me to the headmaster's office for the belt. Donny came from a musically talented and well liked family. Right now, my friendship for Donny was being rampantly replaced by 'et tu Brute' envy. It got worse and worse as each boy effortlessly humbled my performance.

Murdock gave me a wink.

"Keep practising your scale exercises, Hector, make them flow cleanly, with accuracy and control. I want them perfect for next week. Go on and help Meemee with the sandwiches while I finish teachin."

I desperately wanted to be advanced with the other boys, but I obeyed Murdock without question. I poked my head around the kitchen door and could not believe my eyes. Meemee was in a black, silk lace dressing gown, holding a large gin in one hand and a fag in the other, whilst she gyrated against the tumble dryer to the raunchy beat of 'Wild Thing'.

"Have I still got it, big boy?" Meemee boomed.

I prayed to God that she thought I was Murdock. I coughed loudly to save Meemee any further embarrassment. Why I bothered, I don't know. Meemee didn't even bat an eyelid.

"Do you like 'The Troggs', wee man?"

"I do, Miss Meemee, I do."

"Then dance, wee man, dance."

"I'll mark your floor wi ma wellies, Miss Meemee."

"Doesn't matter, dance, wee man, dance. Are you shy now?" Meemee teased.

I immediately began to do the twist at full pelt. It was the only dance I knew. I compensated for my lack of grace with quantity and vigour. After 'Wild Thing' finished we both panted and laughed. Meemee slurped down the last of her gin.

"You'll be Hector?" she panted.

I nodded back and smiled.

"How did you know, Miss Meemee?"

"Oh, just a wild guess. Here, take the sannies in and share them out - you wild kilted thing."

I took the sandwiches in and jealously watched the others finish off. As I left Murdock's house, Meemee pinched my kilted bum and winked.

"The tortoise won in the end, my wee Hector, he did you know?"

"Vive les Troggs, Miss Meemee!" I roared, skipping along the path to catch up with Donny.

Donny cheered me up no end, by treating me to a fish supper and a bottle of Irn-Bru. The hot aromatic steam funnelled out from our fish and chips into the still night air. There is nothing in the world quite like the delicious smell of freshly salt and vinegared fish and chips, to sharpen the pangs of hunger.

We sat on the bench outside the chippy and demolished our fish suppers with ravenous ferocity, neither of us speaking until the last morsel was gone.

"Magic, just bloody magic," said Donny.

"Mmmmmmm," I replied, licking my fingers clean and savouring the last sweet tang of the salt and vinegar.

Our greasy hands finally managed to get the top off the Irn-Bru, with Donny holding the bottle and me twisting the cork. The scrumptious sweet sssssssshhh of the escaping gas hissed and spat into our faces. We guzzled down the sweet sparkling juice as fast as we could, until we could no longer stand the sharp carbon rip against our throats.

"What di yi reckon, Hector, Barr's Irn-Bru or Curries' Red Kola?" Donny gasped.

I flexed my biceps.

"Barr's Irn-Bru, Donny, it's made fae girders!"

Two, small dainty hands suddenly covered my eyes as quick kisses and giggles filled my ears.

"Guess who?" the singing voice asked.

"Well, there are only two girls who would dare to do that. Please God, don't make it my sister," I pleaded.

To my great relief, there she was - my one and only Maggie - unkempt, honest and stunning. She bounced onto my lap and flung her arms around me.

"Hi, lover," she chortled.

I was now postbox red and doing my best to

look disgusted at her advances - as wee boys so often do. I welcomed her teasing open advances and let her know by secretly squeezing her waist.

Maggie was Donny's sister and she was my first love. She had long chestnut hair and, like her, it was beautiful and natural. Her eyes were of the deepest softest brown with long thick lashes, which Max Factor would have killed for. Her smile wasn't perfect, but it beamed warmth and infectious mischief.

A car sped by with a load of drunks hanging out of the car windows.

"Hoy, ya kilted wanker!" came the roar.

"Where do you know them from?" Maggie asked, giggling.

I was about to try and think up a suitable quip when a loud, approaching beagle bay saved me. I quickly thanked Donny, and gave Maggie a cheeky wink.

"Quick! Get in or climb in the back," Dad yelled.

I jumped into the back with Dandy. Dad shot the pickup into gear to make the lights, firing me onto my back and flinging my kilt and legs over my head. I peered through my legs at the chilled midnight sky with its large ivory moon shining down on me. The pickup sped along the old beach road. The air was fresh and sweet with the smell of the sea and holidays long forgotten. I snuggled up to Dandy for some warmth. He was busily engaged in gnawing the last of my fish supper from my lovat jumper, fully aware he was nipping me as well.

Dandy was a simple old soul. He brazenly loved himself with a self-preservation that only a beagle could possess. It was Dandy's unashamed greed and selfish rationality that made him so loveable.

I looked at the chain securing Dandy to the pickup and smiled. It had to be a chain for Dandy, as he would bust or chew through any rope. Independence and freedom were a pre-requisite for Dandy. He was the William Wallace of the beagle world.

Dandy nipped a little too deep, so I smacked him on the snout. Dandy, using Dandy logic, bit me straight back. My hand became wet and sticky with blood and feathers from his muzzle. I had naturally assumed that Dandy had been chained in the back because of his brutal wind. Don't ask me why, but all Dandy's wind stank of the foulest burnt rubber. As my hand searched along his muzzle, more and more feathers began to collect in my hand. I hugged and scolded him, but deep down I knew his fate was sealed.

The pickup stopped. Dad slammed his door shut. My fingers worked feverishly at freeing Dandy's chain.

"Leave him!" came the command.

I shuffled into the house with tears falling down my face. Mum gave me a hug.

"We can kill Dandy now, or we can give him to a hunting pack where he can do what he was meant to do. Dad loves Dandy too, but Dandy's had one too many of Mr Codder's hens. If you truly love Dandy you'll be happy for him. Dandy, being Dandy; he'll forget us within the week."

As per usual, Mum's simple logic was both soothing and wise. Mum handed me a big bag of Scots pancakes.

"Your window's open. Keep it that way as you never know when you're going to have a visitor," Mum whispered.

I knew Dandy and I would never ever share a bag of Scots pancakes again. Well, when I say we would share them, we would share them Dandy style; Dandy would bite anything that came between him and a Scots pancake. Dandy saw all Scots pancakes as his inalienable right.

Dandy's favourite trick was to wait until Mum started making pancakes on the girdle. Once Dandy thought the pancakes were sufficiently cooked, he would charge the cooker and knock the girdle to the floor, ravenously devouring the pancakes and refusing to acknowledge the burning hot pain from the girdle.

You hardly ever saw Dandy's face as his snout was always on the hunt for illicit calories. He could effortlessly cruise at 25 miles per hour all day and track our pickup through towns and even in the rain. His intelligence and hunting skills were boundless.

To Dandy, a chicken coup was nothing more than a feathered pick and mix selection. Dad would beat Dandy with the dead hen until he was just left with the yellow feet. This didn't deter Dandy at all - he just saw us as ungrateful vegetarians.

Mr Codder was a very understanding farmer who loved all animals. The love and care that he had lavished on his bantam hens had been rewarded with top prizes at the Royal Highland Show. They were his pride and joy; nothing was too good for them. Mr Codder could always tell when Dandy had struck, as bantam hens don't normally roost up trees. Mr Codder couldn't stand to see another bantam hen killed, so Dandy had to go - one way or another.

Tears fell down my face as I waited to say farewell to my old black and tan pal. Dandy's experienced paws bounded the six-foot leap to my window then he expertly piloted himself through the narrow gap. He landed on my bed with graceful silent stealth. Dandy immediately snatched the bag of buttered pancakes from me and devoured the lot with his usual uninterrupted passion.

Once Dandy had finished, he proceeded to make himself comfortable by fighting me for command of the bedclothes. After a hard fought campaign, I called a blanket armistice. I went to sleep that night with Dandy's hot breath in my ears and the smell of foul burning rubber in my nostrils.

In the morning Dandy was gone, and that was the last time I ever saw him. It was only years later Mum admitted that Dad had driven Dandy to a hunting pack in Irvine. Dandy immediately escaped and ran the 15 miles back to our doorstep, arriving five minutes before Dad in the pickup. Mum said that if Dad could have given the dog a medal he would have, but Dad had no choice as he had to put Dandy straight back in the pickup and drive him farther away to a really secure hunting pack. I looked at Mr Codder's trees for over a year always hoping to find the odd bantam hen up there.

Dandy is probably dead now, but I like to think that there are a few angels complaining to St Peter of a serious chicken shortage and an overpowering smell of putrid burnt rubber. With Dandy gone, every ounce of my time was now dedicated to hard practise.

The bagpipes are recognised as one of the hardest musical instruments to learn and play. Many people attempt to learn the pipes, but the vast majority are defeated by the cultivation and speed of the finger work and timing.

There are only nine notes in piping, so pipers use movements to embellish melody notes. Movements are made up of many, varied individual finger actions played: separately, in rapid succession, to sound like a single, musical embellishment. This allows pipers to give their melody notes an orchestra of melody and rhythmic accompaniment.

The discipline and mental agility needed to control and develop the vast array of individual finger actions into single lightning movements, is truly breathtaking. It tests the learner's resolve to the very limit and accounts for the high failure rate in piping. It is this skill that sets pipers above all other musicians.

Movements became the unforgiving anvil that Murdock forged us upon. Each week Murdock would order a boy to leave, and each week I would thank God for surviving another elimination. Eventually the teaching circle was whittled down to Donny, a giant bear of a boy who never spoke or played and me.

"Well," said Murdock, "and then there were three."

To my shock and great relief, Donny bravely explained to Murdock, "All I really want to do is play the saxophone. I can't thank you enough for all your time and patience, Mr Dunbar, but it's no for me. I'm really sorry."

Murdock nodded and appreciated Donny's honesty.

"Do you want to wait for Hector?" asked Murdock.

Donny shook his head and wished me luck before he left. This was a wonderful act of friendship from Donny. As we both know to this day, he has never blown a single note on a saxophone.

It was now down to the giant bear of a boy and me. My mind was now going at 1000 miles per hour. Maybe the boy giant was so bad, so thick, that Murdock wouldn't let him play in front of other pupils. I shut my eyes and crossed my fingers, Please God, make him play shite!

"Well, Bear, give us a tune," said Murdock, leaning back in his great chair and lighting up a cigarette.

My jaw nearly hit the deck; the boy wasn't just good, oh no, he was bloody fantastic! The music was sweet and played with such beauty and emotion. It was sheer genius, so any hope of staying had now gone. I hated him.

When the boy finished there was silence. Murdock sighed, exhaling a satisfied blast of cigarette smoke.

"Magnificent, Bear, absolutely magnificent."

I had practised long and hard, but there was no way I could ever compete against the genius of the giant boy's playing. I even considered shooting him with Dad's 12-bore, but realised anything smaller than an elephant gun would only annoy him. I had gambled all and given everything, and I had lost.

I picked up my chanter without a word, trying my best to stem the silent flow of tears. I was so stunned and hurt, for it just never occurred to me that I could have failed. I felt sick in my stomach. My pain soon turned to anger when I heard Murdock's mocking unrestrained laughter. I scowled hard and my face began to redden with rage. I wondered why he'd kept my hopes alive for so long, and why he hadn't asked me to leave before.

"Hector, if I gave you seven years, do you think you could play that well?"

I wiped my face with my sleeve and shook my head.

"The truth is, Hector, I could practise my arse

off and I couldn't play that good either. I can't teach him anything, so a suppose a better teach you!"

I looked up and saw the smiling face of Murdock as he held out a linen hanky. I gratefully took the handkerchief and blew my nose, immersing poor Murdock's hanky with my nasal wrath. The revulsion and horror on Murdock's face immediately made me feel better. I offered Murdock his hanky back, but Murdock refused my offer with his usual candour.

"Keep it, ya mingin wee shite!"

"Thank you, Mr Dunbar," I said gingerly, stuffing the mucus-ridden ball of linen into my sporran.

Murdock started abruptly.

"Listen to me and listen to me well! If you don't practise, you're out! If you lie to me, you're out! If you disgrace your instrument - or my teaching - you're out! Christ on a bike, it's going to take a fucking miracle to make you a piper. If, and I fucking mean if, I'm going to make you a piper, it means you give me everything and I mean everything! Remember, you need me, I don't need you, is that clear?"

I dried my eyes and punctuated each of Murdock's statements with wild smiling nods.

"I'll no let you down, Mr Dunbar, I swear to

God a won't."

"You better no!"

"A won't!"

"We'll see," said Murdock, "we'll see."

For the first time Murdock openly laughed with me. Meemee poked her head around the corner and casually nodded at Murdock.

"Have you asked him if he really wants to learn yet?"

"Oh, God! A do, a do a really do!" I screamed.

Meemee smiled and clasped my cheeks.

"Run hard, my wee tortoise, run hard and true."

I grabbed Meemee's hands and we jigged from side to side along the hall into the kitchen. Meemee knelt down and stroked my hair.

"Murdock comes across as a great block of granite, Hector, but he has the biggest softest heart, and it's been hurt too many times. When he finds a boy worth teaching it just breaks his heart if they give up. If you let him down he'll never teach again, he just couldn't take it. He gives everything and asks for so little in return, so listen and learn. Above all else believe in him, for he has put his trust in you. Learn from him, Hector, not just how to play, but learn the real magic and character that really makes a piper. That's why he chose you!"

Meemee smiled, kissing me on the forehead.

Murdock called me back and laid down the terms of my tuition.

"Every spare hour of the day must be given ungrudgingly to the practise and perfection of your art. In return your pipes will give you the means to travel the world and enjoy all that's in it. I'll make you a piper, Hector, all I ask from you is your best, your honest best!

The price for my services is simple; once you can play, you teach two pupils of your own and when I die, let them know I'm coming - with a strong, bold pipe. Now Hector MacTavish, do I have your hand and your heart sir?"

I shook Murdock's hand as firmly as I could.

"You do, Mr Dunbar, you do."

I sat back down on the couch and clicked my wellie heels with delight. I looked around the room with triumphant glee. My eyes were inexorably drawn to the giant bear of a boy who sat quietly in the corner. Murdock's shrewd eyes caught my stare.

"Hector, meet Roddy Maclean known to one and all as Bear. He is only nine, but I predict that he will be the finest piper to walk God's green earth. You just can't compete against genius, Hector, but you can learn from it."

I nodded to the giant of a boy.

"How did you get so good?"

The boy looked around anxiously for help. I repeated the question, but the boy was now visibly distressed.

"Answer him, Bear, it's okay," Murdock coaxed.

"F-ff-fuck! Fuck! F-ff-fuckin lucky I gg-guess," came the loud agonised stutter.

I stared back with my mouth wide open, too shocked to say anything.

"Bear can't help swearing, he doesn't want to, he just does," Murdock said, patting Bear's shoulder. "But by God he can sure make those pipes talk."

Bear hardly ever spoke because of his Tourette's. He limited his conversation to the few people who he really trusted. Bear was a child protégé who had been ruthlessly and systematically abused by his father and stepmother's parasitical greed. They wheeled him out like a performing monkey to finance their selfish avarice. Once they had received Bear's recital or competition money they would pump him full of alcohol and leave him locked in a car for days on end.

Their shameless abuse had burdened Bear with alcoholism by the age of seven. He would try and escape their abuse whenever possible. He'd invariably run towards the loving arms of his real mother in North Uist, but the blind stupidity of the social services would always return Bear back to his father and stepmother's glaring abuse.

As soon as Bear was freed from the shackles of his captors' greed: he became a typical Hebridean piper, full of modest genius without a care in the world. Money, fame and power meant nothing to him, but God, how he loved to live life. Murdock often hid Bear around various pipers' houses, and did everything he could to protect Bear from the abuse of his parents' greed.

"You know, Bear, you should stay at my house. Nobody can cram more swear words into a single sentence than my Dad can, he really is mental! No one would notice you at all in my house. My Mum would love to feed someone as big as you!"

I nodded, not knowing that I had unwittingly stumbled into the tragic reality of Bear's pitiful hidden existence. Even the youngest of players enjoyed a fly beer, but

Bear needed huge quantities of the hard stuff on a regular basis.

During my first year's tuition Murdock and Bear introduced me to their mutual acquaintance, John Barleycorn.

In my second year, Murdock increased my tuition to two nights a week. I steadily began to notch up some good competition wins.

"No more leavin competitions in a high speeding car!" said Murdock. "From now on, we mount the bar and declare your victories - in the most ungracious manner possible!" Murdock cheered with rampant pride.

It wasn't just the playing and winning I loved. I was hooked on the Rob Roy lifestyle, which all pipers enjoyed. All pipers have an inherent and feudal destiny to live life, like an 18–30 holiday. The piper's ethos of sucking every last ounce of marrow from life was oh so addictive. It was like being transported to a perfect utopia, where all the things I loved in life just got better and better.

In piping it doesn't matter about your age, sex, colour, religion, wealth or position for you are judged solely upon the fundamentals and vital things in life, such as your love of piping, your character, sense of humour, drinking and above all else - your playing ability. I was only nine when I started to compete on the pipes, but I could drink, debate, joke, laugh and play the pipes with anyone, regardless of their age or status. The sheer humour and social adventures that pipers and pipe bands enjoyed made Viking sagas and Greek odysseys seem like 'Janet and John' books.

The fact I was a young piper seemed to excuse the socially inexcusable. This cultural attitude, which I loved so much, also helped to hide Bear's young and tragic alcoholism. If you saw a child of nine drunk as a skunk you would immediately call the police or a doctor, but if you were a young piper folk just looked at you with a fond smile of affection as if being drunk was an intrinsic and necessary part of your training.

"My God that kid's drunk!"

"He's a piper."

"Any good?"

"He's always pissed."

"Oh, he's that good."

Many's the time my poor old Mum had to suffer the embarrassment of the police bringing me home in the back of a police car as drunk as a lord.

"We found him in a rosebush, Mrs MacTavish," the policeman announced.

"It'll no happen again, officer," Mum vowed.

The very next weekend the police would drop me off again, along with the band's battered prizes.

The policeman began to titter and giggle.

"He must have a twin, Mrs MacTavish!"

"Well, you know what it means this time, Mrs MacTavish, don't you?" the superintendent said, frowning.

"I'm really sorry, officer, really I am, Hector's a good boy, really he is! Please don't take him away, he tries so hard," Mum begged.

"No, no, Mrs MacTavish, good God no! That win means the band stands a good chance of winning the World Pipe Band Championship at Glasgow Green and Champion of Champions, Mrs MacTavish, Champion of Champions."

"Would you like a scone, officer?"

CHAPTER 3

The thick depressive air of the hospital filled my nostrils as I approached Murdock's ward.

"He's watchin 'Kung Fu' again in the TV room, Hector."

Sister Cullen inhaled, mimicking Murdock's smoking action to perfection. Murdock and I loved watching 'Kung Fu' together. We would spend endless hours ribbing each other, as master and pupil. I handed Sister Cullen 40 cigarettes, so she could at least ration Murdock.

"See if you can educate his other piping socialites that visiting time is different from closing time," Sister Cullen seethed.

"He's great isn't he, Sister?"

Sister Cullen reluctantly sighed and nodded. You could tell that Sister Cullen had fallen under Murdock's spell, along with the rest of her nursing staff.

I slunk through the TV room doorway and watched Murdock having a sly puff. I slammed the door shut and watched the big man sling his fag out of the window with naughty schoolboy panic.

"The air is thick with forbidden incense, master!" I crowed, assuming my kung fu defensive stance.

"You are young, grasshopper, and you deserve an almighty kick up the arse!" Murdock scowled.

Looking back - slamming a door to surprise someone who has just had major heart surgery wasn't the brightest move.

"Got the incense sticks?" Murdock asked.

"I gave them to Sister Cullen, master."

"She'll only demand more sex of me, the woman's insatiable!"

There was a loud clunk as Sister Cullen gave us the fingers against the window of the door, much to our amusement.

"I've got some good news for you, boy, sit down," Murdock ordered. "You're to represent the Scottish Distilleries over the winter and receive full sponsorship. It's a great honour and it's exactly the experience you need. It will do you no end of good. They only pick the best, but this year they've decided to go with you."

I was ecstatic.

"When do we go?"

Murdock shrugged awkwardly and winced.

"I need to rest up for awhile and give my heart a chance. The lion's share of my work with you is done."

`I nodded reluctantly and slipped a half bottle into Murdock's dressing gown pocket.

"I saw that, you little shite!" said Sister Cullen, as she burst into the room.

"It's watered down, Sister."

"Is it? Kick the wee shite out, Sister!" Murdock roared. "See that you bring me back somthin decent, with a seal on!"

I was going to suggest Lucozade, but I thought I'd better give poor Murdock's heart a chance to heal.

My invitation card and train tickets finally arrived from the Scottish Distilleries. I was only 14, and this would be my first time away from home on my own.

Dad tried to cover every eventuality, but above

all else he had given me strict orders on pain of execution:

"No whisky!"

The trouble was I had acquired a real liking for whisky by the time I was ten. I used to thrash whisky to show off, and was pleasantly surprised to find that I had a real talent for the stuff.

My folks saw me off at the train station. Dad slipped me a few quid and nodded his gleeful farewell. Mum wished me luck and prayed to God that I would leave Glasgow standing - in both senses.

I stepped off the train at Glasgow Central looking like a highland James Bond; no pants and licensed to thrill. It was the first time I had worn my new, piper's, full dress uniform with swords, and I felt bloody gorgeous!

My socks, plaid and kilt were woven in the ancient colours of the Mackenzie tartan. My tunic was a magnificent, deep moss green, trimmed with silver brocade and finished with large, round, silver thistled buttons, which sparkled like diamonds against the moss green of the tunic. My feather bonnet was made of large, bushy, black ostrich feathers crowned with a striking white-feathered hackle.

My broadsword, sporran, plaid brooch and belt buckles shone with pride. They were exquisitely crafted in heavy silver with bold thistles to match my tunic buttons. The large well cut Cairngorm on the top of my dirk stunningly finished my uniform off, and told everyone I was a piper of means (no mine - but means is means in the pipe band world).

I was three hours early and had secretly arranged to meet Bear in the Heilanman's Umbrella before I reported in. The Heilanman's Umbrella was a bridge over the Clyde, where poor highlanders would shelter from the rain when arriving in Glasgow. The pub next to the bridge had adopted the name and attained world notoriety as a piping Mecca of iniquity.

It was my favourite place on the planet for it was packed with piping legends and characters. You were instantly entertained with the latest scandal, patter, gossip, jokes and news. Best of all there was great music played by great people who knew how to love and live life. This could all be purchased by a tune on the pipes, a dram, some juicy gossip, or just you and your company.

I was only nine the first time I ordered a whisky and water there.

"Nane o' yer fuckin fancy cocktails here, sonny!" the barman said, handing me a whisky and pointing to the water jugs on the bar.

It had been a while since I had been there, and

I couldn't wait to renew my patronage.

I looked out of Glasgow Central Station into the people's city of cities. All cities have vibrancy, a soul and a heart, which is given to them by their people. To me, Glasgow's honest heart beats louder and more welcoming than any other city in the world. Oh don't get me wrong, there are still plenty of places where you can end up with your teeth in your back pocket - if you really want to.

The fabulous Scottish rain made me feel like I was driving into it arse naked on a motorbike, so I pulled my new Inverness cape on. Inverness capes are made from some strange alien material, which has the properties of Kevlar and corrugated iron. These ingenious garments protect you from the most atrocious of weather conditions, and cocoon pipers from frozen puddles when lying in beer tents. Inverness capes also aid piping procreation, as they allow pipers to enjoy sex in even the most challenging of Scots weather.

I was only about 200 yards from the Heilanman's Umbrella. I nipped into a tenement close to prepare my grand entrance. I knew if I just walked into the bar wearing my new uniform I would receive the slagging of a lifetime. I had decided to go for a two-pronged assault. I would outflank the main army of abuse by marching straight to the bar with a grim fixed expression. I would then force the unconditional surrender of Minna, their commander-in-chief, with a dazzling display of coolly initiated shock-humour.

Minna was the landlady of the Heilanman's Umbrella. She had been a world class Highland dancer in her day. Minna's angelic looks and grace fiendishly masked her rapier-like caustic wit. Minna was the mistress of the crippling one-liner, and she had slain the bravest of pipers with her tungsten-tipped tongue. I only hoped my plan wouldn't backfire against such a formidable opponent.

I took my cape off and folded it neatly into my case. I removed the two-inch square piece of sandpaper from my sporran and covered the smooth side of the sandpaper with glue. I took a deep breath, lifted my kilt and quickly slapped the sandpaper to the underside of my genitalia. The sharp bite of the rapid drying glue more than woke me up. Ironically enough, the glue I used was All Purpose Bostick.

After a tearful bonding, I made my way to the bar's entrance. I slipped the wee boys practising their chanters, a quid to bring my cases in. I hid some matches in my left hand and a cigarette in my right hand. I was ready.

I took a deep breath and marched into the bar with pace and style. I was immediately greeted with wolf whistles, hoots and jeers.

"Fuck me! It's Moira Anderson with a cock!"

"Look, Mum, a shortbread tin wi legs."

I ignored the pub's taunts and remained coolly aloof. I stared Minna hard in the face.

"A hauf and a half, Minna, and a good hard shag when you're ready!"

Before Minna could say anything, I quickly whipped my kilt up and struck a match off my newly sandpapered loins, lit my cigarette and nonchalantly blew the match out - with a gentle puff of exhaled smoke. Minna and the place exploded into laughter and cheers.

Minna nodded to my crotch.

"I take it you don't want ice, as it looks really cold out, Hector. God you were such a nice wee boy until that old bugger started leading you astray. How is he, Hector?" Minna asked.

"He refuses to stop piping, drinking and smoking, and he's getting ruder by the minute, so he's well on the mend, Minna."

"It's on the house, Hector," said Minna, making it a large one.

I nodded my thanks and took the whisky and my half-pint of heavy from the bar. I peered through the shafts of blinding sunlight that had managed to penetrate the smoke filled lounge. The sweet din of pipes, laughter and rhythm of drumsticks on tables filled the whole bar. I spotted Bear's giant paw wildly beckoning me over.

Jesus, he just kept getting bigger every time I saw him. Before I could speak, Bear hugged the life out of me with his superhuman strength. I managed to get some oxygen back into my lungs.

"You should really learn to express your emotions with speech, Bear. I've only got the one ribcage," I gasped.

"My dear chap you look positively Flora McDonald!" Cassie exclaimed, as he issued smoke from his tortoiseshell cigarette holder.

I have always been really lucky and had the pleasure of having the best and most entertaining of friends, but they broke the mould when they made Cassie Drummond. He was only 15, but you couldn't fail to notice his charismatic, Oscar Wild persona and wit.

Occasionally you would meet some arse who'd mistake Cassie's impeccable manners and speech as a sign of weakness. This was a mistake that they would only make once for, no matter the size or the number, Cassie would unleash his swift retribution with a devastating display of his, divine pugilistic skill. Cassie had been superbly schooled in fist and street fighting by Donald Mor, the Scottish Bare-Knuckle Champion. Cassie's courageous principles could sometimes be bloody terrifying and annoying, but in the end you just had to admire him.

Cassie's full name was Lord Casanova Drummond. His family were the famous whisky barons of Drummond's Famous Highland Malts. He had been educated and expelled from the finest of Scots schools. He had lived a life alone in a world full of privilege because his parents had regarded money as a substitute for parental love and attention.

Cassie was a gifted piper. He had turned the painful void in his life into musical passion and expression. When Cassie played, the world listened to a great piper and not a worthless lord. Cassie and I came from different worlds, but we both shared the same aching dream - to become pipers in the regiment.

Bear and Cassie enquired about the big man's health. I told them Murdock was down to half a bottle and ten fags a day.

"My dear chap that does sound serious," Cassie exclaimed.

I reassured them all that Murdock was far from terminal, as Sister Cullen was in imminent danger of finding out. Bear smiled and nodded over to our glasses.

"Three heavies and three large whiskies with a soupcon of water, my man," said Cassie, blowing out a huge smoke ring with proud relish.

Bear pretended to tug his forelock as he dutifully got the round in.

Time just shot by, as it so often does in good company. I was sorely tempted to stay, but I necked my pint down when the taxi driver called.

My taxi driver was 'Tam the Preacher'. Tam was known as 'the Preacher' because his breakneck driving could make even the staunchest of atheists cry out for religious help.

I had resigned myself to being at least five minutes late but, thanks to Tam's white-knuckle ride through Glasgow's rush hour traffic, we arrived five minutes early. I had displayed some rather impressive bowel control during Tam's kamikaze drive bombing mission. I quickly thanked Tam, but mainly God, for getting me there in one piece.

I checked myself over and climbed the steps of the Kelvin Hall. Giant, art deco floodlight torches lit up the magnificent, red sandstone building. I showed the security my invitation and pass. The security officer smiled.

"May God have mercy on your soul!"

The hall was packed with everyone who was anyone in the world of whisky. My only instruction was to meet up with Mr McFadin, the master blender of all Scotch whiskies and malts. Murdock had described McFadin as a hure of a drinker, with a ginger beard like a bonfire and a nose like a flashing distress beacon. Anywhere else this would have been a precise and succinct description, but at the annual Highland Malt Whisky Ceilidh it was just a generic feature.

The chief barker dutifully announced me, not that anyone noticed or cared. The fiddler's orchestra was in full flow - quite literally. Sets of couples were eightsome reeling like tartan Catherine wheels. From the throng of the crowd, two points off starboard, I suddenly spied the scarlet flashing proboscis of Mr McFadin.

Oh, there may have been other red noses at the ceilidh - but none could match this baby! McFadin's nose was truly the eighth wonder of the world. Every blood vessel in his nose had been burst to maintain its wonderful, nasal, red radium quality. His nose was a testament to his passionate love for his craft and product. He had large Popeye arms and a huge bushy, unkempt ginger beard, which resembled exploded bracken. He was downing whisky as if the entire industry was solely dependent upon his personal intake and consumption. McFadin would occasionally come up for air to give his comments and offer his recommendations.

I waved to McFadin whilst he was in full tasting flow. Before I could speak, he held up his large freckled hand to halt my attempt at introduction. There was a long protracted silence as he savoured every last detail of the whisky. He nodded his head wisely.

"Aye, absolute shite, gee it tae the directors," he scoffed, handing the bottle to the waiter. "You – boy – name – now," McFadin thundered.

"Me – Piper – MacTavish - Hector," I boomed.

McFadin's eyes narrowed into a cold glare.

"Just what I need, a smart arse! Here, make yourself useful and crack open those bottles there."

"I'm a piper," I protested.

"Tell me a piper who doesn't like openin a whisky bottle. Yi have to beat the bastards off with a barb wire whip."

I smiled and passed him the bottles as he required them. Every now and again he would pass me one that smelt or looked a bit lethal. My face would generally relay all the information, which he accepted with a wry smile of gratitude.

During the tour, McFadin and I became inseparable friends. I helped McFadin procure women by acting as a naïve and angelic catalyst. I would broadcast the omnipotent and endless virtues of McFadin to any woman on who he set his sights. McFadin would then play the modest god of a man - and do his best to take the lady in question to heaven and back.

This system had secured him regular carnal conquests throughout our tour. Sadly for McFadin, his one true love, Buxom Morag of Drummore Malts, proved totally immune to his devious courting. She was far too wise and clever to fall for his lustful shenanigans. Morag was all woman and liked her men to be men. She loved McFadin as McFadin, and couldn't stand the ingratiating angel charade or the simpering favours it acquired.

In return for my services, McFadin painstakingly imparted to me a gift; a wonderful, highly lubricated and divine gift. McFadin taught me how to identify any highland malt whisky, purely from the sound of the cork leaving the bottle. McFadin was amazed by my natural aptitude. He decided to show me off and let the directors put me to the test with any highland malt of their choice.

I was carefully blindfolded then I heard the calm words of McFadin.

"You get one guess with one sounding, and

that includes the seals being broken. Are you ready?"

"I am, Mr McFadin, I am!"

McFadin smiled and held the first bottle up to my ear.

Thoomp!

"Glenlivet," I answered confidently.

"Correct, next bottle sounding."

Eeeethumb!

"Glen Ord."

"Correct, next bottle sounding."

Hi! Hi! Hi!

"Screw top, Glenfiddich."

"Correct, next bottle sounding."

Feemp!

"Glen Moray."

"Correct, last bottle sounding.

Thomp!

"Mmm . . . Glen Scotia?"

"Correct! Get in there, ma wee dancin bear!"

McFadin was over the moon as he whipped my blindfold off. "Come tae Dada," he roared with pride.

McFadin gave me a bruising passing out ceremony, where I received full drinking gill honours and my knight of the malt title, 'Hector of the Glens'.

I felt like a Jedi knight with my new-found powers. I promised McFadin faithfully only to use my powers for self-corruption and debauched advancement.

I was now more determined than ever to help McFadin win Buxom Morag's fair heart.

McFadin came close to winning Morag's hand during the end-of-tour ceilidh. The two drank and danced with each other all night, but Morag passed out during a frenzied Scots reel with McFadin. McFadin and I did our best to sneak Morag up to her bed without anybody seeing, but her demise had been noted by some of the directors.

Like a true chivalrous knight, McFadin took full blame for getting Morag drunk. He even offered his resignation, knowing full well that he was far too important to be dismissed. McFadin and I were ordered to leave the tour immediately and forgo our end-of-tour bonuses. Before I left I made sure Morag knew of McFadin's heroic actions and feelings for her.

"He really does love you, Morag, he'd marry you on the spot if you'd let him!"

"He'll take some handling, Hector," Morag scoffed.

"Oh, he will, Morag, but he so desperately wants to be handled by you. He does love you, and he doesn't know I'm here."

Morag smiled.

"When you say your goodbyes to him, give him this box and tell him to meet me at six tonight in the Heilanman's Umbrella - and tell the old bugger to be on his worst behaviour!"

McFadin helped me out of the taxi with my cases. I had about 20 minutes to kill before my train came, so McFadin and I enjoyed a farewell dram together.

"Look Hector, I know you dream of being a piper in the regiment, so I had a word wi ma old pal, Jock Macdonald, at the castle."

McFadin smiled, handing me a rather official looking envelope. I carefully opened the envelope and read the printed card.

> **Please present this card at the time and date stated.**
>
> Mr Hector MacTavish is invited to attend the military piping examinations & audition at Edinburgh Castle on the 28th January at 10 o'clock, with a view to piping employment in the British Army
>
> Yours sincerely
>
> J MacDonald
>
> MAJOR GENERAL J MACDONALD, CBE., MC., DSO

I didn't know how to thank McFadin, so I just placed the small box, which Morag had given me, in front of him. McFadin opened up the box and pulled out a pair of French knickers with the words, 'Open Sesame', written in cherry lipstick. McFadin lit up like a Christmas tree.

"My God, are these Morag's? Ya dancin bear! Yes! Yes! They are fuckin genuine, Hector?"

I laughed and nodded. We had just given each other the keys to our dreams. We said very little to each other, it was one of those fabulous moments amongst friends where very little needs to be said. McFadin gave me a distant strong handshake, then smothered me into his chest with an all-encompassing bear hug. McFadin nuzzled his huge beard onto the top of my head.

"Be lucky, MacTavish, for God's sake be lucky."

I boarded the train and waved goodbye to the only nose in Scotland that was still visible to the naked eye a quarter of a mile from Glasgow Central's number four platform.

I broke the news to my parents. Mum sobbed with pride and remorse. Dad was ecstatic.

"You're definitely leavin! Oh, it's an audition. Well, get practising, Hector. No use in giving us false hope!"

I had only four weeks to prepare for my audition. Every waking moment I could muster was spent preparing and honing my playing skills.

Murdock nodded with satisfaction.

"Well, your pipes are singin and, you're in top form. Remember, Hector, concentrate on the music, nothing else matters! Make me proud, son, and enjoy your day."

I went to bed early that night and practised my tunes in a dream performance.

I stepped off the train onto Waverley Station and looked up at Edinburgh Castle. You could have made me wear two-ton shoes that day and I still would've skipped up the Cannongate. I could hear the sound of the pipes resounding off the castle walls as I presented my pass to the castle guide. The castle guide gave me a friendly nod.

"Good luck, son."

"Good pipers don't need good luck," I boomed.

"Good luck," the castle guide replied, laughing. "You'll do all right, son, they like cocky bastards!"

The corridor signs led me down a maze of tunnels to the tuning room, which was jammed with young pipers. My audition number was pinned to my sleeve. My audition number was 82, and number 12 was on, so I had plenty of time. I had run out of matches, but managed to get a light from one of the pipers who was smoking under the 'No Smoking' sign. I nodded to a few faces I recognised then I heard a welcomed taunt.

"MacTavish! You positive lowland whore."

I ignored Cassie's quip and enquired whether pistols or claymores would be satisfactory. Cassie pointed to the audition board. Number one was Roderick Maclean, aka Bear. Cassie and I pissed ourselves, for the audition was nerve-racking enough without hearing genius first off the bat. Cassie was raw with laughter.

"That poor stunned bastard played after him."

I checked the poor guy out; he was still shell-shocked.

Cassie and Bear had both played and been accepted by the regiment. They stayed with me and tuned my pipes as I warmed up.

"Number 82, MacTavish, you're on now, son."

I marched briskly into the huge stone hall and halted in front of the legendary bench of assembled judges.

"Well, well MacTavish, a march, a strathspey and a reel, if you please."

My pipes were sounding fantastic and I remembered Murdock's wise words. I concentrated completely on expressing the timing of my music. Before I knew it my performance was over. The judges nodded their satisfaction, and asked me a series of questions on theoretical music and why I wanted to become a piper in the army.

"Congratulations on an excellent audition and performance, young MacTavish. Which is your preferred choice of unit?" the captain asked.

"I wish to join the regiment, sir."

"MacTavish, you can't join the regiment, you're too small!"

My brain reeled with shock. I had passed all my army entrance tests and nobody had uttered a word about my height. I had just played out of my skin and answered all their questions intelligently. Now at the last moment they were snatching my dream away. The anger and confusion on my face must have shown.

"The minimum height for the regiment is six foot, didn't anyone tell you?" asked the captain.

I shook my head. All I ever wanted in life, was to be a piper in the regiment. I thought of all the years that I had trained and all the hours I had practised, for it all just to be taken away by my height.

"You can have any other unit or battalion," said the captain.

I shook my head. The judges tried to help me by getting my wrist X-rayed to determine my final height, but the test came back with a maximum expectant height of five foot, eight and a half inches.

"For God's sake, MacTavish, choose another unit!" the captain ordered.

"No, sir, it's all I ever wanted."

I unconsciously collected my things. My brain was still numb with shock as I walked towards the castle portcullis. My mind slowly became consciously aware of someone repeatedly screaming my name out. A hand touched my shoulder and I wheeled around to find a rather out-of-breath, young Argyll corporal.

"They want you back, I think they're gonna take you!"

I was ushered into a side room with Peter Morrison, to await their final decision. Pete was the only black piper I had ever met. His adopted father, the Reverend Morrison of Cathcart had taught him. Like the Reverend, Peter was a beautiful and classical piper. He was something of an oddity because he didn't smoke, drink, swear or compete.

"Good God, Hector, what are you doing here?" Pete exclaimed, shaking my hand.

"I've got to await their final decision, Pete, what you doin here?"

"They said I was a great player. I told them I wanted to join the regiment and they sent me here."

I burst out laughing and slapped Pete on the

back.

"We're both screwed, Pete. They don't take blacks and they won't take me because I'm seven inches too wee."

Pete couldn't appreciate the irony, but then he began to see the funny side.

"I'm the right height, wrong colour, and you're the right colour, wrong height, Hector."

I nodded and we both started giggling out of desperation. Somehow it felt good to be laughing at each other's misfortune.

The door burst open with the awe-inspiring vision of Pipe Major Lachlan MacDonald, resplendent in his Highland full dress uniform. He was the regiment's senior pipe major and every inch the consummate Highland piper. He stared hard at each of us in turn and suddenly his steel blue eyes fixed his gaze upon me.

"Well, MacTavish, you can grow! They'll no make it easy for you, but if you want it bad enough, you'll do it."

I nodded my thanks and shook his hand for all I was worth.

The pipe major from the Black Watch stuck his head around the door and addressed Pete.

"Hell, you were made for us, son! Can you fight as well as you play?"

"I have a black belt in judo and Shotokan karate, sir," Pete replied.

"Aye, but can you fight, son?"

"Yes, sir," Pete replied with a triumphant smile.

"Then join my lot, son," barked the pipe major, shaking Peter's hand.

Pete and I charged down to The Esplanade, clearing each flight of stairs as we went. I kicked The Esplanade bar doors open and waved my acceptance chit to my friends. We hugged and laughed in wild excitement. Pete abstained from drinking, smoking and swearing, whereas I stuck to the more conventional piping methods of celebration.

CHAPTER 4

The morning arrived for my departure to join up. Mum, Dad and I sat in silence as the train carriage buffeted us around in our seats. My face looked like battered mince. Dad had given me a good hiding for nicking his best whisky the night before.

Our train shunted into Glasgow Central. We trudged in gloomy silence towards the London train. You could easily spot the lads who were joining up. Their Scots mums were expressing their love by cramming them with infinitive loads of shortbread, scones and tablet. All the Scots dads competed with each other to see who could look the most disinterested about their son's departure.

My mum was crying hard. Dad looked on with disdain.

"What you crying for?"

"I'll miss him, Dad," Mum sobbed.

"I fuckin hope the Irish don't," Dad muttered.

"Look, he only shared some of your whisky with a few of his friends before he left," Mum snapped. "You begrudged him a drink before he left."

"Five bottles of Glenlivet isn't a farewell drink, it's bloody looting!"

I ignored Dad's barrage, loaded my cases and boarded the train. I slammed the door shut and pulled the window down as the guard's whistle went and the train juddered into motion. Mum waved frantically. Dad couldn't resist one last taunt as the train pulled out.

"Next time you're passing, Hector, we'd be grateful."

Dad and I traded insults as he attempted to run after the train and strangle me. Once I was sure Dad was out of boarding range, I made my way up the carriage. I felt like a midget in the land of the giants, as I couldn't see any recruits under six two.

I made my way along the carriage until I spotted Bear and Cassie. We pretended not to know each other as I offered my introduction.

"My man, I'm dying for a wank, have you got any pictures of your granny handy?"

Cassie remained poker-faced.

"She's dead!"

"Superb, I'll pay double for the wake photos."

The look of sheer horror on the other recruits' faces had us all in fits. After the laughing had died down Cassie introduced me to the boy with his back to me.

"Hector, meet MacFadyen, otherwise known as Fadge."

I stared, open-mouthed.

"You!" I roared.

It was the young piper who had recommended Murdock as a teacher. The boy shook my hand with a loud roar of laughter.

"Well, was I right?"

I smiled and nodded.

"No doubt about it, he is! He is mental! Thank you, thank you, what you havin?"

MacFadyen had clear, grey intelligent eyes with thick, expressive eyebrows. His skin was like well-tanned leather. His hair was a tangle of silver grey, which made him look wolfishly handsome. He naturally exuded charismatic confidence, and you just knew you could depend on him in a crisis.

Women found MacFadyen irresistible. His

incredible success with women came down to his tried and tested chat up technique, rather than his looks. MacFadyen would only ask good looking women, in the most basic terms, if they wished to engage in the most rampant sex of their lives. He generally worked on a one in three slap ratio. MacFadyen could sincerely convince women that his offer was a wonderful and charitable gift that they should gratefully accept. He possessed the patter of a wet flip-flop and could make good on his offer.

Nobody mentioned my bruised face. We all instinctively knew not to ask about our family or home life. None of us really had normal family lives. This was usually the main reason why all of us took the Queen's shilling at 15 and sixteen. The failure rate was high; only one in 150 would make it from recruitment to their battalion. We became our own family, and the army became our home.

We were young, we were pipers and we wanted adventure. Our common adversities and dreams forged great friendship and unwavering loyalty amongst us. Camaraderie and friendship were the keys to survival in the army's harsh world. They say a man's true wealth can often be measured, by the amount of true friends he possesses. If that's the case, the army made me richer than my wildest dreams.

Inevitably our conversations centred on our piping teachers. Most of them were legends. Some were animals, some were loveable characters, some were barking and some were all three. It didn't matter, for we owed them so much and we had nothing but unbridled love for them. Our piping teachers asked for nothing and gave so much in return. They kept piping alive and gave us the chance to enjoy the honour of playing the pipes. In my opinion, these people are the greatest unsung heroes and jewels in the Scottish crown - all too often they are overlooked and undervalued.

We had descended into full exhibition drinking and piping. Our humble mode of transport was soon transformed into a magnificent ceilidh carriage.

The bedlam gradually subsided as we all stared in awe at Bear. He was feverishly composing a tune, blissfully unaware of our enthralled wonder. It wasn't just the sheer beauty of his composition, it was the speed and exquisite neatness of his musical notation. There were no corrections - it was written once with divine perfection. No matter how many times I witnessed Bear's genius, I never once ceased to be amazed by his God-like talents. With a gentle smile of satisfaction, Bear penned the title of his hornpipe, 'The Train Journey South'.

Eventually the train juddered to a halt at Euston Station, to the drunken strains of four pipers playing the hornpipe, 'The Train Journey South'. We manhandled our cumbersome luggage through the tube and onto our connecting train at Waterloo. Silence and tiredness spread their dark wings over us and we began to drift off. We had barely been on the train 40 minutes when we were rudely awakened.

"Recruits! Off now! Move lively! Move, move! One single rank, now move, move!"

It was a voice that, although you did not know to whom it belonged, you knew enough not to question it. We scrambled for our kit and threw ourselves along the entire length of the platform. We stood there in one rank shoulder to shoulder, the cream of Scottish manhood six foot and over, with me, the wee pile of Harris Tweed on the end.

Dull thuds of rubber soled boots became louder and louder with rhythmic synchronised precision. Regimental Police armed with pickaxe shafts quickly surrounded us.

"I shit you not, gentlemen, one fuckin word, one fuckin piece of shite, you'll visit fucking hell tonight! Pick your cases up! Get into three ranks, move! Turn to the right, rri-ight turn! By the right quick march!"

We were forcefully marched with our luggage in the rain for three-quarters of a mile. My arms ached and my hands stung, but I was too terrified to drop my cases.

Eventually we halted out of breath on the floodlit drill square. Steam funnelled from our suits and our grey breath billowed into the jet-black night. The giant, aimless mass of recruits was split into different intakes, companies and platoons.

We were all in Flanders intake, 'A' Company, 9 Platoon. A normal full strength platoon usually numbered about 30 men. For the moment there were 320 men in 9 Platoon alone. We were quickly sub split into sections and trade applications. To my absolute horror, I heard the name that sergeants called pipers.

"Right you fuckin Hectors, surname, Christian name, religion and age."

Cassie turned around, his shoulders uncontrollably pumping up and down with laughter.

"Best of luck, old bean."

Bear tried to hide his smile by nodding sympathetically and pursing his lips. The impending doom of the sergeant finally descended upon me.

"Right, my wee Hector, surname, Christian name, religion and age."

"MacTavish, Sergeant." I crossed my fingers and tentatively offered my Christian name. "H... Hector, Sergeant."

Stifled sniggering broke out.

"Fucking smart arse!" the sergeant sneered, cracking his pace stick off my head. "Last time, Hector, I shit you not!"

It seemed an eternity and totally futile, but I began to reiterate slowly. The word Hector had barely left my mouth when the sergeant's pace stick began to slam into my aching dizzy head.

"That's ma name, Sergeant, honest!"

"Rift the cheek out of the fucker and fire him in the hole!" the sergeant major ordered.

This was my first introduction to army rifting. Rifting consists of being drilled and marched at light speed. The sole purpose of rifting is to disorientate and knacker you. Somehow all of this bedlam is carried out with a swish sadistic genius of regimental ceremony.

I arrived at the guardroom at a rifting factor of warp four. I was flung into the punishment quadrangle and introduced to beasting. Beasting consists of humiliation and physical exhaustion, but with no ceremony. The sole purpose of beasting is to break you physically and mentally in the most inhumane brutal manner possible.

I was beasted to the point of unconsciousness with the insane screaming of my captors ringing in my ears.

"He fuckin is he fuckin well is! We've actually got one."

My chin was forcibly lifted, and through my distorted vision of sweat I gradually began to understand the unintelligible voices and laughter.

"Your name, boy? It's fucking Hector, isn't it?"

I was too exhausted to answer straight away. I just nodded and finally panted a:

"Y-yes, Sergeant, oh God yes."

I was helped to my feet.

"Here's your pipes, come with me my wee Hector," the provo sergeant jeered. He led me over to the sergeants' mess and handed me a large whisky.

"You'll need this, son."

I nodded and gratefully knocked it back. I did my best to concentrate my mind and quickly tune my pipes.

The mess sergeant's introduction sounded like Leonard Sax of 'The Good Old Days'.

"Ladies, gentlemen, guests and mess members, tonight we have a delightful attraction for your delectation, detection, appreciation and interrogation - a Hector! He will give us a wee tune and then you can quiz him to find out his true entertainment value."

I was ejected from the curtains onto a small circular dais. I tried to look composed, but I was still giddy from the guardroom. To my horror the dais began to spin and whirr me around like a demented dervish. I shut my eyes tight and remembered Murdock's wise words, 'You and the music, nothing else matters'.

The dais eventually stopped. I finished playing. I opened my eyes, steadied myself and tried to focus on the blur of red mess dresses. My interrogation of rapid and endless questions began immediately.

"Where are you from?"

"Is Jimmy Cranky your mum?"

"Who do you know in the regiment?"

"Are you a bird?"

"Are you rich or famous?"

"Did the surgery hurt, Lord Lucan?"

Eventually the regimental sergeant major became bored and demanded to know the answer.

"Well, my wee Hector, what makes you so special?"

"Well, Sir, I think it's probably due to the fact

that the regiment refers to its pipers as Hectors and my Christian name really is-"

"Fuck me it's Hector! He's called fuckin Hector!"

"Well, just Hector, Sir."

Their laughter and jeers became a mocking blur as I was escorted out of the sergeants' mess to the cookhouse. The cookhouse was bigger than a football pitch and lit up like Hades. It always puzzled me why the army called these places of culinary hell, cookhouses as the term would lead you to believe that someone with the ability to cook would reside there.

Army cookhouses' sole purpose was to take top quality produce and cremate the shite out of it, and then serve the shite up to you. On a good day they would try and camouflage their gastronomic crimes with iceberg lettuce, or immerse it in some alien hot red sauce. This red-hot sauce was guaranteed to take the roof of your mouth off and generally tasted of atomic waste.

The Army Catering Core initials of ACC were often thought to stand for 'A Canny Cook'. To be fair to the army, they had some excellent cooks, but they never ever let them near a training depot.

I mopped the last of the sweat from my face, straightened my tie and opened the cookhouse door. I was greeted with a crescendo of knives and forks being beaten to the rhythmic chant of:

"What's your name, Hector?"

I gave a mock bow and the royal wave, lapping up the attention. The glad beacon of Bear's arm provided me with a welcoming haven from the sea of strange faces.

"Have you been here before, Hector?" Cassie asked.

"No, but the head waiter is a friend of mine. What's the grub like?"

"It's life, Jim, but not as we know it!"

I collected my plate and approached one of the vast, 40-foot long, stainless steel hotplates. As I queued, I noticed the master chef barking out his hotplate orders to his cremation staff who were fiendishly disguised in chefs' uniforms.

As a result of the sheer volume of numbers, each part of the hotplate is numbered and each tray is named according to the food upon it. As soon as the master chef spotted a tray becoming empty, he'd shout the hotplate part number and the tray names. Cooks would then shoot out and replenish the empty tray.

I waited until the master chef's back was turned and shouted out:

"More shit on six!"

A frantic possession of cooks came flying out of the kitchen like angry wasps with a variety of their incendiary masterpieces. I collected my meal and walked nonchalantly back from the hotplate, feeling a whole lot better.

After our meal we were promptly marched to our barrack rooms, which pre-dated Methuselah by a few millennia. Our barracks were old asbestos spider blocks with badly patched roofs and wall panelling. The corridors gave off a breathtaking and dazzling shine from their highly polished, blue vinyl floors. The pungent smell of Jacob's Regimental Floor Polish reminded us that the shine wasn't accidental.

In the middle of the spider was a square shower and toilet block. Light dazzled from its highly polished, grey stone floor. The floor had been smoothed as a result of decades of frantic recruit polishing. Gallons of sweat and a ton of elbow grease had made that stone floor gleam. The floor's shine radiated pride. It was a frightening reminder that we had entered an alien military world where perfection was the minimum acceptable standard.

Our accommodation rooms were long narrow corridors, which were 110 feet in length and 19 feet wide. Sixteen beds and lockers were placed in perfect symmetry along each side of the room. Everything was uniform in colour, size and design, right down to the amount and size of the ironed starched pleats in each curtain. We were totally in awe of our alien pristine surroundings.

Even the bedding was formed into perfect bed packs. Bed packs are a feat of immaculate blanket construction, not to mention an ingenious way of making your bed a regimental pain in the arse. Bed packs consist of three blankets and two sheets, each folded exactly into two by three feet, completely level, two-inch thick blocks. These are then stacked alternately upon each other and seamlessly bound with a covering blanket. A counterpane is then stretched over the mattress to a high tension with hospital corners and the bed pack placed upon it.

"Jesus wept, check this out!" MacFadyen roared.

We all ran over to him and collected around an impressive black mosaic, which had been painstakingly burned into the brown vinyl floor. It was made up of thousands of precise fag burns, to form the regiment's cap badge. Underneath the cap badge was the intake's name, Cassino, with their pass out date and pass out rate. It was a poignant and powerful monument left by our predecessors. Only 27 had made it out of the original three hundred and five.

MacFadyen's street-smart astuteness switched

on straight away.

"We've got to get rid of this or we will pay for it tomorrow. Don't dismantle your bedding packs just sleep under your mattress covers and use your bedside mats as insulation."

Most of the room nodded at his quick thinking, but one arse called Hern, turned his back on him and wandered off. The remainder of us scrubbed the floor with wire wool until the black mosaic was removed. We layered up the floor with polish and hand bumpered the area repeatedly until it matched. We were chuffed to bits until we realised how long that one small area had taken to buff up. Our minds painfully thought of the miles and miles of endless corridor in the block.

MacFadyen cheered us up by whipping out a kettle and some brew kit, for a welcomed cup of tea, which none of us had had the presence of mind to pack - the man was a genius. It was about eleven thirty when we finished our tea.

Reveille was in seven hours, so we slipped under our mattress covers. The lights were turned off, but the external lights glowed, giving faint yellow fans of pale light into our room. The banter gradually began to fade into silence then all of a sudden, out of the faint darkness, came the rather speculative enquiry:

"Haw, Frank, are you havin a wank, son?"

"Yy . . .yessss," came the unabashed staccato admission.

Nobody could stop laughing. The situation became hysterical as one by one little tents began to spring up under the mattress covers. Cassie crowned the whole surreal experience by starting a chorus of, 'Getting to Know You'. I don't actually know if anybody succeeded in their quest, but it was one hell of an icebreaker. Everybody chipped in one pound towards a £31 sweepstake for the most embarrassing or bizarre wank story.

My mind began to drift back to my long-suffering parents at home. When it came to self-pleasure I religiously adhered to a strict daily schedule of one before I went to sleep, one on waking and, for some bizarre reason, one at 6 p.m. when Reporting Scotland came on the telly. I carried out my cardinal sins in my fixed single bed. The headboard would resound off the wall like a Gatling gun being fired by a gang of possessed woodpeckers.

Poor Dad would try and listen to the news when the bab, bab, bab, bab would start like a pneumatic drill trying to fight its way through the wall.

"Stop it ya randy wee shite! Fuckin stop it! That's it, I'm going to fuckin kill him!"

Dad would storm through and kick my bedroom door open. I would instantly feign comatose sleep. I would feel Dad's spittle bouncing an inch off my face.

"I know you can fuckin hear me, I know you're awake and I know what you're fuckin doing. One more peep and I'm going to rip your cock off! Got it, snookums?"

My face would remain expressionless, without any form of acknowledgement. Dad would storm back through and settle down to watch the news. I would usually give it about a maximum of 50 seconds and then the bab, bab, bab would resume. This form of attrition happened religiously, 365 days a year.

A couple of good stories had been told.

"Whose turn is it next?"

"It's the wee man in the pyjamas."

Bear and I couldn't stop laughing.

Cassie shouted, "Tell them why you're wearing pyjamas, Hector."

I explained to the room about my nocturnal habits and that's why my mum had insisted that I wear pyjamas with her wise reasoning.

"Save you leavin those nasty wee maps of

China on the army's sheets, Hector!"

After the laughing died down I began my embarrassing story. It all started when Mum and Dad had gone to bed. I thought I would watch a bit of telly before I turned in. I had flicked on the telly and there was the most explicit porn I had ever seen in the shape of a BBC's production of 'Moll Flanders'. I turned the telly volume down low and sat on the large, double Queen Anne couch. I was in the mid-throws of enjoying myself, when Mum opened the door to the living room. I grabbed the couch's Black Stewart throw-over to cover my shame. We had no remote, so my right foot flailed about wildly trying to change the channel with my toes. Luckily Mum's eyesight wasn't great, but she was puzzled why I was suddenly wrapped up in her favourite Black Stewart throw-over when the central heating was on full blast.

"Whit yi doin, Hector? Put my good Black Stewart cover back on the couch. Yi know it's ma favourite!"

I remained motionless and nodded back to her with an insane fixed smile. I prayed to God with all my might that Mum would just leave. Mum tried to pull the throw-over off me and replace it neatly back on the couch. I held on with the grim determination of a drowning man.

"Whit's wrang wi yi, Hector?"

I went to offer some insane excuse when Mum suddenly whipped away the cover revealing my morning glory, which had refused to wilt.

"Oh, Dad, Dad he's playin wi himself on oor couch, oh Dad! How could yi, Hector? On oor best Black Stewart cover!"

I heard the sound of my marauding father's resounding tread cantering into a thunderous gallop. Dad stood there with two years of Gatling gun attrition burning in his eyes. He pulled me from my seated position by my manhood until I was upright then punched me back to the seated position whilst screaming:

"Dirty, dirty fuckin Hector!"

This was repeated until Mum interrupted him, quite oblivious to my plight.

"Does the Black Stewart have any white in it, Dad?"

Dad smiled a cold smile of revenge and lied.

"No white in it at all, Mum, why?"

"Oh, Dad, he's ruined it, there's white stripes all over it."

Years of forced attrition were now being vented onto me as Dad laid into me. Needless to say the rhythmic bab, bab, bab, was never heard again in the House of MacTavish; well, at least no by me.

Convulsive laughter, wolf whistles and applause rang out. I was confident of winning the £31 sweepstake, but I hadn't counted on Frank the Wank with his top tip for early morning rustic masturbation.

Frank began his reverent words of wisdom.

"Well, what you dae is get up on a cold morning with a stonker on and head for a herd of cows. Now make sure you find a cow with a really, really snotty nose then you get your welt right up its nostril."

By this time everybody was in kinks.

"Shut it," Frank shouted, "am no finished!"

Frank could hardly talk through the hysterical laughter, but did his best.

"Once you've got your welt up the coo's nose, you wait for her big old rough tongue tae lick yer baws!"

No contest! Frank had won and he carried on mooing until he was handed his winnings.

The room door burst open.

"I suggest you get some sleep, you'll need your strength for tomorrow. I know. I've been there before. Nighty-night!"

"Who was that?"

"Remember the shit who walked away and didn't help us, that's him, his name's Hern. They made him room senior because he's been back squaded."

"Cannae be that good if they back squaded him, watch out for that shite," warned MacFadyen.

During training we were barred from using the phone. All our communication had to be by letter, which was always read before it was sent. I turned my bedside light on and wrote Mum a quick note to set her mind at ease.

Dear Mum,

Just arrived and everybody seems to know my name, so I'm famous already. I'm sorry for doubting you every time you said that the shops had sold out of mugs with my name on, as I am surprised how common my Christian name is down here.

The sergeants have been very kind making sure everybody knows my name. They even threw a party for me in the sergeants' mess to celebrate my arrival.

Cassie & Bear are here too, so I'm in good company. I'll have to go, Mum, I'm up in six hours.

All My Love,

Hector

PS

Cheers for the PJs, avoiding maps of China at all costs!

CHAPTER 5

"Wakey, wakey, rouse, rise and shine, hands off cocks on with socks. The birds are singing, the sun is shining, now let's invade some neutral, defenceless Third World country and kick the livin shite out of them! Wash and shave petals, schnell, schnell! Your first day in the British Army, you lucky, lucky bastards, move, move!" the duty corporal screamed.

We all sprang out of bed and grabbed our washing and shaving kit. The cold sharp breath of the corridor draughts chased us into the toilet block, which was known as 'Ice Station Zebra'. The freezing cold water of the shower instantly woke me up and turned my genitalia into inverted walnuts. I now resembled a wee, blue Greek statue with a token attribute. For the first time I went through the farce of pretending to shave. I patted my face with admiration at the removal of all the thick manly stubble that had never existed on my smooth adolescent face.

When we returned to the room, Hern told us to get into olive green coveralls and to make our beds. When we had finished we stood at ease by the foot of our beds.

"When I call 'room', come smartly to attention," Hern ordered. "Right, here we go - room!"

Sergeant Wallace casually swaggered in, his precision eye looking over the expert bed packs and knowing full well that we could never have made them. He stopped where the mosaic had been. Sergeant Wallace's face lit up and a wise smile washed over his face.

"Well, gentlemen, somebody's no daft! You've just saved yourself from a savage session of beasting hell. Intelligence should always be rewarded. You've just bought yourself an easy morning. Enjoy it, gentlemen, you won't get another. Three ranks, outside, move!"

We marched at the double to the cookhouse where we feasted on an army, no-holds-barred breakfast. Without question the best meal the army can produce is breakfast. The only drawback from an army breakfast is the fact that it produces a strange, opaque and inexhaustible flatulence. It is a hard subject to endure, but not grasp. The anomaly about 'Army Breakfast Farts' or ABFs, is the sheer density of their odour and how prevalent they remain for the rest of the day. It actually feels like you have released some solid wild entity into the world.

I once boarded a train at Liverpool about one in the morning, rather the worse for wear after a poteen drinking competition with some Irish Rangers. The train carriages were the old fashioned eight-seater compartments without a corridor. There were no lights in my compartment and I could just make out the black silhouette of someone lying across the opposite seats. I quickly stowed my gear and gratefully fell into the four vacant seats. As I rolled over, I kicked my shoes off and let an ABF go.

After a while a voice came out of the darkness.

"You're in the fucking army!"

I was just about to enquire how he knew, when the voice explained he was a para and he'd recognised the unmistakable aroma of my ABF. We discussed the matter at some length and concluded that after some training you could probably narrow down the guy's regiment and posting. In my mind, ABF forensics is an area much neglected by army intelligence. I feel this subject could have been explored and developed in the interest of military intelligence.

I imagined a scenario going something like this.

"Sergeant MacTavish, Sir, Army Bowel Intelligence."

"Hand Sergeant MacTavish the ABF test tube exhibit."

"Ah yes, an Aldershot Paratrooper, newly

returned from (sniff, sniff, sniff) north of the Rhine, with a passion for extra fried eggs and bread with double sausage. Judging by the filtration of the upper stench elements, he wears both long johns and puttees."

There again, those marvellous words 'Military Intelligence' always seem a contradiction in terms to me.

After breakfast we were formed up into a squad and doubled down to the medical centre for a training medical. We had all undergone stringent and thorough joining up medicals two months before. This was basically another check-up to make sure we were in peak condition to have the shite kicked out of us. This was my first introduction to running in a squad after an army breakfast, and the ABFs came thick and fast. I was near the front, thank God.

We halted outside the medical centre, gratefully facing into the cleansing wind. We were ordered to strip naked and queue in single file. Everybody stood speechless and opened mouthed, as Bear unleashed his mighty highland caber. Bear's mammoth phallus strangely resembled the Wallace Monument in both shape and scale. Hell, if I had a cock that size, I would have wanked with the lights on.

Cassie was the first to speak.

"Bear, does that thing stick buns up your arse?"

Bear tried to look nonchalant, but you could tell he was a proud highland boy. Bear may have had Tourette's, but God had more than compensated him with outstanding gifts.

There were about two lines of doctors, 18 on each side. It was like running a medical gauntlet. One moment you were saying, "Aaaaah," with a tongue suppressor, and the next minute you were screaming, "Christ!" with a gelled finger up your arse.

At the end of the gauntlet there was a voluptuous nurse with a polio sugar lump. Everyone tried to ignore her sensuous cleavage and see-through uniform, but it was useless. Within seconds I was walking towards her with beetroot cheeks and a huge stonker. Needless to say, there was more than a bit of talk if a guy walked towards her still limp.

I stuck my tongue out for my polio sugar lump from Nurse Lusty Busty. She pulled me in close and interlocked her hands with mine, placing my hands on my hips. I thought my luck was in when about eight male nurses suddenly appeared like an iron maiden, each of them plunging two syringes into my arms and arse with sadistic smiles, as they sincerely uttered the words:

"This will hurt!"

My arms became dead lumps of numb throbbing flesh and my arse felt like it had just taken part in a nude, cross-eyed leapfrogging competition.

Still, we had some token revenge when Bear walked down the line. The nurse's calm superior look soon turned to an embarrassed lustful blush that could have torched asbestos.

The army, with its typical sick humour, sent us on a mission that would have been hell if you had two good arms, a trailer and a Land Rover, never mind being on foot with dead arms and a paralysed bum.

We queasily doubled away from the med centre. We ended up in a giant quadrangle surrounded by the clothing stores. Once again there was a conveyer belt system of issuing us with all our uniforms and equipment. As the recruits slowly advanced down the line, shouting out their clothing measurements, a cold wave of inevitability began to wash over me. The regiment specialised in recruits with heights of six feet and over. I prayed to God, that they would have some mortal clothing sizes in stock for me. I gulped hard and began to state my measurements, which were blatantly ignored by the staff sergeant.

"Head size?"

"Six, Staff."

"Eight, pluke heed, chest size?"

"Thirty-six, Staff."

"Forty-five, melon tits, inside leg?"

"Thirty-one, Staff."

"Forty-six, you stumpy arse shite, boot size?"

"Eights, Staff."

"Tens, trotter feet, now fuck off!"

We trudged along ridiculously overladen with our suitcases, kit bags, webbing and large packs. It seemed an eternity before we limped the half mile to our block. My arms were burning and throbbing. I felt sick to my stomach and as dizzy as hell. Nobody went to dinner; we all just lay on our beds as the various inoculations and jabs kicked in.

The training corporals decided this would be an ideal time to do our kit checks with us. Most of the equipment was self-explanatory, but the army terms for them were completely alien. 'Suit, man's, one, distressed, general European purpose', meant a combat suit. My personal favourite was, 'Man's, times drawers two, perforated, olive green, military, short, utility'. This succinct description meant two pairs of pants.

My brain began to wonder if in a war situation would you shout, 'Sergeant, I've just shit my man's, times drawers one, perforated, olive green, military, short, utilities. Oh, don't worry they're dry now'?

We searched our kit repeatedly and nobody could find any pants whatsoever. The training corporal held up the offending articles of sartorial elegance. As he did so, everybody forgot their nausea and fell about laughing. They resembled green perforated duffel bags and looked absolutely nothing like pants. The design had obviously been modelled on Private John Merrick. The waistband was designed to give you all the comfort of a starving boa constrictor. The material had a murderous filing action, ideal for pot scrubbing, but merciless and insensitive to your genitalia. The crotch also doubled as a hod and could easily house half a dozen Wimpy bricks without detection. These darlings were referred to as 'passion killers'. If you could pull a girl while displaying them you were automatically afforded free drinks from the boys, and a girl who really meant business.

After our kit check we were ordered into fatigue order with No. 2 dress macs. You could see the feverish pride as everyone donned their uniforms. For the first time we began to look like soldiers, well, apart from me. I was completely drowned in my oversized clothing. I looked more like Bozo the Clown instead of a lean, green killing machine. In five minutes time, I knew I would also have the luxury of the regimental sergeant major's opinion on my new ensemble - nothing I did made any difference.

I decided to show off my new sartorial elegance

by mimicking a fashion model, using the gap between the beds as my catwalk. Cassie provided the running commentary in an extremely camped up Pepe Le Pew accent.

"Mon amies, from de fashion house of Jee Ten, we bring you, killer fashion! Notice the extravagant extra foot of coat, which manages to sweep the floor as he walks. The beret doubles as a landing pad for helicopters - and can even affect planetary orbits - giving the whole sartorial elegance a je ne sais quoi quality. The surplus four inches of jumper cuff highlights the extra six inches of mac sleeve. The whole ensemble says, look out, Ivan, I'm a diva packin mama with attitude!"

Before I go any further I'd better explain the general rank system of the army, just so you can understand my panic about meeting the RSM.

On the bottom rung of the British Army's hierarchy are privates. Privates are the grafters, fighters and characters of a unit. They live for the moment and believe in booze and sex in that order. Without a doubt they are the essence of a regiment's courageous heart, tradition and pride.

Corporals are next, their primary purpose is to defile, corrupt and live life by the seven deadly sins. They worship anything that will advance their career or give them a cushy posting.

Next up the rung are sergeants. They are the linchpins of the army and basically run the army. Generally most sergeants are either mercenary or cavalier. Sergeants thrive on inter-regimental one-upmanship.

Sergeant majors are demonic entities - either all inspiring or bloody life crushing. Their chief purpose is to dream up new obscenities to reduce grown men to tears.

Regimental sergeant majors are the devil incarnate. They are not born, but are omnipotent and self-generated. The key syllable of their rank is the word 'mental'. They are insane! Their main purpose is to make sure the world sadistically conforms to 'Queen's Regulations'.

The main function of officers is to keep the national industries of Labrador and Pimms production going. However, they do have excellent morale boosting properties, as their stalwart incompetence makes everyone feel positively professional.

Last of all there are pipers, who see the army as an 18 to 30 holiday with a wage. Although they wear army uniform, they remain indignant Celtic troubadours. The piper's chief purpose is to amass as many army two five two charge sheets as possible, whilst boldly pushing back the chemical barriers of alcohol consumption in the interest of scientific and social endeavour.

Sergeant Wallace brought us up to attention and doubled us around to the edge of the drill square, as we were only crows and deemed not worthy to touch its hallowed ground. Crows was the army terminology for raw recruits, as all their new equipment still bore the government stamp, which resembled a crow's footprint, hence the name crow or rookie.

The drill square was an acre of smooth, black onyx tarmac, which was known as 'The Golden Acre'. A never-ending procession of recruits marched onto the square. You could tell each squad's state of training by the uniforms they wore. The entire drill square was almost filled, apart from a small section at the front.

There was a smack! It was the wonderful sound of a drill squad shouldering arms in perfect harmony. The single crack resounded from the tarmac as they executed a perfect right turn. You couldn't see them, but by God you could hear them. The sharp resounding crack of their drill boots became louder and louder. The marching rhythm was in perfect defiant unison. It was Cassino intake, the 27 who had made it from the original three hundred and five. Each one of them was a testament to human endeavour and spirit. Only soldiers that had been to hell and back can look that good.

They were magnificent. Their uniforms were

tailored to perfection and their turnout was immaculate. Every action was precisely styled and uniform. This was their final parade and practise before their passing out parade. It had been well planned by the regiment; the new and raw witnessing the seasoned polish of the highly trained military elite.

The RSM inspected each squad as they came onto the square. The RSM went to leave the square when his telescopic eye suddenly caught me in its sights.

"Aaahh! What in God's bowel movements is that fucking thing?"

I knew he meant me, but I just prayed to God he was referring to someone else.

"Which fucking thing, Sir?"

"That fucking, khaki gnome shite defecating Her Majesty's uniform!"

I was swiftly identified as the RSM's source of rage. Sergeant Wallace simply stopped in front of me.

"Go and meet the RSM, laddie."

I marched as quickly as I could. My coat dragged along the square and the sleeves of my mac flapped over my hands. I looked like a demented scarecrow with Elizabethan ruffles. The RSM was an immaculate, imposing khaki monument to blanco and bulling. He could have been standing there in a pink thong with a red feather boa on and you would still have known he was the RSM. I could see the scornful contempt in his eyes.

"What and who the fuck are you, sweetheart?"

I waited until I had composed myself and the jeers had died down.

"Am going to be a p-piper in the regiment, Sir."

"D-d-d-don't bank on it, sweet pea! What's your name?"

"Hector, Sir."

"Fucking what?"

"MacTavish, Sir."

"No, the first bit again."

"Hector, Sir."

"You again! Fucking Hector, fucking Hector! Your parents must fuckin hate you almost as much as I do! Get off my fucking square before I stick my pace stick through your ears and ride you about like a motorbike! Now, disappear in a puff of smoke - and get off my fucking square!"

"Y-yes, Sir!"

I resumed my position in the platoon at warp factor four. Just as I thought my ritual humiliation was finished for the day I was given a further boost when our sergeant major decided to address us. Sergeant Major MacLachlan paced up and down delivering his timeless introductory speech, which had probably been delivered to him in Latin by his first cohort commander.

"Only between 20 and 30 of you will make it. Don't be ashamed if you don't make it, but by God be proud of yourself if you do! What turns a recruit into a successful soldier? I'll tell you, gentlemen, always give 200 per cent, never think and always follow orders without question. Never take your eyes off your target of becoming a professional soldier in the finest regiment in the world.

Now, tallest on the right, shortest on the left, move!"

The line stretched interminably with me on the end again. In the regiment your height determines the company you join. Six feet four inches and above went to Kings Company, six feet two up to six feet four went to Queens Company and six foot up to six foot two went to Centre Company. HQ Company was usually formed from long-serving soldiers and senior ranks. If you were built like a brick shithouse and superhumanly fit you went to Mortar and Recognisance Company. Mortar boys had to be fit, as they had to carry additional backbreaking mortar equipment, which would have crippled a Clydesdale horse. Needless to say, they needed a joie de vivre and a military zest for life, which would have made Alexander the Great look like an anaemic Boy Scout.

Pipers are front line soldiers who can also be called on to play the pipes if they are so commanded. They are usually in the thick of battle and are famed for their heroism. Pipers often act as ambassadors for their regiments. For this reason, they carry out one year of infantry training and have to go through ruthless selection.

Once a piper successfully completes his infantry training, he must also successfully complete another year of demanding musical training before he is allowed to join the Drums Company in the battalion. The Drums Company can fight as an independent company or it can be used to bolster other companies within the battalion.

Each company within the battalion chooses a piper to be regularly attached to them when on active service or in a theatre of war. This is why pipers command so much respect within their battalions.

Sergeant Major MacLachlan touched each recruit on their berets with his pace stick and announced to which company they were likely to go to.

"Kings, Kings, Kings, Queens, Kings, Mortar,

Queens."

He finally came to me at the end of the line. Without hesitation or change in his voice the sergeant major glibly touched my helicopter-landing pad of a beret and announced:

"Back to Civvy Street!"

I was a bit hurt, and as the sergeant major turned to walk away I managed to blurt out:

"I've got heart, Sir!"

The sergeant major carried on walking and shouted over his shoulder:

"Trust me, you'll fuckin need it!"

So far my reception had been less than cordial, but fairly tongue-in-cheek. This was all about to dramatically change. The regiment only wanted the best and it was determined to receive it by any means.

Over the next six weeks, 9 Platoon was reduced from 320 to 150 recruits. This was achieved through constant ruthless attrition and 24-hour barbaric training. This unforgiving process was acceptable, but a more sinister unacceptable process reared its horrific head. Trumped up false charges and routine beatings began to happen with increased ferocity and frequency.

Bear had been on alcohol so long he needed it

every day just to function. Although Bear secretly drank through the day, he was never drunk or the slightest bit intoxicated. Four cans of lager and a bottle of vodka were planted in Bear's locker during a routine room inspection. This gave the Regimental Police the excuse to check his luggage, but to no avail. If by some remote chance they had checked the toilet systems, their search would have been far more fruitful.

Bear was jailed and beasted with sadistic fury. His only hope of redemption was to sign his release forms. Every morning he would refuse, so the cycle would continue.

MacFadyen was stitched up for failing to report for guard duty, which was never posted, and was being hammered in the same way. Cassie was beasted daily without reason and given all manner of physical punishments.

My hell began at three in the morning when my mind swirled into painful consciousness. My arms had been bound and lashed over the toilet cubicle beams in the crucifix position. My mouth tasted and reeked of carbolic from the rag that had been forced into my mouth. Through my blurred swimming vision three gas-masked figures came towards me. The left-hand side of my rib cage had been smashed and my stomach had been beaten to a pulp. I was repeatedly ordered to sign my release forms. Each time I refused I received another beating. I believed I was going to die and wanted one last throw of the dice.

The next time they asked me to sign, I just mouthed words without speech. The gas-masked figure turned his ear to my mouth to hear better. I bit down hard on his entire ear with every last ounce of strength. My mouth was full of blood and most of his ear, his screams were deafening, but I was past humanity and remorse.

It was then they made their second mistake. They struck my face and head with a baton to release the ear from my mouth. Up until then they had concentrated on my Byprox soaped body, to hide their handiwork. Byprox detergent soap was used as it clogged the skin pores and stopped bruises from showing. By marking my face they had made their crimes visible.

We never reported our beatings because you didn't grass and we did not know who sanctioned or carried them out. Now one of the beaters was easily identifiable and the anonymity of their terror could be broken.

After some more blows to my head I completely blacked out. A shot of pain brought me around, as Cassie and Big Rab cut me loose when they come off guard. There were tears in Cassie's eyes.

"A wee bit of S & M, darling?"

I tried to nod and smile. Cassie and Big Rab eased me into the shower then gently sponged and washed the Byprox off my body. My torso began to turn an ugly black and purple paisley pattern. The right-hand side of my face was cut and swollen like a Belfast ham.

My ribs were taped up and supported by cardboard. I could just about stand, but I could not move my arms or upper body without pain. I swallowed huge amounts of Brufen and tried to prepare for room inspection. Cassie and Rab helped me to stand to attention by my bed, to save me the agony of coming to attention for inspection. I made my mind up; I was going to have revenge without conscience or consequence.

I scoured the faces of my room-mates to see if I could determine if any of my adversaries were in the room. The one person I couldn't stop staring at was Hern. Hern had been back squaded and he was the one who had separated himself from us on our first night. He sycophantically kissed training corporals' arses and was given all manner of privileges. He had two ears, but he couldn't look me in the face and he was visibly nervous.

"Room!"

Sergeant Wallace strode into the room. His eagle eyes quickly honed in on my face. Sergeant

Wallace smelt the Byprox and shook with rage.

"Everyone into the shower block now! MacTavish, stay here."

The whole room charged out through the doorway to escape his wrath and displeasure. Cassie remained and never flinched. Sergeant Wallace stared hard at him.

"If you think I've got anything to do with this, think again, Drummond. Wait outside the door - he'll need your help soon enough. If I'm going to help him I need to speak to him now, alone!"

I nodded to Cassie. Sergeant Wallace remained calm and waited patiently for me to speak, but I said nothing.

"I thought I had stamped this shite out," Sergeant Wallace sighed, pulling a beautifully worked silver notecase from his top pocket.

"No, Sergeant, I'm still very much alive!"

Sergeant Wallace smiled and offered me a fag.

"You know, Hector, I wouldn't blame you if you thought I might be in on this type of crap. Maybe you think that grassing is not so heroic or maybe you fancy yourself as a tartan vigilante. Have a think, son, this crap has to be stopped even if you are still breathing. Can you walk?"

I shook my head

"I'll get a Rover and get Drummond to take you to the medical centre and take this note with you. It must go directly to the medical officer and no one else, understand, MacTavish? Here, you'd better read it first."

Medical Officer

Sir,

Request thorough medical examination of Junior Piper MacTavish. Possible court martial action to follow for imposed injuries, full confidentiality essential to prevent contamination of evidence disclosure, all visitors and communications to be strictly monitored and recorded. Junior Piper MacTavish to be allowed full NAAFI stores and privileges. All costs to be billed to my mess bill.

Sergeant Wallace, 9 Platoon, Flanders Company.

"That'll stop any of the shits getting to you. You show that to the MO and no one else! You must only speak to him or me about this, is that clear? Let me know if any bastard does otherwise," warned Sergeant Wallace.

The MO examined me. My rib cage had been broken in several places, I had suffered abdominal rupturing, kidney bruising and internal bleeding. The left-hand side of my skull and jaw were both fractured. The MO admitted me to the MRS, which was a small depot hospital.

I was just about to be wheeled into my isolation ward when I noticed Lance Corporal Lindsay. He was having a large dressing placed on the remains of his ear. I saw the shocked look of horror on his face when he saw me. I smiled and nodded to him as he backed along the wall and ran off.

Lindsay now knew I was on to him. I swallowed a mountain of tablets; anti-inflammatories and painkillers given to me by the MO. My pain soon vanished under the welcomed cool of the MRS's, crisp linen sheets.

We were worked so hard with so little sleep we would fall asleep at any opportunity. This fact had not escaped the very Christian padre, who just turned the lights off during our religious education. As soon as my head touched the pillow I was out for the count.

I awoke a few days later, still bloody sore, but well rested. My newly employed valet brought in my meals.

"Ah, young Drummond, you're late!" I

complained.

"I've been busy buggering your family, your Lordship," said Cassie.

"Thank you, Drummond. I trust pater wasn't too hard to dig up?"

After a fortnight my ribs felt a whole lot better and my guts were starting to heal, although I made damned sure I appeared completely immobile at all times. I hadn't wasted my time in the MRS. I had come up with a plan that would either destroy them or me.

Cassie informed me that Bear and MacFadyen were out of nick and that Lance Corporal Lindsay and his stubby misshapen ear had returned from his conveniently taken leave.

I needed to punish Lindsay with such terrorising retribution he would be forced to give up the identities of his other two accomplices. I didn't just want to cause them pain, I wanted to destroy and humiliate them. In order to complete my plans I needed to get hold of some quite bizarre and dangerous gear. The bizarre items I obtained from mail order via one of Cassie's Chelsea cronies.

MacFadyen got the dangerous objects at great personal risk to himself. His courage and devotion never ever wavered. Breaking out of barracks was daring enough for MacFadyen, but what I had asked him for was bloody suicidal. MacFadyen, being MacFadyen, carried all this out with cool calm professionalism.

All the props for my payback were now in place and hidden in a sewer outlet near our block. I was terrified of them being discovered as just one of the items meant an instant dishonourable discharge.

Each stage of my plan took agonising effort and painstaking rehearsal. In the beginning my progress was thwarted by pain and lack of mobility. I needed to knock a whole seven minutes off my time if I was going to get away with my plan. My whole alibi depended on speed and the physical impossibility of being in two places at once.

My salvation came through the duty sergeant carrying out the night check of the MRS with the duty medic. After their rounds they would have the obligatory cup of army tea. The duty sergeant did his barrack round checks on a bike and rested it in the MRS bike shelter. His bike would allow me to break the all-important five-minute barrier, providing absolutely nothing went wrong.

Cassie brought good news in with my dinner; the conditions were near perfect for tonight. I was raring to go, so I gave Cassie the go-ahead for tonight.

Every hour seemed to drag, but eventually it

was time for the ten o'clock bed check. The fan of torch light passed over my head as I pretended to sleep. As soon as I heard my ward door shut I shot into action. I already had my coveralls and gloves on, so I carefully swivelled from under my bed covers into my boots.

I crept along the corridor and pushed the heavy maintenance locker with my legs, just enough to allow me to work on the disused fire exit. Slowly and surely I managed to force the redundant fire exit open again. The sweat was pouring down my back when the door finally popped open. I packed mud along the door to keep the door shut and stop it from totally closing. I silently pulled the pushbike out of the shed - time was now ticking against me.

I quickly peddled off, taking care to cut straight through the centre of the camp to avoid the perimeter barrack guard. I collected the necessary props and carefully made my way to Lindsay's bunk.

I peered through the window into the darkened room and I could just make out the silhouette of Lindsay sprawled across his bed asleep. If Lindsay awoke or called for help I was finished. I pulled my face veil up, turned the lock slowly and silently opened the door. I closed the door methodically behind me, never taking my eyes off Lindsay. My heart was pounding and my body shook with coursing adrenaline. I pulled the packets from my pocket and purposefully placed them into his locker, and emptied one measured sachet into his bedside water bottle.

Lindsay was now in the foetal position with his knees facing me. I gulped hard and slowly drew the weighted chest expander spring from my coveralls. I slipped my knuckle knife on my hand and gripped the taped chest expander end with both gloved hands. I interlocked my fingers and raised my arms slowly and deliberately above my head. I aimed the weighted end carefully, to make the blow as telling as possible. I was only going to get one crack at this - it was all or nothing. I began to fill with panic and dread. I wanted to pull out. Lindsay yawned and lazily opened his eyes. I drove the spring down with all my might and threw my weight forwards at the same time. My boot stamped down hard on Lindsay's throat, and as the chest expander smashed the weight mercilessly into his kneecap he immediately spasmed and tried to twist upwards. I bore down hard on his throat with my boot to stop him writhing and stifle his screams. His pained face was frozen with fear. Lindsay's horror came to a climax when I calmly pulled my face veil down. Lindsay's eyes widened.

"Please don't," came the strained whimper from his restricted throat.

His eyes flashed from my knuckle knife to the weighted spring aimed at his mouth.

"If you want to live, who else?" I asked.

"Hern and Corporal Haling, I didn't want to."

I placed my finger to my mouth.

"If you want to live, keep your eyes locked to the wall and answer a few of my friend's questions."

Lindsay nodded without a word, his panicked eyes becoming transfixed to the wall. I calmly left the room and slipped away while Lindsay pleaded with his non-existing onlooker.

My bluff worked for about 30 seconds. I heard Lindsay's distant screams as I rode off. The pain was terrible, but time was of the essence, so I willed myself on. I threw my clothes and gear down the large, flowing sewer drain and then slipped the bike quietly into the shelter.

The fire door was a swine to close, but it had to be jammed shut, making it unable to be opened. I pushed the locker back up against the fire door and buffed away the slide marks. My stomach and ribs were pulsing with pain from all the effort of pushing the locker back. My head swam with nauseousness as the MRS phone went. The ward door burst open and the lights were quickly turned on.

I squinted my eyes sleepily in a strained fashion, from my bed. The duty medic shot back and answered the phone.

"No, he's here, anyway he can't fucking move, we even have to take him to the toilet. Yeah, no problem, the duty sergeant is here."

I quickly slipped my pyjama bottoms on under the covers and rubbed the last of my sweat off on the sheets. The duty medic came in.

"I'm sorry, MacTavish, but you have to get up and answer some questions."

"Can I no answer them in the morning, staff, my guts are really bad."

"No, now!" the duty sergeant boomed.

The duty sergeant and medic both helped me from my bed into my wheelchair.

"Take it easy, you're hurting him," the medic warned.

Just to make their day I insisted they took me into the toilet cubicle. The MRS security buzzer sounded and the duty medic went and opened the door. Lindsay was carried in wailing like a banshee and cursing like a gypsy.

Military police came streaming into the toilets. The cubicle door flew open.

"Stand up, fucker!" they ordered.

"I can't, you'll need to help me, I can't get up."

"Up now, or you'll spend a lifetime in the hole. Get fucking up!"

"I can't get up, you'll have to help me," I begged.

"He can't move, moron, fucking touch him and you'll be the one in the fucking hole, Okay?" warned the duty medic.

The green-faced military police were forced to wipe my bottom before they wheeled me out of the toilets to face Lindsay.

Lindsay had his leg heavily strapped and packed with ice. He was waiting to go for X-rays. I kicked the proceedings off.

"What the fuck's that bastard doing here?"

This just incensed Lindsay into a white rage as he ranted on incoherently. I sat calmly and waited until he had finished.

"You're no quite the full shilling are you?"

The more I remained calm the wilder Lindsay became. I carefully guarded against looking too smug. I had to remain calm, angry and bemused.

The military police were doing a fine job interrogating me and proving it was impossible for me to have left the building, never mind attack Lindsay. My plan was working so well; the military police were now asking why Lindsay was doing this to me. Lindsay was almost at absolute breaking point. It just needed another little push to send him into barking mad land. I felt honour bound to simply oblige him.

At exactly ten minutes past eleven, a phone call came through to the regimental guardroom. The voice threatened if Lindsay didn't hand the gear over, he would get a lot more than tonight's beating. This message was relayed to the military police and then Corporal Lindsay.

If Lindsay was incensed before, he was now completely deranged. His face only reflected sheer disbelief and insane wonder. Thanks to Cassie's phone call things were going to get a lot worse for Lindsay. I prayed to God that Cassie had got back to our block safely.

The SIB (Special Investigation Branch) officer ordered Lindsay to have blood samples taken before he was allowed to have any treatment.

"I want him kept under close escort and he's to remain in the MRS for questioning," the SIB officer ordered.

At twenty-five minutes past eleven our block swarmed with drug sweeper dogs and military police. The first bunk to be searched was Lindsay's. Wee packs of cocaine and smack were found hidden all over his bunk. He also managed to test positive for cocaine, which shocked the hell out of him considering he had never taken drugs in his life.

By some strange quirk of fate Bear had been first on the scene to help Lindsay. Bear treated our poor wounded lance corporal for shock, making sure he took regular sips from his drugged water bottle whilst the others ran for help.

"Is there any way MacTavish could have left the MRS?" asked the SIB officer.

The duty medic shook his head.

"All the windows are small top windows and all the fire exits are alarmed. There's just no way he could have left."

My prints were taken and my bedside locker was searched. The SIB officer asked for the fastest man in our company and one of his men to run from Lindsay's bunk to the MRS. Cassie ran the time trial and came in at a rather too impressive eight minutes and four seconds. The SIB man came in at nine minutes and five seconds.

"Our man runs for Colchester district," the

SIB officer said, nodding. "Five minutes is the maximum time elapsed from the attack to the duty medic checking on MacTavish. Can't be done, there's no incriminating evidence. Why are you in here? Let me see your injuries."

All the exertion had pumped the bruising up into grotesque swelling.

"Jesus, get him dressed and get him to bed," the SIB officer said, wincing and turning his face away from my injuries.

The duty medic gave him the details of my injuries.

"He can't even walk, Sir, never mind run. Look at that internal swelling and that's just with assisted movement. There is no way he could do it. Lindsay's up to no good!"

The SIB officer nodded and carefully watched me being dressed and lifted into my bed. He stared hard into my eyes searching for guilt. My eyes reflected only clear and genuine pain.

It had been a long night and I welcomed the chance to take some painkillers and rest. Fate delivered me a surprise bonus. Corporal Haling was found stoned in his bunk with shit loads of Afghanistan Black. During his interrogation, Haling had a fit of the munchies and ate the guard's sandwich rations, so he was given the additional charge of stealing another man's rations.

Lance Corporals Lindsay and Haling were both given dishonourable discharges after a year's military prison at Colchester.

That just left Hern, our treacherous so-called roommate, to be taken care of. We were determined that Hern would be made to suffer a long, drawn-out, humiliating dishonourable discharge. Unlike the others, Hern would have to be dealt with by cunning alone. The hunter would now become the hunted. It was Hern's turn to be alone with no chance of redemption.

.

CHAPTER 6

Sergeant Wallace strolled into the MRS with a happy contented smile. He carefully checked we were alone.

"I'll ask you this once. Were they the ones?"

I didn't want to lie to Sergeant Wallace. He had been brilliant. He had visited me most days and had taught me weapon handling while I recuperated. He even had me kitted out from the neighbouring ordinance depot. Not only did he get me uniforms that actually fitted, he also sent over the officers' batmen to make my turnout immaculate. Now I had perfect kit and I knew how to make it sparkle. This was an absolute godsend in training.

I paused for a few seconds and nodded to him.

"I don't know or want to know how it was done! Never ever speak of it again, 'cause that's how they'll nab you, son. Always remember the great salmon; as soon as he opens his mouth he gets hooked," Sergeant Wallace warned.

I owed Sergeant Wallace so much and wanted to tell him the whole truth, but I just nodded my understanding.

"I take it you still want to go on and be a piper in the regiment?"

"More than ever, Sergeant!"

"Good, 'cause there's a few things we've got to get straight."

Sergeant Wallace made it clear to me he did not allow favouritism and it would be business as usual. On the contrary, he told me if I was going to make it he expected me to willingly volunteer for every shite detail going. Rather reluctantly I agreed to my new terms of servitude.

It felt good to leave the MRS and to be reunited with my friends again. The platoon now fondly referred to their pipers as, 'the four must-have-beers'.

We never spoke to the rest of the platoon about our little coup. Most of the platoon still believed Hern had power and influence with the training staff. We had to be very careful and take our time about destroying this myth, if we were to successfully discredit Hern.

Hern had set up and systematically beaten his fellow recruits just to feather his own nest. He was the shallowest and most selfish quisling of all. There was no use in involving the rest of the platoon in Hern's demise; it would only complicate matters and warn Hern off.

I started the ball rolling by eating huge breakfasts and letting rip with brutal flatulence in Hern's bed space just before every room inspection. Of course, I would always thank Hern and explain I didn't want to stink up my own bed space.

"Hern, you and your bed space fucking stink! Parade behind the guard!" Sergeant Wallace barked.

Hern suffered Ralgex in his gas mask filter and repeated orders to those companies who advertise their grotesque plates in the Sunday magazines. These plate companies sent Hern copious supplies of plates depicting Geronimo, Elvis and Lassie. Their sales department hounded Hern remorselessly to settle his spiralling account. Cassie and I would always congratulate Hern on the exquisite brushwork of his latest plate.

Hern would not dare any form of open or physical retaliation. He could tell that we were all more than willing to oblige him. Occasionally he would attempt a stitch up, but people were becoming less scared of him now, so we were always well warned.

I had shrewdly invested in some extreme gay

boys' toys, apparel and some perverse gay S & M mags, which would have made Caligula's toes curl. Sending mail wasn't possible, as all incoming and outgoing mail was opened and read. Cassie's Chelsea friends obliged us by sending the gay S & M mags to Hern - in nice clear plastic envelopes.

The British Army had zero tolerance for drugs, homosexuality and cruelty to women or animals, so if you were a transvestite trying to rape an Alsatian bitch whilst under the influence of LSD your ass was grass. Mind you, murder, GBH and insanity were all seen as highly respectable career-enhancing qualities.

Hern was lucky, as he managed to convince the sergeant major the gay porn was a sick joke, by proving he was seeing a NAAFI girl, but the more times the mags appeared, the more suspicious the training staff became. We needed to distance Hern from the NAAFI girl.

This was MacFadyen's territory. MacFadyen worked his magic on Cora the NAAFI girl, who was only too willing to get rid of Hern. We had to do MacFadyen's duties and kit each night, so he could do the fair Cora. MacFadyen would creep in late at night and smear the scent of his fingers under our noses.

> "MacFadyen! You could at least have the decency to bring the girl's pants home instead of your fucking, Captain Birdseye, nicotined

fish fingers!" Cassie exclaimed indignantly.

"Think yourself lucky. Last night it wasn't his fingers the bastard belted off my nose," I seethed.

Fair Cora turned out to be a spectacular nymphomaniac from Kilmarnock. She completely loved cock and super lager, but not always in that order. MacFadyen had kept his cards close to his chest, making out that Cora was a hard nut to crack, instead of a hard-drinking socialite, with a highly accessible aperture. When Cora found out why we wanted Hern so badly, her feline mind engineered the most sublime coup de grâce for Hern.

Cora told Hern she wanted him back, but she needed him to abuse her with more extreme and adventurous sexual fantasies. Oh, and would it be okay if she brought her extra big chested friend around for some group sex? Amazingly enough, Hern didn't need to be acquiesced too much.

The only drawback to our plan was that we had to suffer Hern's incessant crowing about being a sexual studmuffin. MacFadyen was near breaking point and wanted to strangle Hern. We managed to console MacFadyen by planting some more obscene props to incriminate Hern.

My personal favourite was when I managed to elude Hern's safety checks by securing my masterpiece onto the ceiling above his bed space. My magnum opus consisted of a poster of a naked beefcake with the commandant's head superimposed onto it. I tastefully finished the poster off with a stupendous papier mâché phallus, which made the poster come to life - with a wonderful 3-D effect.

Even the poker-faced and unshakeable Sergeant Wallace finally cracked when he saw the poster during room inspection.

"Let's get something fuckin clear, Hern! The title of Camp Commandant doesn't mean the man's fond of women's clothing, or he wants folk to raid his fuckin chutney locker! Do you fuckin get me, Hen?"

Hern desperately protested his innocence.

"It's fucking him, Sergeant, it's fucking MacTavish!"

"I'm very flattered, but that picture doesn't look anything like me, Sergeant."

Sergeant Wallace looked at my 3-D masterpiece and then nodded.

"Hern! Parade behind the guard for the rest of the week."

"It's not me, Sarg-"

"Sarg! Fucking sarg! There are only two types

of sarg in the British Army, Hern, sau-sage and fuckin' dres-sage! Call me by my fucking rank of sergeant or I'll stick my pace stick up your arse and open it!"

"I doubt it would touch the sides-"

"Shut it, MacTavish, or you'll be parading behind the guard with him!" Sergeant Wallace thundered.

"It's just that I am on guard tonight, Sergeant, and I would feel a whole lot safer if Hern paraded in front of the guard," I reasoned.

Sergeant Wallace ordered me into the toilets. He was no fool; he could tell that I was turning from gamekeeper to poacher. Sergeant Wallace eyed me carefully.

"No fucker likes Hern and no fucker likes a smart-arse. When I bollock someone I do it alone! I don't need anyone else jumping on the bandwagon. Do you understand me, MacTavish? Now get ready for guard."

Tonight was the night; it just needed the wonderfully feckless Cora to give Hern the bait.

Cora was brilliant. She waited when Hern was on his own, just before the guard came out. She opened her coat to reveal her red PVC catsuit to Hern.

"Come in through my window. Read the note on my bed and then join me and Busty Babs in her bed next door," Cora cooed.

Hern nodded with the intoxication of a rabid dog on heat. Cora left her window open and sure enough, Hern crept in. Hern read the note that Cora had left on her bed, obeying it with ecstatic glee. The note had been cleverly composed by Cora to make Hern as rampant as 12 bears.

My Dear Hern Man,

I've bought a little something for you, it's in the wardrobe. Hurry up and get dressed. Leather and PVC send me insane. I can't wait for you in your masterful uniform. Each garment of leather means one more fantasy with Busty Babs and me. Don't forget to bring our toys. We're under the covers next door. Hurry up, we need it now!

Cassie and I waited until Hern had left the room in his leather apparel. We leaped through Cora's window, I snatched the note off the bed and immediately chewed and swallowed it. Cassie turned the volume of his radio to whisper. We pressed our ears to the door and waited with baited breath.

"AAAAAAAAhhhh! What the-"

Cassie and I charged into the corridor. Cassie booted the door open, catapulting Hern across the room and off the far wall. I slapped the lights on and addressed the rather rotund and now completely stunned NAAFI manager, Fat Dave.

"Oh, God! Why Dave - tell me why?"

"I was havin a kip in my bed when this freak tried to stick that fuckin thing up my arse!" Fat Dave yelled.

Hern's panic-filled eyes shot from side to side under his PVC masked helmet. His black PVC waistcoat, pants, thigh-length boots and cape, made him look like a cross between a leather gimp and Batman.

Cassie played the concerned law officer.

"You mean to say you didn't invite him in? You're saying he tried to violate you, Fat Dave?" Cassie asked, nodding sympathetically.

"Well, yeah," Fat Dave agreed, gratefully exonerating himself.

Cassie wheeled around just missing Hern by a hair's breadth with his night stick.

"What's Batman's name?" Cassie asked Fat Dave.

"I don't fuckin know," screamed Fat Dave in desperation.

"I think it's Bruce Wayne," I chipped in.

Cassie nearly corpsed into laughter, but just managed to hold his composure.

"Are you sure you didn't ask him in, Fat Dave?"

"I swear to God a didn't, am not a poof!"

Cassie now focused on Hern.

"Okay, Mr Wayne, put the whip down and step away from that monster of a dildo. Hello Zero this is Alpha patrol, we have a leather intruder called Mr Wayne who's tried to violate Fat Dave, the NAAFI manager - over."

There was a small silence.

"This is Zero! Alpha patrol, is this a fuckin joke?"

"Alpha patrol, no Zero this is not a joke. No duff! Repeat, no duff. This is an emergency! We need an RP escort and the barrack guard at the NAAFI manager's bunk."

"You fucking know who I am," Hern snarled.

Cassie calmly addressed Hern.

"I assure you, Mr Wayne, I'm not in the habit of socialising with homosexual rapists."

Hern lunged at Cassie and tried to smash Cassie with the large two-foot brute of a dildo. Cassie left it to the very last second and smacked Hern in the solar plexus with excruciating force. Hern was winded and flopped helplessly towards Cassie. Cassie grabbed Hern's hand and viciously jerked it towards Fat Dave, as if Hern was trying to stab Fat Dave with the dildo.

"Leave Fat Dave alone, Mr Wayne, David doesn't want you to play with his bottom," Cassie snapped.

Fat Dave, for all his size, shot out from under his duvet and pressed his arse firmly against the wall, like a rocket-propelled limpet.

"For God's sake, Dave, get dressed. You're just teasing Mr Wayne," I ordered.

The room was quickly filled with RPs and the barrack guard. Fat Dave was led away for statements.

"I don't know what I would have done if those boys hadn't heard my screams," whimpered Fat Dave.

The barrack guard now slammed Hern into the wall and unzipped his leather helmet. I used my best Scooby Doo accent.

"Why, it was Hern all the time. So you really

are an Arab's Dagger!"

The army's judicial system is a rather one-sided affair called Orders. You are presumed guilty until proved otherwise. The verdict is already decided along with the sentence. The evidence is given in documentary form with little or no chance to defend yourself. This worked brilliantly in our favour. Both the NAAFI girls were on duty that night, and nobody saw them with Hern. The note could not be found and his track record of gay porn didn't help. He had also been caught by the barrack guard in the out of bounds NAAFI quarters trying to violate Fat Dave.

The documentary evidence from Fat Dave proved damning. I watched Hern being dishonourably discharged. He collected his luggage under escort.

I shouted after him, "Catch you later, Cape Crusader!"

Hatred burned in Hern's eyes as I snogged the glass of the window and waved him goodbye.

It was now coming up to the eleventh week, which meant leave was due in two weeks. Out of the original 320 we were now down to ninety. Sergeant Wallace's policy of making me volunteer for every shite duty was starting to pay off.

I made sure I carried all the ludicrously heavy anti-tank equipment, the gun and the radio. I went first on every confidence course, wall and rope drill. My lack of height was starting to lose its stigma.

MacFadyen and Cassie would also delegate me, much to the rest of the platoon's amusement. They would usually employ an over-exaggerated Dickensian style.

"Oh, Sergeant, this seems a positively sublimely perfect task for Tiny Tim MacTavish. I happen to know he would relish the challenge of carrying the gun and the radio."

I would nod with fervent enthusiasm.

"Please, Sergeant Wallace, let me carry the gun and radio, please. I feel positively guilty just running in my normal 30 pounds of webbing."

The rest of the squad would join in.

"Oh, go on, Sergeant. We don't mind - honest to Betsy, we don't."

Sergeant Wallace would complete the cycle by adopting the persona of a Dickensian benefactor.

"Capital idea, young MacTavish. Now you enjoy your run with the gun and the radio, mi young scallywag."

The remaining 90 of us were now given the regiment's training name of Celt Platoon. Celt Platoon was responsible for filling the regiment's shortfall each year. It was the only bloodline to the regiment and that's why it would only accept the very best.

Many different units used the divisional training camp. In the beginning we felt slighted, knowing we ran farther, faster and worked harder than any other platoon, but through time we began to welcome our hellish training and tougher targets. Heads would turn and all would stop as Celt Platoon ran or marched by. It was a great feeling and it instilled incredible pride and effort within us.

At the back of all our minds was the terrible knowledge that a further 60 would not make it. It was a constant war of physical stamina and attrition against the training staff and us. It was all or nothing and nothing else mattered. We had given and taken so much, none of us wanted it to amount to a lifelong defeat. When someone finally cracked or someone else was forced out, your heart went out to them but, deep down, you were relieved it wasn't you.

There were no farewells to any recruits who cracked or failed, as all failed recruits were immediately separated from the platoon and discharged. This process was swiftly administered with brutal efficiency.

Before we could go on leave or have the option

of returning, we had to pass the vast array of weapon and shooting tests. I was fairly confident I would pass, as it was the one area of soldiering where I displayed a natural aptitude. I loved target shooting no matter what the weather, and thanks to Sergeant Wallace's efforts whilst I was in hospital, my weapon handling skills were slick and confident.

Most folk were panicking over the weapons and shooting tests. Any spare time I had was spent drilling Bear, Cassie and MacFadyen on their weapon handling. MacFadyen and Cassie were certs to pass, but big old Bear was struggling.

I could see the comical looks of superiority on Cassie and Fadge's faces at Bear's awkwardness.

"Ff-fuckin shite! P-p-poofs!" growled Bear.

"Well, you can't argue with that," Cassie nodded.

Even the disgruntled Bear managed to stop frowning and crack a smile.

Desperation began to set in as time marched on. All the weapons had been signed in and Bear was still hopeless. His panic and desperation made it impossible for Bear to progress. Bear and me had been through thick and thin and I was determined I wasn't going to lose my best friend because of a few weapons tests. I used posters and made weapon replicas from broom shafts, cartons and tape. Bear was becoming more and more frustrated with failure staring him in the face.

I told Fadge and Cassie to go to bed, so they were fresh for the morning. I needed time with Bear on his own, so he could concentrate. Fadge and Cassie understood and reluctantly left us to it. I gave Bear a break and asked him to bring some brews in.

"It's me, Bear, I've figured it out where I'm going wrong, it's no you – it's me. I'm thick. I promise you'll get it after we've had our tea."

Bear's eyes began to flicker with a ray of hope. The truth was I had no answer or time to get the answer. Bear was so naturally brilliant it never occurred to either of us that some basic weapon skills could cause him so many problems, then suddenly the light began to dawn upon me. Bear's whole life had been dedicated to the pursuit of musical perfection. I quickly referred to all the working parts as musical terms and piping parts. Using familiar musical terms instantly relaxed Bear the transformation was amazing and instant. Bear's weapon drills became smoother and slicker, and he even started to show off. At that point I knew he was back on form. He overcame every testing trick I could throw at him with effortless glee. He was ready and more importantly, he knew it.

It was half three when Bear and I finished, and

it would be gone half four by the time we finished doing our kit. This meant we would only have two hours' sleep before our weapon and range tests.

We trudged wearily into our room to begrudgingly start our kit, but to our joy we found it all immaculately pressed and polished ready for muster parade. It was a welcomed act of kindness from two tartan piping elves who were pretending to be asleep. Bear swept Fadge and his mattress up in one effortless single movement. Bear was about to whisper his thanks into Fadge's ear when his Tourette's kicked in.

"W-w-wanker! Wanker! W-w-wanker!"
Bear roared into poor Fadge's ear.

Fadge didn't stir at all and carried on pretending to be asleep. With comic genius Fadge waited for the laughter to die down, and yawned:

"Night, Mum."

Breakfast came and went in a blur as we were marched at the double to the testing huts. We arrived just before seven and the tests weren't due to start until half eight. We sat on the hut's cold stone floor. Most of us obeyed the soldier's first law and started to kip straight away.

The soldier's first law was all about strength conservation; allowing you to fight through, long arduous campaigns. Quite simply, the soldier's first law stated, 'Don't run when you can walk, don't walk when you can stand, don't stand when you can sit, don't sit when you can lie down and don't lie down when you can sleep'.

I could never quite come to grips with how the army prioritised time. The army specialised in rushing you around at ungodly hours of the morning, just to make you wait around interminably for the rest of the day. I would estimate that at least half a soldier's life is spent queuing or waiting.

I looked up from my nap and saw Horatio Blake standing rigidly to attention with a look of total dejection in his eyes.

"You okay, young Hornblower?" I asked.

Horatio was ordered to get his eyes front and I was ordered to shut up. Horatio should have gone to Sandhurst or at least some academic branch of the army. Horatio hardly ever spoke, but when he did, you listened. He was six feet seven and painfully thin with small National Health glasses and an almost corpse-like pallor. Although he kept himself to himself he was well liked. This was mainly due to him going along with the platoon's obsession that he looked like his namesake, Blakie, of On the Buses. Horatio had even grown a small one-inch moustache, and when he wore his forage cap and No. 2 dress mac, the resemblance was priceless.

Fadge whispered that Horatio had failed his weapon test and was awaiting a dreaded resit. Resits were dreaded, as they were much harder to pass than the original test, and they were your last and only chance to redeem yourself.

I recited the weapon drills and stoppages over and over in my mind until I heard my name being called.

"MacTavish – in now!"

I pulled my feet in and stood at the door awaiting permission to enter.

"Aw right, stand at ease and relax, MacTavish, just toss us that weapon and we can get started."

I quickly thought of Horatio and did anything but relax, as this was the ideal opportunity for the regiment to get rid of their undesired piping midget.

The rifle had a mag on, so I let my fingers feel the blind side of the rifle. The safety catch was off. I quickly snapped it on, removed the mag and cleared the weapon. The bullet spat onto the floor. I picked up the bullet, mag and rifle, and presented the open breach to the sergeant.

"Clear," came the grudging reply.

From then on I was a paragon of musketry excellence, much to the annoyance of the testing sergeant. I went from room to room until I had successfully completed all my tests. After two hours of solid, mind-numbing weapon tests I was finally ushered outside into the bright sunshine and ordered to wait. I sat on my webbing and prayed that Bear, Cassie and Fadge would pass.

One by one they trooped out and we rejoiced in each other's success. We fell asleep on our webbing in the warm summer sun. We were awakened by the sound of the failures being doubled away. There were about ten failures - at the head of them was the dejected figure of Horatio Blake. The failures would now be separated from the platoon to await their discharge. We nodded our brief farewells with a strange mixture of distraught relief and pity. We fell into our squad positions, making the necessary changes because of our diminished numbers. We were then marched off onto the ranges for our APWT (Annual Personal Weapons Test).

The test shoots were split into two sections. The first part consisted of hitting 100 electrical flip targets and the second part was 20 advance-to-contact targets. We were allocated 120 rounds and five magazines, which held 20 rounds each. This was a very clever test as it meant you had to hit your targets, count your shots and reload magazines between targets.

Surprisingly enough, this demanding test was passed by the whole platoon.

Electronically marked targets fall when hit and have some delightful quirks for a crafty shot. If you aimed low, your bullet would either strike the bottom of the target or cause a fan of gravel to strike the target, which the computer would blindly record as a hit. The one, two and 300-metre targets were spaced across the full width of your firing lane. This was to stop the same bullet hitting targets at different ranges. However, it was possible to angle your shot to hit two targets with a single shot, which allowed you extra shots if you missed. These well-noted quirks accounted for our platoon's high, first time pass rate.

We also won the inter-platoon competition with a perfect score of 901, which included the anti-tank target. The anti-tank weapon was the 84mm Karl Gustov, which fired high explosive anti-tank shells. A special shell was developed to fire sub-calibre bullets for range purposes. It was notoriously hard to use and completely inaccurate at long ranges. The anti-tank teams were given four sub-calibre rounds to try and hit the tank target from the 300-metre point. The anti-tank score was usually the deciding factor in range competitions.

Every time I managed to hit two targets with a single bullet the tank target divinely received a perfect hit. Our tank target managed to score four perfect hits without the anti-tank gun being fired!

Our victory was made all the sweeter when our closest rivals were ludicrously caught cheating. They had placed their worst shot in the corner of the range woods, only 150 metres from his targets. He was such a bad shot he accidentally managed to shoot the safety Land Rover's windscreen out. Their myopic Daniel Boon stumbled out of the woods at the end of the shoot and calmly asked the range warden if he had hit anything. The range warden nodded slowly and drove him off to the guardroom - in his new alfresco Land Rover.

It had been a great day; we had passed our weapon tests and won the inter-platoon shooting competition. We were celebrating in style with some of my bathtub gin. I wandered into the toilets to get the last few bottles of gin from under the bath. All of a sudden I heard wild thrashing, like a door being repeatedly kicked in. I locked the bath cubicle and re-hid the bottles by re-screwing the bath panel back on. The thuds gradually stopped.

I gingerly crept out of the bath cubicle and began to advance slowly towards from where the thuds had come. I usually have a cool head, but the sight before me chilled my heart. Horatio's lifeless body swung from the shower head - he had used his rifle sling to hang himself. I flung my arms around his legs and took his weight. I tried and tried to take him down from the shower head, but I couldn't gain enough height to release him. I screamed and screamed for help, as I desperately fought to keep Horatio alive.

My screams and calls for help were eventually heard, but for poor Horatio it was too little, too late. We lifted the limp dead body of Horatio and laid him down on the impersonal stone floor. His face was contorted with desperation. I closed Horatio's eyelids to cover his haunting eyes, which reflected the tragic circumstances of his lonely death.

The platoon packed into the toilets, nobody spoke, we just gawked in shock and disbelief. Eventually the barrack guard filtered in and hurriedly took the body of poor Horatio away. The area was sealed and the SIB were called. We were thoroughly briefed and given strict orders never to speak of the incident again; anyone who breached the order would be jailed and discharged. We decided to say goodbye to Horatio at church parade, in our own way.

Church parades were compulsory, as in training no day was a day off. However, on Sundays we were given the welcomed luxury of finishing at one o'clock. The job of giving the Bible reading was voluntary, but it was so dreaded it was usually imposed as a form of punishment.

I volunteered to read the passage and promised the platoon I would give Horatio a fitting farewell straight after my reading. I only hoped that I wouldn't break down, or ruin the occasion.

Church parades were usually boring, highly regimental and seldom religious. For a start the regiment's religious bigotry would come to the fore.

"All those lesser mortals who don't belong to the superior one and only Church of Scotland, one pace forwards. RCs, you rat catchin fuckers, fuck off to your chapel, you demonic fucks!"

This was usually greeted with hearty cheers and gleeful acceptance from the dozen or so Roman Catholics, which included Bear. The army kept a strange control of its religious sectarianism by openly ridiculing its own bigotry.

On church parades you halted silently, paused two three, removed your headdress and held it over your heart, marching silently into the church without any arm swinging. You then marked time in the pew until the pews were filled, then a parade sergeant would signal a halt and seat the pew.

On one legendary church parade, a tired recruit had forgotten to remove his headdress in church. This was noticed by a rather over-excited cockney parade sergeant. Amidst the hallowed silence of the vast military church, came the cockney sergeant's bludgeoning rebuke.

"You! Get your 'at off in the 'ouse of the lo'd, Caaaannnnt!"

This order reached its full hilarious climax when most of the wives immediately obeyed the order by removing their hats.

Sunday came all too quickly and the dreaded church parade with it. I read the reading and then cleared my throat and addressed the congregation in a loud clear voice.

"'Then out spake brave Horatius,

The Captain of the gate:

To every man upon this earth

Death cometh soon or late.

And how can a man die better

Than facing the fearful odds,

For the ashes of his fathers

And the temple of his gods'."

I waited to be marched to jail, but nothing happened, so I left the lectern and took my seat. I was oblivious to the pats on the back and the handshakes. I was filled with nauseating dread about my intended fate.

After the service I was escorted to the commandant. He was a tall, athletic Irishman with an impeccably groomed handlebar moustache. His perfectly tailored pinstripe suit told you at one glance he was an officer and a gentleman.

"Thank you, Sergeant, no need for cuffs, I'll take it from here."

The commandant waited until the sergeant left and gave me a knowing wink.

"A beautiful recitation, MacTavish, a trifle reckless though. Where did you learn it?" the commandant asked.

"My father used to recite 'The Last Lays of Rome' and my old headmaster gave me Macaulay's Essays as a leaving present, Sir, and I couldn't think of a better epitaph for a soldier, Sir."

The commandant nodded.

"You won't be going to jail, MacTavish, only because you showed genuine discretion. Come on, follow me to the officers' mess."

When we arrived at the officers' mess the commandant gave me a mess chit and told me to collect a couple of crates of beer from the bar.

"Discretion is the better part of valour - and it saves 252 action, MacTavish," said the commandant with a warm chuckle.

The army's law system of charge and punishment was called 252 action. It was the commandant's way of telling us to have the beer discreetly without any riotous aftermath. I thanked the commandant and nodded my understanding. Horatio was sent off in true Celt style; celebrating his life and not mourning his loss.

One week and our first leave would be in sight. I mistakenly thought no more tests, no more problems. I wrote Mum a letter telling her I had passed all my weapon tests and would soon be home for three weeks' leave. I begged her in the letter to give me minuscule portions of food, so I wouldn't have to run the food off, but as I penned the letter I could feel the scones spot-welding themselves to my ribs.

It was a bright sunny morning and the first time we had been allowed onto the main drill square, 'The Golden Acre'. Our chests were puffed out to their maximum with our heads were held high as our arms swung shoulder high with iron flesh rigidity. Everybody had put in the extra effort; our kit gleamed and our eyes shone with pride and superiority. We halted magnificently and left turned with rapid crack precision. I was just savouring how magnificent we all looked when it happened.

The RSM had just finished his 'what not to do on leave' speech, when the RSM smiled an evil smile - an evil, evil smile. He unbuttoned his breast pocket and unfolded a small blue piece of writing paper.

"We have a letter; a letter from Mrs MacTavish."

Oh God no, maybe just maybe it was another Mrs MacTavish.

"Mrs MacTavish from Ayrshire!"

Well, it was still a pretty common name in Ayrshire.

"It's about oor Hector, Junior Piper Hector MacTavish."

"Aaaaah shite!"

"Get your fucking arse oot here, oor Hector!" the RSM ordered.

It was bad enough constantly being at war with the training staff without having my own mum handing them the nails to crucify me. My wee moment of being a highly trained, lean mean killing machine - just vanished. I halted immaculately and stared at the RSM with a look of a faithful spaniel about to be shot. The RSM's eyes had the look of a killer shark; expressionless and incapable of mercy or clemency. The RSM read my thoughts and body language.

"No chitty - no pity!"

It was an old army adage used against malingerers, but it had been beautifully levelled at my imminent demise. The drill square suddenly turned into an amphitheatre with the gladiatorial crowds baying for blood - my bloody blood.

"About turn," the RSM ordered, "and face your public, oor Hector."

The RSM allowed me to sweat on the rack of the crowds' jeers before he began his merciless monologue.

"Even the address is testament to the pedigree of this trained Scottish assassin, for oor Hector lives in a quarry, Dundonald Quarry, a known breeding ground and home of this Caledonian killer."

The laughter and jeers were deafening and never-ending. The RSM had them all in the palm of his hand and they were loving every minute of it. Even in humour he commanded their respect and laughter.

Eventually the cheering and laughter began to die down. I just wanted the ground to swallow me up, or for someone to have the decency to shoot me and put me out of my misery. I smiled, knowing that every word of my mother's letter was about to mercilessly lash me to death with untold embarrassment.

The RSM cocked his head and winked at me.

"I will now read the letter!"

Unbridled cheers rang out across the square.

"Dear Sir,

Oor Hector has just turned 16 and he's an awfy, awfy boy. He was bad enough as a wee boy with knives, catapults and a bow. I cannae help but think how dangerous it would be to let him play with real guns.

Yours faithfully

Mrs Mary MacTavish

When you go to war MacTavish, you will find an enemy with a similar letter from his mum, and you awfy, awfy boys can beat the awfy, awfy shite out of each other with broom poles. Now get off my fucking square!"

I've often reflected that mums and not their sons should settle wars. Mums wouldn't kill, they'd just have vicious baking competitions against each other. God help any nation who took on Scotland's feminine SAS!

.

CHAPTER 7

We had survived seven months of hell and passed all our drill, weapon, navigation, tactics, signals, NBC and first aid tests. Our relentless and gruelling regime had ground the platoon down to 50 men. Only five more months with one more battle camp and we had done it!

For the last two months of basic training all pipers are sent to the Regimental Piping School to rejuvenate their playing and band drills. This meant we would be free from the training staff's autonomy two months before our passing out parade. This fact had not escaped the training staff's notice. The instructors were determined that only Bear and Fadge would hold the coveted rank of 'Piper'.

I was still considered genetically inferior as I was still five inches under the regiment's six-feet height restriction. Sergeant Wallace's master strategy of volunteering myself for anything naff or arduous had earned me some much-needed grace and favour, but there were still many who thought I had outstayed my welcome.

Cassie's obstinate willingness to express his unflinching principles meant he was at constant odds with the training staff. Cassie was a defiant symbol, which the training staff were determined to crush. They made sure the PTIs (Physical Training Instructors) remorselessly hounded Cassie with physical beastings, which would have finished any of us off. We were all super fit and in peak condition, but Cassie was bloody super-hero fit. It gradually began to dawn on the training staff that normal physical beastings might not work on this remarkably fit and principled young Scot.

Cassie would always position himself at the back of the squad during platoon runs. He would run up and down the line helping the weaker runners in the platoon. Cassie would carry their kit and sometimes even the runner. He was truly incredible.

It was a scorching hot day and we were on the most draconian of punishment runs. The PTIs had banned Cassie from helping anyone. The bastards wanted to make us crawl.

The PTIs were forcing us to run in full NBC (Nuclear, Biological and Chemical) suits and gas masks. NBC suits are made of fabric lined with charcoal, to protect soldiers in nuclear, biological and chemical environments. They do not allow air in or out, which generates terrific body heat and sweating. The NBC suits and gas masks made the run lethally intense. Four runners had collapsed and were now fighting for their lives in the med centre. The med staff fought to bring the recruits' temperatures down and rehydrate their tortured and parched bodies.

We were remorselessly driven on by the PTIs for a further two miles and were now dangerously beyond all human limits of endurance. We lost control of our bodily functions, with desensitised urinating and defecation. Brutish hyperventilating took hold of our souls. We were now frying our own bodies and entering into a fatal death cycle.

Our minds became numb and deaf to the cries from our bodies to stop. Spluttered gagging and choking from the sweat in our gas mask chin cups occasionally tortured us back into our hellish reality. Another mile was added on to the run if you stopped, or lifted your gas mask. Nobody wanted the honour of prolonging this insane hell or killing someone.

Eventually the punishment run was abruptly halted when the PTIs panicked at the rapid collapse of bodies fighting for air. Most of us were numbed with senseless exhaustion or thanking God the hell had ended. We ripped our gas masks off. Our starved lungs gulped down the unrestricted air like marooned fish on a riverbank.

The PTIs were ranting on how next time they would kill us and that this had better be a lesson well learned, when they noticed Cassie standing defiantly to attention with his gas mask still on.

"You get your fucking mask off, prick!" the PTI screamed, ripping off Cassie's gas mask.

Cassie looked him square in the eyes and calmly stated, "If it was a punishment run, why not tell us why we are being punished, staff?"

The PTI smashed Cassie hard in the guts. Cassie hardly flinched and calmly repeated his question.

"Mask up, shithead," said the SMI (Sergeant Major Instructing).

"Don't," the PTIs warned, "he's mad!"

Cassie smiled and winked at the SMI, knowing he would have to be punished without mercy.

"You won't be wearing a gas mask, Sir?" Cassie asked. It was a direct taunt and challenge to the SMI.

"No, I won't, shithead," the SMI snarled.

The PTIs urged the SMI to stop, but he ignored all their warnings, after all he was the sergeant major in charge of physical instruction, and who the hell was this sprog to challenge his authority?

Cassie had run six miles in full marching order

(that's 80 pounds consisting of webbing, rifle, ammunition and field pack) in his NBC suit with a gas mask on. The SMI had barely jogged three miles in just his vest and shorts.

"Is it up and down Heartbreak or on the flat, Sir?" Cassie enquired.

This was insane; Cassie was virtually asking to be run up the hell of all hills.

"Up Heartbreak, shithead, until you're a fucking puddle, now mask up!"

Cassie now played his masterly trump card. Instead of letting the SMI dictate the pace and beast him, Cassie exploded like a panther out of starting blocks, making it a race. He was incredible! The SMI was left in the wake of Cassie's blistering and relentless pace. The cheers of the platoon were quickly quelled when PTIs threatened to mask us up again.

Heartbreak Hill and the inclined run up to it was one mile long with a one in five gradient of hell. The first 300 yards were sand, followed by 400 yards of shingle, followed by leg sapping mud. Cassie bounded up Heartbreak as if he was rocket propelled. The total return circuit came to two miles.

Cassie sprinted over the line to tumultuous cheers. When the SMI eventually stumbled over the line, he beheld the gas-masked figure of Cassie standing resolutely to attention. The crowd grew as more and more people came to watch the incredible 'Flying Scotsman'.

They gave Cassie press-ups and sit-ups to tire him out between each race, but it made no difference. Cassie resoundingly thrashed the SMI every time. Hell, they even tried different PTIs, but nothing could defeat our Cassie.

Cassie had run an inhuman 14 miles in blistering heat, carrying 80 pounds in his NBC suit and gas mask.

"You're not all there, Drummond, are you?" the SMI snarled.

"No, not entirely, Sir!" came the muffled shout from Cassie's misted and heaving gas mask.

Cassie jogged away casually, but he was fatally dehydrated and delirious. He stubbornly refused to go to the med centre.

"If I go, they win - and they will break me!"

It took all three of us to overpower Cassie and his deliriousness. We threw him into a bath of cold water and ice. It took all Bear's incredible strength to keep Cassie pinned in the bath. Desperate, blood-curdling minutes seemed to last forever until Cassie finally relented from exhaustion. I held a block of ice against the back of his neck and mopped his tortured face. Fadge forced honey and salted orange juice down his throat to rehydrate him, while Bear held him fast by straddling him in the bath. We watched over him, caring - and praying.

We wanted to take Cassie to hospital, but he was right; if we had taken him to the MRS, the training staff would know he was broken and they'd have finished him off with sadistic fury.

At zero three thirty hours, Cassie's eyes opened. He stared at me for awhile then a roguish smile appeared.

"No med centre, MacTavish?"

I shook my head.

"No med centre, Drummond."

Cassie had almost run himself to death, but his principles and vanity were still firmly intact.

Cassie closed his eyes.

"Make sure I'm first out for morning muster parade," he whispered. "I want the bastards to know I'm unbowed."

Cassie stood defiantly to attention for morning muster parade. His turnout was immaculate and his kit gleamed with unrepentant pride. The moment was made all the sweeter when the platoon spied the SMI limping sheepishly towards the medical centre.

Sergeant Wallace smiled.

"A mere mortal, Drummond, a mere mortal!"

The training staff had earmarked ten of us for definite discharge and a further 20 for crippling selection. The final battle camp was the means by which the training staff would force the excess recruits' discharge.

The four-tonner lorries coughed their way along the never-ending road to battle camp. Nobody spoke for we were all painfully aware that battle camp was going to be the hell of all hells. The four of us had made a pact to dedicate our actions for our own personal survival. This was an intelligent decision as it was almost certain we were going to be split up and pitted against each other. It was vital we did not let our friendship be used as the means of our own destruction.

The unmistakable dreaded features of the exercise area began to come into view. British MOD exercise properties have a unique, bleak godforsaken quality. They are usually vast desolate areas, peppered with vast pine forests containing insects that can be classed as livestock. Wind, rain and sleet are always present to lash the British soldier.

The four-tonner lorries lurched to a stop. The 50-strong platoon was formed up and then split into three groups. One group was made up of recruits whom the regiment more or less wanted. The remaining two groups consisted of maybes and undesirables. Cassie and I were in the undesirables. Fadge and Bear were in the desirable group. Anything went here, as this was the final sift. It was going to be four weeks of hard, dog-eat-dog exercise.

We were being pitched against some of the regiment's top soldiers and the training staff. For the first three weeks we were subjected to constant attacks, route marches and digging in. The name of the game was survival and the secret to surviving was rest. We were constantly on the go with very little food or rest. Any chance to sleep was grabbed with yearning arms. Defiant souls fell by the wayside as their last hopes were ground into failure.

The training staff had selected sleep deprivation as their way of forcing my discharge. Sleep deprivation is a slow, painful leeching torture, which makes even the simplest of tasks torturous. Your will and wits cease to exist with horrific fatal certainty.

Some of the platoon had been negligently issued live rounds instead of blanks. Their tired minds and inexperienced fingers loaded their deadly magazines.

Blanks bullets are very similar to live bullets except they have pinched tips instead of the copper bullet tips. Blanks let out an explosion to simulate live firing. The barrels of the rifles are plugged when firing blanks, which concentrates the small explosive gases of the blank rounds and allows them to re-cock the breach for firing. The temporary metal barrel plugs are known as BFAs (Blank Firing Attachments).

We now had the deadly cocktail of tired inexperienced recruits with live bullets and plugged rifle barrels. The stage was now set for a horrific bloodbath. A recruit called MacMann had been toying with the trigger and safety catch, out of boredom, on the night patrol. MacMann negligently discharged his weapon. The barrel splintered, the BFA shot off and split a tree.

A few recruits panicked and returned fire, as they thought they were under attack. Streaks of yellow and orange flashes pierced the jet-black night with deafening explosions.

"Cease fire, you fuckers, cease fire!"

Amazingly enough nobody was injured, but heads had to roll. MacMann and the other seven who had returned fire were mercilessly beasted and discharged. The drunken sergeant who had issued the live ammunition in the first place got off Scot-free. Recruit negligence was listed as the cause of the catastrophic error, with sleep deprivation and drunkenness being conveniently omitted. After the almost fatal night patrol, we were re-formed to help make a company defensive position. This meant more back-breaking and exhaustive digging in.

For the first time on exercise I got a fantastic break by being teamed up with Boris. Boris was an enormous South African of Scottish descent. He had been a gravedigger before he joined up. The man was a human JCB. The earth seemed to jump on Boris's shovel and throw itself out of the trench in no time.

I was close to breaking through lack of sleep.

"They've really been fucking you bad, Hector," said Boris.

I nodded, too tired to even answer or think of an answer. Boris proudly nodded to the finished trench. We jumped down into the trench with our webbing and rifles. I was just about to savour some much-needed sleep when I was ordered out of the trench.

"MacTavish, go and join Morrison. Youse two can have the honour of digging the command trench."

I was now devoid of all hope - I couldn't go on much longer. I grabbed my trench shovel and trudged wearily to the command post area. I stared at the vast area of the command trench, which had been marked out with white mine-tape.

A command trench is an enormous excavation with various trenches shooting off the main command tunnel. It would take five fresh men a day to dig a command trench. Asking two exhausted wrecks to dig a command trench was like asking us, to empty Loch Lomond with teaspoons.

I looked at what was left of Morrison. He resembled a grotesque figure of death. Even cam cream couldn't hide his gaunt drained pallor. I laughed at his shocked horror when he saw my face, and wondered if I could possibly look worse than he did.

My punishment of being made to work while others slept was now par for the course. We dug on, shovel after shovel, stupefied by exhaustion and the unforgiving sun. The day painfully crawled into interminable night. We were given no rest or rations, and knew if we stopped we were out.

"Remember, if the trench is not finished by daybreak you're out, so give up now and get some rest. If the shovel sounds stop, it's bye-bye too," the corporal mocked as he left.

Morrison and I struggled on with grim determination, but we both knew we couldn't last much longer. Now, I don't know if it was exhaustion or the hellish situation that made Morrison come up with his insane idea - or desperation that made me listen to him.

"Here's how we'll do it," Morrison began. "We'll sit at opposite corners of the trench and take our steel helmets off. As soon as one of us goes to sleep, the other'll smack him on the head wi his trench shovel."

Morrison could see that I was struggling to see the positive benefits of his master stratagem.

"Look, the guy who gets hit with the shovel gets evacuated from the exercise with a couple of days' rest or a battle camp pass, and the guy who twats him with the shovel will be stopped from digging in. Are you in?"

I was finished, and just nodded my agreement to Morrison. We took opposite corners of the trench, removed our steel helmets and waited. After a couple of uneasy minutes' silence I wanted to call the whole thing off when I heard the faint snores from Morrison. There was about a 20-second lull before the dull 'dunnng' rang out from the flat of shovel. My face was immediately splattered in Morrison's blood and scalp as blood fountained from the top of his head.

"Fuck, I've killed him! Sergeant, sergeant! Medic, medic!"

I whipped my field dressing out and tried to

stem the bleeding with direct pressure, as Morrison convulsed in my arms.

The training staff were panicking; this was yet another blunder on an already chequered battle camp.

"How the fuck did this happen?"

"It was dark, Sergeant, he walked by me when I was hacking a root out."

Morrison was hurriedly stretchered onto the back of a four-tonner. Christ, what if I had turned Morrison into a vegetable? What if I had killed him – God, what had I done?

As the four-tonner pulled away I wondered whether I would be charged with manslaughter or murder when Morrison's hand popped out of the four-tonner's gun port. Morrison gave me a V for victory, before turning his hand to give me the fingers.

"You dickhead! Stop digging in and go and join Boris!" the corporal snarled.

I was so tired I just collapsed into the trench and slept where I fell. For the first time in four days I was allowed to sleep. My mind tumbled into a deep unquenchable unconsciousness.

I was awakened at four o'clock to take my turn on the gun to guard the company position. I had been given an incredible, straight 12-hours' sleep. I was still shattered when I took over the gun, but my mind was a lot more alert. As my mind sharpened, I realised my 12 hours of uninterrupted sleep hadn't been an act of generosity. They had deliberately placed me on the gun at stand-to. Stand-to is the time just before dawn when soldiers silently take up their defensive positions, as this is the usual time for enemy attacks. Stand-down is when soldiers quickly prepare for dawn inspection. You only had half an hour to quickly re-clean your weapons, wash, shave, clean your boots, change your socks and apply fresh cam cream. If you failed dawn inspection you were out. By letting me sleep 12 hours and placing me on the gun during stand-to and stand-down, they had ensured I would fail the dawn inspection. If I wanted to survive I would have to gamble all, and break the sacred vigil of guarding the company. If they were watching me I was a dead man.

I stripped and cleaned my rifle with trembling guilt until it was spotless. I had no water and was forced to wash my face with bracken and spit. I hacked into my raw face with a painful dry shave, reapplied my cam cream and cleaned my boots. I packed my gear into my webbing with panicked haste, and took hold of the gun knowing I had just placed my own personal survival above the lives of the company. I had become the lowest of the low.

I had very little time to feel guilty, as the training staff were now waking up the company for stand-to. Stand-to was silently signaled. Everybody scanned their arcs of fire with their weapons at the ready.

Half an hour after daybreak everybody was stood-down. The company flew into a hive of activity preparing for the dawn inspection. I was under constant scrutiny. I could feel the vengeful anticipation of the training staff's eyes. They were longing for the chance to fail me.

I was relieved from the gun and called over first for the dawn inspection. I could see the hatred in their faces when they saw my freshly applied cam cream and shaved face.

"Show me your fucking weapon!" the sergeant ordered.

My rifle was as clean as a whistle, never mind battle clean. The sergeant repeatedly inspected my weapon. His livid face told me I'd passed.

"When did you clean your kit, MacTavish?"

"Before I went to sleep, Sergeant," I answered, trying to look dutiful and puzzled.

After a long silence the inspecting sergeant ordered me to go and get my breakfast. For the first time in three weeks I received hot rations. After breakfast I powdered my feet and put on fresh socks.

I leaned back on my webbing and savoured my black mug of hot army tea.

It never ceases to amaze me at the metamorphic powers of fresh socks, powdered feet and a drink of hot tea. This strange little comfort can turn a beaten man into a victorious soldier. A good soldier never accepts de-feet, but he does appreciate comfortable ones in his boots.

A four-tonner lorry containing the desirables pulled up. Bear and Fadge ran over.

"Well, you look hellish, but what's new?" Fadge chirped.

I was too tired to answer or avoid Bear's vertebrate-popping embrace.

"Have you seen Cassie?" Fadge asked.

I shook my head.

"Not for two days. He's on permanent beat-up runs. Not even Cassie can take that!"

The others nodded back in silent agreement. The distant whirr of the beat-up Land Rover made its way to the company rendezvous. The company fell to a deathly silent hush. Five of the missing six crawled from the Rover. They were broken and ready for discharge.

As the Land Rover dust settled there came a terrific roar from the platoon. Over the hill came the silhouette of a lone runner, unbroken, but staggering from exhaustion, his rifle still defiantly held correctly in the shoulder.

Cassie stumbled into line with the Land Rover. He looked like a ghost of a man. The poor wretch marked time at the double for five minutes until they halted him.

Cassie was eventually dismissed after another fruitless attempt by the training staff to get rid of him. We propped Cassie against a tree and gave him water. When Cassie was properly revived, I handed him a mess tin of breakfast and a mug of tea.

"Tardiness is not a virtue of today's modern army, Drummond," I teased.

"MacTavish, you lowland whore. I hear you're now in the business of removing feline genitalia. Having poor Morrison spayed, how perfectly wicked," Cassie chuckled.

I nodded, took Cassie's rifle from him and gave it a good clean while he ate his breakfast.

We now had eight hours to prepare for the last escape and evasion part of the exercise. This final stage meant living off the land for four days and marching to a given destination without capture. We would be hunted by foot patrols and Land Rovers. If you were caught, you were subjected to a type of torture that you would have gladly inflicted upon any MP or estate agent. Our game plan was simple - we were going to cheat. This had two distinct advantages of gaining us eight hours' sleep and a realistic chance of surviving.

Our detailed preparation and planning now started to pay off. While all the other members of the platoon ran about like headless chickens preparing their equipment and replenishing their webbing with fresh rations, we calmly cleaned our weapons and enjoyed eight hours of glorious uninterrupted sleep. For the first time in three weeks I felt refreshed and ready to go. I smiled at the others optimistically preparing their webbing.

We knew we would be stripped of all webbing and stores. That's why the four of us had taken time to secrete small, but well thought out, survival stores into our uniform before we had even set off for battle camp.

The adrenaline and our nerves began to take hold. This was the training staff's last chance to get rid of us, so it was do or die. Escape and evasions were my area of expertise. I had picked up some cracking tips from the troops who had hidden in our garden sheds over the years. We kept our preparation and knowledge a secret to stop our precious advantage being squandered and lost.

We were going to work as a four-man group until the final assault, but after that it was every man for himself. As individuals our stores were scant, but as a group we possessed a clever list of equipment.

Our last meal arrived in large, square Norwegian containers. As they were cracked open, hot steam wafted the sweet aroma of army compo; chicken curry and boiled rice. Contrary to popular belief, army compo or 24-hour ration packs are bloody good eating. Compo ration packs are the food issued to soldiers when they are in the field. We greedily crammed in as much as we could, as we knew it might be our last meal for four days. Bear picked the Norwegian container up and quaffed the last dregs of the curry before being beaten off with an angry cook's ladle.

After our meal we were ordered to stack our webbing on the four-tonner and sign our weapons in. Any personal kit or money were listed, bagged and tagged. The only thing they left us with was our ID cards. We were given 30 minutes to study and memorise the area's boundaries and land features from the land model of the area. We were then formed up in three ranks for the RSM's final briefing.

"Hurry up, petals, time's a wasting and we need to interrogate you little weasels once you've been given your mission. Your mission is to deliver the words, 'the victorious never recognise defeat' to your allies in the Red Army, whilst you are in their HQ. I repeat, your mission is to deliver the words, 'the victorious never recognise defeat' to your allies in the Red Army whilst you are in their HQ.

The Red Army's HQ is 30 miles due north from your final drop zone between the Carlton marsh and the mighty Carlton river. The Red Army's HQ consists of two four-tonners marked with red flags. You will only be considered safe and free from harm once you are in the back of the Red Army's lorries.

The Blue Army is your enemy. Divulge your mission to any member of the Blue Army and it's good night Vienna, hello job centre! If you're caught more than three times, you're offski. Fail to complete your mission within 96 hours, bye-bye, you've failed - Dear Deirdre, life's a bitch!

All firing ranges, the River Carlton, civilians and civilian buildings are out of bounds! If you are caught out of bounds you will do nick and be discharged - how sad, never mind!" The RSM smiled with sadistic relish. "Now let slip the dogs of war!"

Interrogation bedlam exploded and descended upon us with all the fury of hell. Everywhere you looked there were recruits being terrorised and tortured. These ranged from physical tortures like having your testicles whipped with nettles and gorse, marking time in freezing rivers or being dragged along behind Land Rovers. Cruel physiological tortures were constructed, where you honestly believed you were going to die. It looked like a cross between the Spanish Inquisition and something from the Marquee de Sade's repertoire.

My head was quickly sandbagged as I was kicked to the ground. A noose of D10 cable was pulled tightly around my throat. The other end of the cable was wrenched behind my back and bound to my feet, which had been forcibly folded against the backs of my legs. I had to keep my back arched like a rocking horse to counteract the ferocious choking force of the cable. My head was held fast as water was poured through the hessian of the sandbag. My choked mouth spluttered and gagged for air. I twisted and fought desperately to avoid the relentless stream of drowning water.

"Let the dumb fucker go, he'll no say anythin!" said Sergeant Wallace, in an appalling Russian accent.

After our interrogations we were blindfolded and searched. Our hands were windlassed behind our backs with 14-gauge wire then we were thrown onto the back of the four-tonner lorries. We landed on top of each other like dead fish from a trawler net.

"First bastard who moves gets stiffened, so don't fucking move!" the voice warned, as the tailgate slammed shut.

We waited until the four-tonner started to

move then we sprang into action. I kicked and bucked like a madman until I was free from the squirming mass of protesting bodies. I frantically slid my hands down my legs and managed to wriggle my windlassed hands over my dumb awkward boots. I whipped my blindfold off and worked the wire off my hands using my teeth and the tailgate handle.

Cassie and Fadge were nearly free, but Bear was pinned under a mass of writhing bodies. We desperately threw bodies off him. The blood soaked wire had cruelly bitten deep into Bear's huge broad wrists. I worked fast untwisting the wire until he was free at last. Bear grinned that big old bear grin and nodded his grateful thanks.

We were the only ones free and we weren't going to waste the opportunity. I peered out through the thick road dust as the four-tonner bounced its way down the dirt road. The lorry sharply braked at a crossroads and whirred its way along a rifle range. Before I gave myself too much time to think I leapt into the range's pine trees. Thoom, thoom, thoom, came the sound of Fadge, Cassie and Bear as they hit the pine brush. The pine was perfect; it took out quite a bit of our momentum and gave us a reasonably soft landing.

The four of us lay on the deck giggling like wee school kids as we watched the four-tonner thunder on. As things stood we were in a pretty good position. We cleaned and bound Bear's wrists by cutting up a field dressing.

Cassie looked at me like a faithful, but disconcerted, butler.

"We're at least four miles outside the operation limit, Hector. Has anybody got a map?"

I nodded and reminded Cassie we were also four miles away from enemy search patrols, with a plentiful supply of water to cook and wash with. Cassie began to look a lot more relieved, and nodded his approval.

"Right," I said, "let's see what we've still got."

We took it in turns to display our contraband stores.

I went first and tried to imitate the suaveness of a gentleman conjuror. I pulled a small Silva compass from one shoulder epaulette, a neatly folded MOD map of the area from my other epaulette and nine square yards of parachute silk from my jacket lining. I was just about to crow when Bear casually pulled a fully-stocked mess tin from his army Y-fronts. We all fell about; I had tried to be so fly whilst Bear had just blatantly stuffed a fully-stocked, five by seven inch mess tin down his pants. Anyone of us would have been caught, but old Bear with his legendary undercarriage had obviously been overlooked.

At long last the enigma of the army Y-front design had been broken. They had been specifically designed to help smuggle fellow prisoners and extra rations out.

Fadge stepped up next and handed over parachute cord, snare wire, sweeteners, a canvas bucket, curry powder and razor blades. Fadge casually smiled, opened his flies and flopped his Scots love wand out. Bear began to snigger.

"You'v-ve nn-no got much then!"

"All right, Mr Donkey Cock," snapped Fadge, "how much do you think it weighs? If you're within one pound - I'll give you a week's wages!"

Bear whipped out his own monstrosity and cupped his hands around it to judge its freakish caber weight. He registered its weight and then looked at Fadge's mortal piece. Bear paused for a long while and then nodded after deep thought.

"I was right, you've-ve gg-got ff-fuck all!"

Our laughter was finally quelled by Fadge holding his hands up for silence. Fadge gingerly began to roll back his foreskin.

"Wrong - it weighs 50 pounds," he beamed, triumphantly holding up a £50 note, which he had craftily folded around the tip of his manhood.

Once again we forgot about our tactical situation as we cheered our resourceful hero on with wolf whistles and laughter.

Cassie's clothes had been torn from him and meticulously searched, so we weren't expecting much. Cassie winced.

"I'm sorry, chaps, but they left me with nothing – well almost nothing."

Cassie smiled, lowering his pants like a provocative stripper. After some bizarre fidgeting, Cassie finally whipped out a remarkably clean credit card and announced it had been anything but a flexible friend. This was the last straw; we all fell into helpless fits of laughter. It had been a great morale booster, but we had to make tracks.

We carefully crept our way around the range perimeter to ensure our safety. Once we had made our way to the river, we washed the mud out of our kit and did our best to clean ourselves of cam cream. The camouflage cream, which the army used, was actually defective mascara made by a very famous cosmetic company. When you were on exercise you applied cam cream daily to darken and camouflage your face, hands and neck. This clogged your skin pores and made your skin feel like leather.

We lit a small fire to brew some tea up and

discuss our next move. My plan was to gradually make our way by travelling in the out of bounds area near the River Carlton. Cassie came up with an extremely ludicrous and impractical plan of lording it up in a hotel in the nearby town of Aprington. My plan was simple to implement, militarily superior and tactically sound, so we naturally chose Cassie's lording it up in a hotel plan.

We spent the rest of the early morning wading through bushes and scrub, and eventually made it to the town of Aprington. Fadge bought some cheap tracksuits, a couple of duffel bags, a rope and some washing gear. After some searching around we eventually found a nice wee B & B.

For the first time in a month we had the luxury of long, steaming hot showers. After a ton of scrubbing, the hot water began to penetrate and revive my skin back to normal. The indescribable luxury of a long hot soak in bubble bath made me feel and smell human again. I volunteered to launder our uniforms while the rest carried out a recce to replenish our kit and rations.

I sat in the kitchen chatting to a nice old Irish boy called Connor while the washing machine got to grips with our uniforms. Connor was ex-Enniskillen Rifles and he helped the landlady to clean and run the B & B.

Connor laughed his socks off at the coal-black water coming out of the washing machine. After the second wash the water became a normal soapy grey. I pegged the washing out and enjoyed a nice glass of stout with Connor. Connor was due to knock off about four o'clock.

"You'll be glad when I do, Hector, you'll get to meet the landlady, a fine woman from Taunton called Dolly."

Connor smiled, accentuating Dolly's curves with his hands. I began to blush and thanked Conner for his tip.

Dolly made her cheerful entrance and Connor introduced me. Dolly was voluptuously buxom and deliciously all woman. She effortlessly oozed sex. Her feminine curves were perfectly accentuated by her white summer dress and stilettos. Dolly had beautifully cut platinum blonde hair, a warm smile and large, blue crystal eyes that sparkled with life.

My hungry eyes gazed in lustful wonderment at her tanned sensual cleavage.

"Ain't nothing wrong with your eyesight is there, my lover?"

I turned scarlet and did my best to address Dolly's face and not her chest.

"I don't usually do supper, but I'll do you a nice stew with some nice big dumplings. You do like nice big dumplings, Hector?" Dolly teased.

"Oh, God, I do, I do, Dolly," I said, nodding enthusiastically.

I did my best to talk to Dolly as a friend, but I couldn't blind myself to her obvious charms. I tried so hard to look suave and collected. Unfortunately my loins had decided to give Dolly a rampant, unconscious 21-gun salute through my tracksuit bottoms. Dolly nodded down to my crotch and winked.

"Nothing like seeing a growing lad."

I tried to apologise, but the two of us couldn't stop sniggering.

Dolly was completely unfazed and set me at ease in the most accommodating and pleasant way I had ever experienced. We lay in bed and Dolly teased me about my clumsy experiences with girls. She couldn't stop laughing at my graphic open honesty.

"Don't grow up into a bugger, Hector, most men do and that's their downfall. Just stay the way you are and you'll do just fine."

For the first time I was completely relaxed in a woman's company where there was more than just friendship at stake.

By God, Dolly had lived. She had been a go-go dancer and travelled the world five times over. She possessed a sincere and down-to-earth honesty, which I found irresistible. The unwelcomed noise of my friends meant I had to leave.

"Can I see you tonight, Dolly?" I whispered.

"Don't worry, Hector, I'm not that wanton am I?"

"God, I hope so, Dolly," I said, giving her a quick kiss before I slipped out of her room.

I brought our uniforms in and sat down in the tele room. Fadge, Bear and Cassie were arguing over the map about our next move, but my mind was elsewhere.

"Are you listening, Hector?" Cassie snapped.

"Are you okay, Hector?" Fadge asked.

I nodded, stretching my arms.

"Yeah, I feel - fantastic!"

"You've had a shag, you randy little bastard, haven't you?"

I was just about to deny the accusation, when the sweet dulcet tones of Dolly chorused through the door.

"Has he ever, Trevor," Dolly laughed, skipping through the doorway in her white blouse and knickers.

Dolly placed a large tray with four bowls of thick, sweet meaty stew and dumplings on the table. She jumped onto my lap and gave me a large exaggerated smacker on the lips.

"Let it cool down, boys, it's a bit hot, like myself."

Normally I would have been so embarrassed, but my open-mouthed friends made me feel like Don Juan.

"Not so shy now, my Hector, are you?" Dolly teased.

"Hell no, Dolly," I replied, blushing.

Dolly correctly guessed everybody's names from my descriptions and I could tell she liked them.

"Now, you boys eat up and we'll have a party. The bowl with two large dumplings is for my Hector - he does love his dumplings. Oh, I do love it when he goes nice and red," she cooed, giving me a quick farewell peck.

"MacTavish you lowland jammy whore, she's bloody marvellous!" said Cassie.

I nodded with satisfied pride. The stew was

lovely and just what the doctor ordered. We partied late into the night. Dolly and I slipped away, leaving my friends to demolish the last of the whisky.

In the morning Dolly skilfully drove me up a small secluded track just up from the exercise finish point. The target area had been well selected. There was only one real way in and that was across useless, open flat ground. One side was guarded by the menacing Carlton marsh. The other two sides were protected by the vast, powerful sweeping bend of the River Carlton.

A few of the platoon had already made bold charges towards the sanctuary of the four-tonners parked by the river's edge. All of them had been caught; some were imprisoned in a corral whilst others were returned to the daunting start line. Two unfortunate recruits had been staked out on the riverbank. Their faces and backs had been plastered with sweet sticky jam, so they were being eaten alive by ferocious Scots midges.

The Scottish midge can be easily distinguished from the English gnat, as the English gnat leaves annoying bites whilst the Scottish midge tends to bugger off with a limb. These 'Tigers of the North' were obviously starving after their long flight from Fort William, and had wasted no time in making their bloodless victims look like they had just gone 20 rounds with Rocky Marciano. I looked down at my own badly bitten hands and gently rubbed them out of sympathy.

The tied up recruits in the corral looked pathetic and tragically broken. They had been caught three times and were awaiting discharge. Amongst them was the bandaged head of Morrison. The bastards had only given him one day's rest and had sent him straight back out on exercise. My heart went out to him; he had gambled all - and had lost everything. Each day the recruits would be taken away and each day Morrison would reappear in the corral.

The River Carlton went right by the safe haven of the four-tonners. The river was wide with powerful deep currents - the most dangerous option of all. The marsh and open ground had failure stamped all over them. It would have to be the river option if we wanted to be successful.

Dolly warned me about the Carlton's deadly reputation. I pointed to the broken, dejected figures in the corral.

"Anything is better than that, Dolly, besides, we're all really strong swimmers."

After awhile I spotted a very wide section of river basin, which was perfect for our departure and river entry.

Dolly climbed over and straddled me.

"I'm in desperate need of some more military manoeuvres myself, Hector," Dolly giggled, hitching up her dress and pulling it over her head. "Don't want my Hector going off – half-cocked," she cooed.

Duty was indeed a lustful cruel master.

It seemed like an hour instead of a day when Dolly drove us out to the drop off. I made all the usual idiotic schoolboy promises to Dolly, but Dolly was too wise to take any notice of them. She could see the hurt and dismay in my face.

"I've loved being with you, Hector, and the boys are lovely too, but life goes on and let's live it as it happens," Dolly said, smiling.

"I'll no forget you, Dolly, I won't," I promised.

"Go on, you daft bugger, give it a month and you'll not give me a second thought, but if you do, I would love to see you again."

Cassie hugged Dolly.

"Madam, both you and your hospitality have been truly divine."

Dolly thanked Cassie. Bear stepped forwards.

"Now, you go gentle with me my big old Bear," warned Dolly.

Bear's large paw cradled Dolly's head as he kissed her tenderly on the forehead.

"Now, you listen here, Fadge my old fox, you look after these boys and your wicked old self."

Fadge nodded and gave her a tight squeeze. I held Dolly close and playfully squeezed her bum. Dolly laughed and clasped my face in her hands.

"Go now, lover, and don't ever change my little red faced piper. Let me know when you all make it."

Dolly's eyes began to water, she kissed me quickly and ran off to her car. I watched her car's headlights drift away into the distant darkness.

We quickly stripped to our trousers and put our kit into our duffel bags then slipped silently into the cold black waters of the Carlton. We swam hard to try and keep our muscles warm, but the freezing water quickly stiffened and numbed them. The current became faster and faster. Its strength started to sweep us away towards the far bank, so we had to swim for all we were worth just to stay on a true course. As we rounded the bend we could see the four-tonners bathed in moonlight. The intense din of skirmish fighting became louder and louder.

We swam desperately for a small eddy and dip in the bank. The bank was sheer and loomed six feet above us with no floor or footing. Bear was the tallest, so he dug his hands into the mud of the bank and braced himself. I was by far the lightest, so I scrambled onto Bear's Scott's Porridge Oats shoulders. There was no time for pleasantries, so I trampolined straight off Bear's startled head. The bank was slippery. My legs and hands frantically scrambled like a wheel spinning car until I managed to get an arm onto the top of the bank and swing my grateful body onto the flat of the bank.

Manic screams and shouts erupted like the sounds from some hellish Armageddon. Everywhere you looked there were recruits being caught, beaten or repelled. I silently slithered along the rough ground and focused on the four-tonner's front wheel. I carefully peeled the rope from around my waist, knotted it around the wheel and flung the rope over the bank into the grasping hands below.

One by one they popped up. I untied the rope and let it gently fall into the river. We laced our boots up and quickly got dressed. Our minds raced, trying to decide the best tactic to bypass the enemy and gain our sanctuary.

The training staff hadn't banked on anybody approaching from the river. They had parked their lorries right next to the river with all their defences facing away from us. We now had a superb strategic advantage, which we could exploit. We cautiously climbed up the cab and slithered onto the canvas roof.

"Search around the four-tonners in case any of the bastards have slipped through," a sergeant ordered.

We pulled the camouflage nets over us and held our breaths. The dogs barked feverishly; they knew we were there. Probing torch beams flashed all around us. The dogs pulled their handlers towards a sudden rustling sound from the undergrowth near the other four-tonner.

Young Scots burst from all sides in a wild Bannockburn charge, forcing the perimeter guards into a tight cordon around the four-tonners. Vicious, determined hand-to-hand fighting exploded all around us - desperate recruits fighting for status and survival. We used the chaos to slip through the canvas roof flaps. We had done it - we were safe. The feeling of accomplishment was fleeting and quickly quelled by the cries of fellow Scots fighting on.

I crept up to the tailgate and knelt down. Fadge smiled and took the other side of the tailgate. I gave him the nod and we ripped the tailgate pins out. Bear and Cassie's boots launched the tailgate open, firing the cordon guard to the ground.

"Now boys! Now!"

About ten made it onto the lorry before the training staff initiated a murderous flanking action to stem the exodus and protect the trampled cordon guard. We managed to rip the canvas cage off the lorry. Recruits flew in from all sides. The tide had turned; it was now the Blue Army who were overwhelmed.

We fought with impassioned belief and courage - we fought like true Scots soldiers. The brilliant flash of the Endex flare erupted and signalled the end of the exercise. Uncontrollable rapturous cheering rang out in tribal triumph.

The training staff made vain attempts to silence the celebrations. The sergeant major halted them and admired his bloody, but unbowed, platoon.

"Let them have their moment, they've earned it!"

Eventually the cheering was utterly quelled by the unquestioning voice of the sergeant major.

"Shut the fuck up and well done, in that order, gentlemen. Call the roll from the trucks and let's see who's made it."

Twenty-six of us had made it into the truck and a further four were granted passes for outstanding action and gallantry. I was overjoyed when I spotted one of them still sporting a large field bandage. I kissed his bandaged head and hugged him.

"Morrison, you bastard, how the hell did you make it? You were shipped off."

Morrison, the cunning bastard, had not been caught at all. He had had the genius of mind to make for the corral and not the haven of the four-tonners. He sat there pretending to be dejected and tied up. When it came to shipping the prisoners out, he simply disappeared into the brush and because his name wasn't on the capture list he had escaped detection. He repeated this action for two days. On the last night he had been caught freeing two prisoners. Morrison had fought like a highland wild cat, until the Endex flare had gone off. His ingenuity and courage had been quite rightly rewarded with a pass.

The poor wretches who hadn't made it were marched at the double never to be seen again. A horrible chill ran through us as we thanked God we weren't one of them. Our gloating was dramatically replaced with silent sorrow.

Bright field lights were suddenly turned on, revealing the training staff and the regiments' soldiers who had acted as our enemy. Many of them were bloodied and bruised, but all of them smiled and shouted:

"The victorious never recognise defeat!"

The sergeant major brought us up to attention.

"Gentlemen, they have sweated, they have bled. Without them you would be nothing, this would mean nothing. A victory is never a true victory unless you truly appreciate the cost. I would now ask you to show your appreciation for them."

It was a fantastically poignant and simple speech.

Loud applause was instantly showered upon the staff. The field kitchen was opened and ravenous recruits scrambled to receive their hot tatty stew. I sat down against a tree watching the others gulp down their stew with animated gusto. I puffed away on my fag and drank the cool water from my water bottle. I had battled for nine months against all the odds, and I had endured! A strange overwhelming pride took hold of me as I savoured my victory. I still had to survive one more year's harsh training at Regimental Piping School - but life was good!

I listened to the various adventures of the platoon's mushroom eating, rabbit catching and sheep rustling. Cassie smiled and winked at me.

"Lord, we were lucky - Hector had something simply divine on him, which made the most exquisite dumplings."

Sergeant Wallace came over to me and nodded.

"Well in, MacTavish! Now go and get someone

to have a look at your hands or just paint them brown and join the boxing team."

CHAPTER 8

Celt Platoon swept all before them in the depot competitions. I won the Rifle Challenge Cup. Cassie blissfully set two new army records for the battle and combat fitness tests, and was begrudgingly awarded the Depot Physical Education Prize. It was official - Cassie was now the fastest man in the British Army. We constantly reminded him of this fact every time we dispatched him to the distant Naafi.

As a wee aperitif, Bear won the shot and the hammer for the army in the Inter-Service Athletics. For his main course, Bear made it to the final of the Junior Inter-Service Heavyweight Boxing Championships. Bear's opponent, ran at him on the stroke of the opening bell. Eleven seconds later Bear's opponent was being stretchered out of the ring, deliriously asking why the venue had taken place on a level crossing. Bear's boxing triumph was immediately signalled to all points of the military globe.

Out of the depot's surviving 2,500 recruits, Fadge had won the highest award of Best Depot Recruit. He had come top of command and leadership, drill, field soldiering, NBC and first aid. Fadge had to go in front of the commandant and explain his reasons for turning down his prize of commanding his own passing out parade, as Junior Regimental Sergeant Major. Fadge spoke bravely and honestly to the commandant.

"Sir, in the army's eyes I am a soldier first and a piper second, but you are a piper yourself, Sir, and I know that you know there is no greater honour for a piper than to play his pipes for his regiment. This is the honour, which I've fought for and it's this honour, which I wish to cherish, Sir."

The commandant shook Fadge's hand firmly.

"Bravo, Piper MacFadyen! Enjoy your day in the band - dismissed."

Sergeant Wallace didn't seem to care about any of the platoon's achievements – something was wrong. He grimly led the platoon up the long winding stairs of the record tower. We filed into the circular room and stared at the surface of the wall with dumbstruck awe and wonder.

A continuous photograph of the original platoon stared back at us from the wall. It had been taken on our first day, which seemed a lifetime ago. Three hundred and twenty faces, still innocent, still hopeful and so untried. There was a sea of heads circled in red, with their discharge dates written beside them. It was a haunting reminder to those, who had fought and lost. I wandered around the great wall tracing each person with my finger. There were some I had forgotten, some I wanted to forget and some old pals I sadly missed. I asked Sergeant Wallace if I could have the photograph as a keepsake.

"Jesus, no! They are sent straight to the regiment after you all sign the bottom, but a bottle of the good stuff to the chief clerk might get you a copy," Sergeant Wallace said, nodding shrewdly.

In the centre of the circular room was an immense tower of McEwan's Export Ale and Tennant's Lager. Tied around the tower of cans was a large banner bearing the simple inscription, 'Celt Platoon Drink Me Dry!'. The instructors strolled in and joined the celebrations.

Sergeant Wallace turned to us.

"Let's have a tune from the regiment's newest pipers."

Bear ran and got his pipes and kicked the party into life. I could hardly play, as my hands were still infected with insect bites from battle camp, so I shared more than a few beers with Sergeant Wallace.

"Well, well, our wee Hector, you made it! You actually . . . fucking made it," Sergeant Wallace marvelled.

"Did you ever doubt it, Sergeant Wallace?"

"Oh, fuck aye!" He smiled, clinking my can. "I doubted it, Hector, by fuck aye . . . I doubted it!"

With typical sick training humour, we were woken up two hours before reveille to have the booze run out of us.

Sick irony and frustration humour was constantly used to subdue recruits during training. My favourite example of frustration humour happened on a dreaded Wednesday.

Wednesday afternoons were reserved for beasting us within an inch of our lives, so when we found out we were going sailing on one of those dreaded afternoons, we were over the moon. We were informed it would be only inland sailing until we got hold of the basics. We arrived at the most idyllic of lakes and were immediately beasted up and down the surrounding hills with heavy assault boats on our shoulders. The instructors ably accompanied this feat of sadism by bawling in our sweating ears:

"Rule number one! Boats work best in water."

After our sobering run we spent the rest of the day moving our kit out and making the room sparkle. Once the room had been thoroughly inspected

Sergeant Wallace gave us a carton of fags and a wooden stencil of the regiment's cap badge. We took meticulous care to burn the cap badge onto the floor, along with our intake name and pass out rate.

As we lit our fags and puffed away, we remembered our first night in the block. I wondered if the new intake would have a streetwise Fadge of their own - or would they get a rude early morning beasting as their welcome to the British Army?

The stencilling was perfect, and our uniforms were pristine and ready for the RSM's parade. The cycle had been completed and tomorrow the room would have new guests to entertain. I went to sleep praying that the RSM wouldn't have any further correspondence from Mum.

Our No. 2 dress uniforms sparkled and gleamed in the warm, morning sun. We were young, strong, conditioned and bloody bullet proof. Sergeant Wallace marched towards us wearing his full regimental number ones. His chest was criss-crossed with medals, including full Oak Leaves and the Military Cross. Along with his sergeant's chevrons, his arms proudly displayed the insignia badges of SAS, Commando, Para and Sniper. He halted immaculately with a blaze of sparks from his heel plates.

"Some sneaky shites have replaced my chromed issue drill cane with this poofy, silver . . . girlie piece of shite! From the bottom of my army Y-fronts, I thank you. Now make me proud! This is the last time you will march as Celt Platoon because today . . . we lose those fucking, flute-playing whisky-swilling pipers."

Celt Platoon came to attention, with one of those single drill cracks that only ten months of arduous training can produce. Our arms swung in perfect unison like rigid pendulums of flesh. Chests were filled and heads were high with arrogance and self-belief. Our heels smashed into the tarmac with defiant echoes of pride and passion. Celt Platoon just oozed panache.

"Lookin good, boys! Harder! Harder yet!" cheered Sergeant Wallace.

We could feel the heads turn as we approached 'The Golden Acre'. At the side of the square was the regiment's new intake for next year. They stared in awe, as we had stared the year before. Their fresh faces were full of hope and wonder. A strange sense of pity came over me as I looked at their expectant faces - I knew that they would all go through hell and only a handful would make it.

After the parade the four of us went to the clothing store and handed in our No. 2 dress uniforms and drill boots. We received our piper's brogues, trews and glengarries. Last of all, the store safe was opened and we were presented with the piper's silver cap badge.

We all got changed into our piper's barrack dress. Fadge was up to some skulduggery and handed the store man a wedge of money. We marched past our platoon wearing our new piper's uniforms. Sergeant Wallace was the first to speak.

"Morning, Pipers!"

It was the first time we had been addressed by the rank of Piper. The regimental courtesy was echoed by the rest of our platoon. We marched along like four Jacobite lords. In the distance we could hear the sweet sound of the depot's pipes and drums.

The depot pipe band was truly world class. The four of us listened and nodded with professional admiration. We rounded the corner and the full power of their music made me rise with pride. The band was formed in a pipe band circle. The sheer geometric perfection and spacing of the circle seemed to defy all human endeavour.

There at the centre of the top arch of the circle was the unmistakable figure of Pipe Major Benjamin Macmillan. His vengeful gaze had earned him the apt nickname of the 'Benbecula Medusa'. In the interest of safety most folk abbreviated the pipe major's nickname to the BM, as it could be easily mistaken for the rank of P/M (Pipe Major).

His Medusa stare could issue its displeasure at the most microscopic of mistakes, turning the offender and his chanter to lifeless stone. His granite-like glare could penetrate the most ardent shields of deception. God help any piper who transgressed Pipe Major Macmillan's sacred commandment of piping perfection. We lived for piping, but piping was a religion to Pipe Major Macmillan, a religion that demanded total commitment. When Pipe Major Macmillan came across a musical heathen, even hell quaked.

The pipe major led us into his office and closed the door firmly behind us. He was sweating heavily. He mopped his sandy balding brow.

"You have a day to move your kit into the piping block and prepare your pipes. I'll listen to you all tomorrow." Pipe Major Macmillan pulled our army records from his in-tray and casually glanced at his penned notes.

"Which one is Maclean? I'm expecting great things from you. Which one is Drummond? Mmm, as long as you keep your tongue in check, you should be okay. MacFadyen? A good training record, keep it up! Hmmm . . . oh . . . hmmm . . ." Pipe Major Macmillan's intimidating face began to soften, into a perplexed grin. He bit his lip and averted his gaze from us, "Which one is MacTavish? You're eh-" he was laughing with tears in his eyes. "Your Christian name is eh-"

"Hector, Sir."

He nodded gratefully towards me.

"By God you're going to have a busy time here, son! You know that all pipers are called Hectors?"

"Yes, Sir," I said, nodding back with a resigned sigh.

"All right, lads, stow your gear and get your pipes ready for my inspection. I'll listen to you tomorrow morning. You've got a lot to do and not much time to do it in, so get cracking!"

We moved our kit into the pipers' block and drew our bag covers, cords, ribbons and army pipe boxes. We began the painstaking job of getting our pipes ready for Pipe Major Macmillan's inspection.

The bagpipes are notoriously temperamental instruments to maintain. The binding on all the slides and joints are bound with hemp. Hemp is made from nettles. It expands when wet and contracts when dry, which means all the joints need constant maintenance. The bags themselves are made from hide or sheepskin, depending on the player. Wet blowers play sheepskin and dry blowers play hide. As the bags are made of skin, they have pores, which can open and cause leaks. Our pipes hadn't been played for a long while, so they were going to need a lot of restoration work.

We started off by testing the bags and stocks to make sure they were airtight. The actual bag was made airtight by corking the bag's stocks and pouring in heated seasoning. Seasoning is a foul tasting and smelling concoction, which is heated and poured into the bag. The bag is then kneaded and massaged to work all the seasoning into every part of the bag. The bag is then blown up as hard as possible, to force the seasoning into the pores to test that the bag is airtight. Once the bag is as tight as a drum, the corks are removed. The bag is then drained and the drone stocks cleaned to stop excess seasoning from ruining the reeds.

Our pipe slides and joints had to be rehemped, as Pipe Major Macmillan insisted that all joints had to be bound by a single length of pitch-rosined hemp and finished with a light film of Vaseline to give the precise tolerance of friction.

The blow stick valves were hand cut leather flaps made supple by chewing and shaping the leather. We lightly greased the valves with Vaseline, to make sure the valves were completely airtight. We placed our new regimental pipe cords and bag covers on. Once our pipes had passed inspection, the pipe major fitted our drones with Lumsden drone reeds, which gave our drones a rich harmony of sound. The pipe major then issued us all with wonderful Sinclair chanters. The Sinclair chanter is still one of the finest chanters a piper can play. It has a clean crisp tone, which is superb for band and solo playing.

The pipe major made us carefully bind our chanters in front of him. Once he was happy with our work, he reeded our chanters with powerful MacAlister reeds. All the hard work paid off - our pipes sounded fantastic.

Keeping your pipes in peak condition is a full-time job and it is the hallmark of a professional piper. The simple truth is when your pipes sound great, you enjoy playing and you naturally play to the best of your ability.

At the end of the morning a tall sergeant looked at our creaseless trews and unbulled brogues. He stared down at his trews razor sharp creases and immaculately bulled brogues.

"By tomorrow's muster parade, your kit will match mine."

This was the last thing I wanted. I needed the rest of the day to work my fingers back into condition. If a piper does not practise regularly his fingers lose their accuracy, control and speed. My swollen hands meant that I had a mountain to climb. I had counted on a long practise session to get my fingers back up to speed. I needed time to practise and a blessed miracle to heal my hands.

"Come over to the block, Hector. You'll be amazed what a cup of tea can do!" Fadge said optimistically.

I couldn't see what good a cup of tea was going to do, but I went anyway. Fadge opened our room door to reveal his miracle. On each of our beds was a pair of trews, with creases you could have shaved with. Beside each pair of perfectly pressed trews was a pair of brilliantly polished brogues. The brogues' cleanly punched out holes accentuated their dazzling, black mirror shine.

Fadge grinned and winked.

"Get the teas on, oor Hector, I'm fuckin magic you know."

Fadge's uncanny ability, to out-think any problem in advance was truly a magical thing to behold. I tried to think of when and how Fadge had achieved this feat of genius, when I remembered the sizeable bung given to the storeman. We always gave Fadge at least a quarter of our weekly £10 wage allowance without question. Sometimes it would disappear, but more times or not it would come back as a godsend, or a bloody big windfall.

Fadge grinned at me like a panting fox and pulled me to one side.

"I know your hands are bad and you need to practise, but for God's sake don't stay up all night. They're not daft! They can see how bad your hands are. Just batter your exercises and get a good night's sleep. We can fix the order of play tomorrow. That'll buy you some more time as well. What do you think?"

I nodded towards Bear.

"Well, as long as I don't have to play after wonder boy there. He makes me sound shit on a good day!"

"J-j-jealousy g-gets y-you n-no w-w-where!" said Bear.

"Second thoughts! By the time Bear gets a sentence out, I think my hands will have healed."

Bear gave me one of his light friendly taps, which sent me flying from my seat and bouncing off the wall.

"One lump or two, darling?" Cassie quipped, pouring out the tea. "Bear, old thing, please don't bounce Piper MacTavish off the wall. It makes such a frightful mess of the decor. Besides, you have absolutely no idea where he's been."

We savoured our tea from our army pint mugs and started to work on our polish-ridden cap badges. Pipers' cap badges are different from all other badges in the regiment. They are made of solid silver and are preserved in a heavy polish, which has to be burned out. As the glinting silver started to emerge from the molten polish the cap badge began to reveal its true brilliance and beauty.

I lovingly buffed the cap badge to its full glory and fitted it to my glengarry. I loved how it sparkled against the proud black of my glengarry. The cap badge's spell was broken by the sound of stampeding brogues and laughter.

"Well, that's either the lads from the piping school or the Avon brute squad," said Fadge.

The pipers from the piping school began to file into the room; they were immaculate and a credit to the regiment. Most of them were friendly and welcoming, a few were aloof and a bit wary of Bear. The first to cut to the chase was Gunny. Piper Gun was one of the finest players to have graced the regiment's piping school in many a long year. He glanced at Bear's pipes.

"MacDougall's, ancient, no silver or ivory, just plain wood."

Bear smiled at the accurate, but clinically cold,

evaluation.

"I pp-play them because I love the sound. No pipe can match their sound."

Bear picked his pipes up. They had belonged to his grandfather. MacDougall, the legendary pipe maker, had forsaken all ornamentation and had poured every ounce of his unmatched genius into producing a sweet and unsurpassable sound. When the great MacDougall had finally triumphed, he painstakingly carved spectacular Celtic designs into the drone slides, to mark his masterpiece from all other pipes. This made Bear's pipes a rare thing of beauty, in both sight and sound.

Gunny looked the pipes over and started to really appreciate the genius of their simplistic splendour.

"No need for silver or ivory. Would you mind if I played them? I've never seen their like before."

Bear nodded and carefully slid each of the drone slides onto their hemp lines.

Bear smiled.

"J-just play them. D-don't touch them, they'll stay in tune for a good 20 minutes. Th-they'll settle themselves!" Gunny looked a bit dubious and puzzled, but did as he was told.

The chanter reed, which provides the pipes' melody, sharpens the more it is played and flattens the longer it is rested. This means the harmony of the pipes' drones needs to be constantly retuned to match the chanter's ever-changing pitch. The pipes' tuning can be drastically thrown out by minute changes in temperature, humidity, moisture and pressure. Bear's pipes had been painstakingly set up to defy all of these infuriating tuning problems. The beautiful tonal consistency of Bear's pipes, in all conditions, made them an extraordinarily rare and a highly prized instrument.

Gunny carefully struck Bear's pipes in with expert grace. I liked Gunny's easy style. He wasn't trying to show off, he was just enjoying a superb musical moment. Right from the start Gunny managed to capture their great sound. Minute by minute the pipes' tone became sweeter and sweeter.

"They're amazing! What a sound." Gunny sighed. "Right from the start. They just get better and better. Is it the reeds or the pipes?"

Bear smiled.

"A l-little of both."

A tall rat faced boy with a personality to match, jealously sniped:

"Gunny can make any pipe sound good."

"He probably can, but you would have to go a long way to beat this man."

I smiled as I watched the rat faced boy mimic my statement in ridicule.

"I'll cover any bet you offer, that Bear is the finest player - that anyone has ever heard!" I said confidently.

Bear shouted to me.

"Sss-Stone, fuckin S-Stone!"

Bear was right, the rat faced boy was Roland Stone, the boy who had been thrown out of Murdock's teaching class.

Fadge looked at me and winked.

"Even if there was the slightest chance that Bear could beat Gunny, do you really think that rodent boy has got the sort of money you carry?" Fadge taunted, secretly palming a tight roll of notes in my pocket.

"You're still on your £10 training allowance. We bet with real money here - no copper!" Stone sneered.

"The whole thing's irrelevant as you don't have the balls or the cash and besides, Bear hasn't had time to get ready." Cassie chirped, sneaking a small ball of notes into my hand.

I slipped the money into my pocket and smiled coldly at Stone.

"I'll bet you half the money in my pocket, and the loser has to do four pieces of kit for the winner - and I mean, *immaculately*!"

Stone's eyes flashed around, looking for solace and weakness, but he was greeted with cold glaring silence.

Stone's face reddened with rage.

"You're on!"

Stone's crimson face began to turn rather pale as I calmly counted out 140 quid from my pocket.

"That's a hell of a lot of bulling and 70 pound of paper I'm betting - still game?" I asked.

Stone nodded back.

"What do you want to play?" asked Gunny.

"Anything you want, and the room can judge," I suggested, and so they began in turn: march after march; strathspey after strathspey; jig after jig; polka after polka; hornpipe after hornpipe; reel after reel.

Gunny was truly fantastic and his technique was faultless, but he only had mortal talent. He wasn't blessed with the divine genius of my incredible friend. Eventually, after a valiant attempt, Gunny conceded defeat.

"You're not even trying are you, Bear? Show us what you can really do."

Bear effortlessly slipped his playing up a few gears and played a dazzling selection of jigs at breakneck speed. The finger work was godlike and the timing perfection. It was the unsurpassable genius of something wonderful called Bear. Bear finished his matchless playing with his usual nauseating modesty.

Gunny was the first to speak.

"My God, he's something special isn't he?"

We all nodded with proud futile acceptance. I placed all our new brogues in front of Stone.

"There you go, my man. Four pairs of nice new brogues for you."

Stone's face was seething.

"Just the brogues, my man, we don't need the cash," I said, with a simpering smile.

Stone snatched the brogues from me and began to work on them straightaway. I handed the cash back to my friends and sat down on my bed with triumphant glee.

The piper next to my bed space was Ronnie Douglas. He had the mannerisms of a meerkat on speed. His slender face possessed two, dark soulful eyes and one hell of a nose. I liked Ronnie's, open cheerful introduction.

"I'm shite! No, no a really am. Am just packed wi nervous energy, that's ma problem."

"Don't worry, Ronnie, we're all crap against folk like them," I said.

"Thank Christ, somebody that's human. It's hellish being mortal an livin on Olympus, Hector."

"I know what you mean, Ronnie," I said, smiling and nodding towards Bear.

Ronnie began to explain who was who, and who to look out for. Ronnie was instantly likeable and we all warmed to him straightaway. In about ten minutes Ronnie knew all there was to know about us.

"I'm fae Paisley, ma Dad kills folk for a livin, but he's in Barlinnie, so he's sort of between jobs at the moment."

I choked on my tea at Ronnie's child-like honesty.

"Jesus, your hands look rough, wee man," Ronnie said, using his nose as a pointer.

Battle camp had left my hands looking like balloon toys. Bear examined my hands and stared at me hard.

"I cc-can hh-help you, Hector, but it will sss-sting."

If there was one thing I knew about Bear, he had a talent for understatement. I nodded and so the fun began. Bear opened up my infected bites and cuts with nicks from his reed razor. He then poured an oily concoction and two kettles of boiling water into the sink. The blistering steam wafted up the pungent herbal aroma from the oil. Bear added a little drop of cold water and whipped his fingers in and out, to test the heat. Bear nodded.

"It has to be hh-hot, Hector, the hotter the better."

Before I could argue, Bear plunged my hands into the sink. The heat was excruciating. Streams of bright blood billowed into tormented red clouds. The intense scalding heat was beyond any pain I could withstand. I tried to wrench my hands free from Bear's iron grip, but it was useless.

"A f-f-few s-s-seconds m-more! A w-wee b-bit m-more," Bear pleaded.

At this moment I can't tell you how much I hated having a friend with a stutter.

I was close to fainting when Bear whipped my burning hands out. My relief was short-lived as Cassie and Fadge plastered my hands with a hot bread and soap poultice. They quickly bound the hot poultice to my hands with layers of lint and gauze bandages. My hands throbbed with heated pain. Bear watched me like a she wolf all night to make sure I didn't remove or slacken the bandages.

In the morning, Bear carefully unravelled my bandages. Each layer contained deep, dried, green and brown discharge. The final lint layer contained a solid ball of poisonous jelly. Bear skilfully cleaned my hands with surgical spirit. The swelling had completely gone. He massaged some waxed menthol ointment into my hands. It was cold and soothing; my hands felt supple and pain free.

"Jesus, Bear, that's amazing. Over two weeks of antibiotics, scalpels and dressings at the medical centre, with bugger all change, and you heal me in one night. How did you know what to do?" I asked.

Bear cleared his throat.

"W-well, it f-fuckin works on sheep!"

The whole room burst into fits of laughter as I gawked in disbelief at Bear's naive innocence. I shook my head and wandered over to the piping school.

We formed up in open ranks and were

meticulously inspected.

"Good turn out. Keep it that way!" the inspecting sergeant barked.

The piping school was an old prison, which was ideal for the purpose as the cells made excellent practice rooms. As we entered the piping school we were issued with our blue books and told to warm up our pipes.

At the piping school a piper has to learn a new tune every day. The piper has 24 hours to learn, memorise and play the tune to the pipe major's satisfaction. If the pipe major is satisfied with the interpretation, he signs and dates the tune in the piper's blue book, then writes the next tune to be learned along with its date of issue. This unforgiving cycle tested and forged us into tempered steel.

In one sense your blue book was a testament of your ability to learn and memorise tunes, but it could also be your hellish downfall, as the pipe major would test each piper on all their blue book tunes at least once a month.

These sessions were a real trial of memory and nerve. If a piper failed to play all his tunes to the pipe major's satisfaction, he would be stripped of all liberty privileges and locked in the cells until he could play all his tunes correctly.

Your blue book was also used to allow officers and members of the royal family to select tunes from your repertoire when playing at regimental or royal functions. God help you if you couldn't play the tune they selected. The blue book was a demanding harsh system, but it is amazing what the human brain can achieve once it has been correctly conditioned.

By now I'd been playing my pipes for about two hours on and off. My pipes were sounding terrific and my fingers were beginning to hit form again, but I welcomed the rest when Naafi break was called.

The Naafi was miles away, so we went next door to the camp's religious café. Five pipers had been incarcerated because of their blue book sessions. Ronnie was ecstatic.

"First time in two months I've no been locked up."

Ronnie began to sing 'Born Free' to the packed café. "You're soundin really good, wee man," Ronnie nodded to me.

"Don't sound so shaggin shocked," I snapped.

"We ff-fuckin are?" Bear sighed with genuine wonderment.

"Shut it, Daktari," I said, wiggling my fingers with sarcastic defiance.

The man serving behind the counter was badly cockeyed.

"Five mugs of tea, Clarence," Fadge chirped, squinting his eyes at the poor man.

"Fuckin ten bob," the man growled, slamming the mugs of tea down. I went to pay with a £10 note. The man behind the counter was infuriated.

"Can you no whip out anything smaller?"

"Aye, I could, but this is a religious establishment."

The man behind the counter began to grin.

"Fuckin pipers!"

All of a sudden, the café manager leapt to the counter.

"Mr MacNab, what did you say to that piper? I hope you're not swearing again, this is a religious establishment, Mr MacNab!"

"Muckin! Yes! 'The Muckin of Geordie's Byre' is the correct name of the tune, Mr MacNab, although I have heard it referred to as, 'The Cleansing of George's Cow Emporium'," I said, nodding reverently.

The café manager squinted at Mr MacNab in disbelief and wandered off. MacNab nodded his thanks to me, and grumbled on to the next customer. We finished our teas and returned to the piping school.

Fadge and Cassie played first then came the words that I had been dreading.

"MacTavish, bring your pipes into the pipe major's office!"

The pipe major was puffing away on a sweet-smelling, horned smoking pipe.

"Whell, oor Hector, tune your pipes, and let's hear what you can do."

I smiled my recognition of the joke and tuned my pipes up. Once my pipes were in tune I turned to face the pipe major and played my best march, strathspey and reel. There was a slight pause as the pipe major puffed away on his horned pipe.

"Christ, that's some volume from your chanter, MacTavish, and a nice sweet tone you've got too. Your expression is good too, but I think your fingers still need to heal a bit more. But time and a swift brogue up the arse works wonders. Over all - I'm very pleased. Now, what about giving me a lovely piobaireachd?"

"I'm afraid it would have to be 'a 6/8 Donald Dhu', Sir. I've only really learned light music."

"Piobaireachd is the classical music of the pipes. You must learn it. It is the ultimate test of a piper. As a regimental piper you must know at least two. Don't worry, you're not alone. You'll receive the necessary tuition once you're ready. Now sit down and we'll discuss your future.

I will give you your duty picket tunes first then I will develop your overall playing. If you're up for it, and don't mind some extra work, I need some strong, experienced band players for the competition band then we'll start your piobaireachd instruction."

I couldn't believe that a pipe major called the 'Medusa' could be so human.

The pipe major must have read my mind.

"Just you keep in my good books - and you might not turn to stone, or did you think I didn't know what they call me?"

I laughed and nodded my understanding. The pipe major relit his horned smoking pipe.

"I love all pipes." He winked. "Now, I need you to help me to help young Maclean. You're his friend, tell me about him."

"Well, Sir, he is my best friend, and I don't deserve him really. He's loyal and as strong as an ox, and if you want proof there is a God - listen to him play!"

The pipe major laughed and nodded

sympathetically drawing on his pipe.

"That's not exactly what I meant, but it's a damned fine recommendation all the same. I want to help him, MacTavish, but I can't - unless I know the boy's troubles. Everything you tell me will be in the strictest confidence.

All I want to do is help him! You have my word on it."

I could tell the pipe major was sincere, so I told him about Bear's parents' abuse and neglect. He shook his head in disgust.

"Do they still bother him now?"

"Not since he's been in the army, Sir."

"By God, if they try, they'll taste my broadsword. I promise you that!" The pipe major remained in deep thought. "Is that the cause of his stammer and his swearing?"

I fell silent.

"It's on his record, MacTavish. I want to help!"

"It's just nerves, Sir. He doesn't want to, he just does it when he's nervous or excited, but it's a lot better now."

"Well, it will make a nice change to hear it to my face." The pipe major's eyes suddenly widened,

"What if I was to introduce him to the Queen Mother?"

"I'd make sure the old girl was wearing ear defenders, Sir."

The pipe major roared with laughter.

"Well, we'll see what we can do." He winked. "A bit of care and help can work wonders. I'll just need to use my brains and a wee bit of horse sense." The pipe major tapped his pipe tobacco into the ashtray. "And his drinking, how bad is that?"

"He's a lot better now, Sir, the odd wee nip to keep himself steady, and each month it becomes less and less. It's no his fault, Sir. You wouldn't want any other man at your side and you can count on him when all others would falter. He's - well he's – Sir, he's-"

"Calm down, MacTavish. I'm no lookin to harm the boy's potential - quite the reverse! He won't be the first or the last piper to throw his God given talent to the bottom of a whisky bottle - and I don't intend to let him do that, especially if he's half as good as you say he is. Confidence and fresh focus is all the boy needs to curb his liquid appetites, do you understand me? Now give me your blue book," the pipe major ordered.

The pipe major wrote 'Johnny Cope' as the first tune in my blue book (the tune played for reveille).

"Now call Maclean in and let's hear how good he really is," the pipe major ordered.

Bear walked into the office as the pipe major relit his horned smoking pipe.

"I want to hear music, real music."

Bear nodded and sounded his wonderfully sweet sounding pipes. All pipers in the piping school stopped to listen to the hypnotic genius of Bear. Bear opened with the beautiful piobaireachd, 'The Lament for the Children'.

Piobaireachd or Ceol Mor means great or big music and it is the classical music of the pipes. A well-played piobaireachd is the hallmark of genius, and Bear played his to perfection.

Enthusiastic cheers and tumultuous applause shattered the disciplined regime of the piping school. Even the pipe major could not contain his admiration.

"That is the finest rendering I've ever heard, and I've heard the best! Young man, you are a very gifted player, you play with a genius of emotion, so curb your piper's vices. Get some work done on your social skills and who knows - if you are truly friendless, black hearted and incapable of compassion or reason, you could become a great pipe major!"

Bear nodded and realised the implication of the

pipe major's thoughtful assessment.

We spent the rest of the day learning our new tunes. I was struggling to try and learn the first parts of 'Johnny Cope'. Bear had nauseatingly learnt the whole tune in a matter of minutes. I could see the pain and concern in Bear's face as he watched me using the repetition method to memorise the tune.

"Hmmm," Bear began, "w-we help each other d-don't we, Hector? And you d-don't hold back none, do you?" Bear asked.

"No, I don't." I was half-enjoying Bear's painful attempt at diplomacy, but I decided to put him out of his misery. "Just say it, Bear, what's wrong?"

"W–w-well, it's all wrong!"

"What do you mean?"

"Y-you can't learn to p-play a t-tune a day with the r-r-repetition method. It w-won't work! Y-you need to develop a strict c-c-canntaireachd system, which you can learn and p-play from."

"That means I have to learn canntaireachd and the tune in a day. I'm not like you. I can't do it, Bear!"

"T-trust me I've got a really easy c-canntaireachd you c-can use for light music, a-and we'll only concentrate on the bits of canntaireachd for 'Johnny Cope'. A-a promise you, it'll work! T-trust me."

Canntaireachd is the ancient system of phonetic song especially developed for the pipes. It uses phonetic sounds to represent piping movements, and song to capture the tune's melody and expression.

Bear spent an hour going through my movements and exercises. He took meticulous care to make sure I could fluently recite and play all my movements to his canntaireachd. He then spent the next half hour teaching me to recite the canntaireachd for the first part of 'Johnny Cope', making sure my fingers matched the canntaireachd.

"N-now play the f-first part on the chanter r-reciting the canntaireachd a-a-as you p-play," Bear said, smiling with glee.

I was completely stunned. The tune sounded fantastic. I felt like I'd known the tune all my life.

"That's bloody fantastic, Bear!" I gasped in wonderment.

"D-do the same for the second part. The k-key is to learn the song with just fingering first, only one bar at a t-time! A-and keep singing while studying the music. I'll w-watch and l-listen to make sure you don't go wrong."

By dinnertime I had the first two parts of 'Johnny Cope' firmly fixed in my mind.

"Bear! You're a genius, and I am glad you're ma pal."

Bear smiled.

"M-me too!"

"Come on, let's skip dinner and learn the third part!"

"N-no, just keep s-singing the song for the first two parts. It's easy to g-go wrong with trying to learn t-too much too quick. You sing and I'll eat," said Bear, with hungry enthusiasm.

By the end of the day I was playing 'Johnny Cope' like a seasoned veteran. Over the next few weeks Bear polished my canntaireachd. Bear's canntaireachd made it nearly impossible to forget tunes. It was an absolute godsend in overcoming the piping school's harsh regime of learning a new tune every day, which was just as well as I spent half the day sprinting from room to room every time a piper was addressed as Hector.

After a breathless first week, the pipe major called me into his office.

"To save confusion and the school's carpet, you will only answer to the call of 'oor Hector'. Is that clear?" asked the pipe major.

"Yes, Sir!" I nodded gratefully.

"Well, oor Hector, sit down beside Piper Douglas."

Poor Ronnie was nervously seated at the pipe major's table with a look of battered panic. The pipe major ordered Ronnie to play the strathspey, 'The Braes of Tullyment'. Ronnie played the tune nervously and timed it appallingly.

"Cheasus Christ, Douglas, is there no music in you at tall!" screamed the pipe major.

Poor Ronnie had been through the tune repeatedly and was so nervous he was all over the shop.

"MacTavish, play the tune."

I studied the music carefully and then played the tune with Bear's canntaireachd to capture the tune's timing.

"That's how a strathspey is played, Douglas, it's all in the timing."

Poor old Ronnie nodded to the pipe major with his usual meerkat ferocity.

"Tell him the accent of a strathspey, MacTavish," the pipe major ordered.

I stared blankly at the pipe major. I had never heard the term 'accent' before. I could feel the Pipe major's dreaded Medusa rage about to erupt. I began to panic, and my mind began to whirl at 1,000 miles an hour. The only thing I could think of was how you would say the word 'strathspey'. I cleared my throat and announced the word 'strathspey' in my best Highland accent.

"The accent boy! The accent for a strathspey," the pipe major roared.

This time I tried really rolling my Rs like Harry Lauder.

"Strrrrrrrrrrrrrrathspey."

"No!"

"Strathththththththththspey."

"Fucking no!"

"SSSSSSSSSttrrrrrrathspey."

"You're fucking mad!"

"Strathsspaahaaaaay."

"Shut the fuck up! If you say the word 'strathspey' again I swear to God I'll kill you!"

Ronnie ran out of the room in blind terror.

"Don't speak, just listen to me. How do you time the accent beats of a strathspey?" the pipe major asked, through firmly gritted teeth.

I finally realised that the Pipe Major wanted me to express the strathspey's beat pattern. I also noticed, with some alarm, that his hand was now placed firmly on the handle of his dirk.

"It's a four-four, Sir, strong, weak, medium, weak. I thought you meant how to pronounce the word 'strathspey', Sir."

The pipe major stared at me with incredulous awe. I couldn't hold my laughter - the more I tried, the worse it became. The Pipe Major vented his frustration by whipping me with his chanter.

"Get your strathspeying arse out of my office! Get out! You ignorant lowland lunatic! Oor – Hector, my arse! Get out, get out!"

I beat a hasty retreat and sought sanctuary in the main practice room, but I received hoots of laughter from all the other pipers as I rushed in.

It was strange, but that little event sort of cast the die for my relationship with the pipe major. The Pipe Major liked me and let me get away with a lot more than most pipers. My inability to hold my laughter, and shameless corpsing, made me a firm favourite with him. I learned so much from him. I was one of the few pipers who actually looked forward to my sessions with him. He was one of those people you could learn a lifetime of wisdom from if you listened to him for only a second – and I listened to him with a willing heart.

The pipe major was also extremely generous to Bear. He tirelessly groomed Bear and taught him all manner of useful protocols, to bail himself out of trouble.

Bear had played for all the crowned heads of Europe by the time he was six, but a lot more was expected from a regimental piper.

As regimental pipers, we had to obey regimental custom and observe all royal and social etiquette. Bear would have us all in stitches when he had a swearing fit during etiquette training. Our laughter, far from discouraging Bear, seemed to relax him. The hours of extra rehearsing and repeated mess functions groomed Bear into a seasoned, regimental piper.

By far the greatest change that befell Bear came from Cora, the insatiable Naafi girl. Cora had learned of Bear's biblical genitalia and had practically dragged the poor boy, by the Wallace Monument, to her bed every night for bouts of prolonged lust, which can only be described as rampant siege sex.

Bear and Cora were made for each other. She was courageously extrovert, socially confident and outward going. She began to transfer these attributes to Bear. Bear's modesty and easygoing nature seemed to soothe Cora's insatiable appetite. Maybe it was their positive contribution to each other, or maybe it was their gruelling sex life from the Kilmarnock–sutra, but whatever it was, Bear - just blossomed.

.

CHAPTER 9

Our passing out parade was only two weeks away. We had learned all the band tunes and the pipe major had drilled us to perfection. The pipe major nodded with satisfaction.

"Go to the tailor's, lads, and collect your uniforms. You've earned them."

We couldn't get into our full dress uniforms quick enough. All the pain, beastings and torment seemed to pale into insignificance when we saw ourselves in our full dress uniforms. Our luscious, black feather bonnets, regimental plaid brooches, belts, horsetail sporrans, high leg spats, dirks, sgian dubhs, broadswords, kilts and plaids were perfect. The magnificent regimental splendour of our uniforms just reminded us why we all wanted to be pipers in the regiment.

The master tailor surveyed his work with professional relish.

"Aye . . . you look bonny, boys. Would you like

a photo cause youth fades fast?"

"We would, Sir . . . how much?"

"Spoken like a true piper, Piper MacTavish. For ten pounds I'll give you four portrait photos and one group photograph."

"Is that four portraits and four group photos, altogether Sir?"

"Christ, there's no flies on you, Piper MacTavish. Aye, that's one portrait and a single group photo for each of you. Now, do you want them or not?"

"Sir, what would happen if I could get everyone in my platoon to buy at least . . . four copies of their platoon photograph from you Sir?"

"Well, a wouldnae retire Piper MacTavish, but a would give you another group photo - each!" the master tailor said before I could interrupt him. "And - a copy of each other's portrait, for the same money, but a'd have to see the platoon order form first."

I pulled the platoon order form from my trews pocket. The master tailor squinted at me with admiration.

"Where are you from, Piper MacTavish?"

"Ayrshire, Sir."

"Remind me no to set up business there. Christ, they'd have the breeks off me in a week! You have a deal, Piper MacTavish, and if you're here tomorrow, for half eight sharp, I'll give you your photos. Okay?"

"I'll be here on the dot, Sir."

"A had a feelin you would be."

The master tailor double-checked and corrected our uniforms, giving advice as he went.

"A piper's uniform is the bonniest uniform of them all, but it's the hardest to get right, so here's how to get it spot on. Always work in pairs when you get dressed or you'll never get it right. Allow a minimum of 30 minutes to get dressed. Always start from the bottom up, and check each other as you go. And remember! How you stand affects the whole lie of your uniform, so stand to attention the way you will when you're inspected, and if you've got a mirror there, use it! Last of all, gentlemen, never, ever, blame the tailor."

The master tailor took our individual photographs first.

"That's it, just turn your left shoulder a little more, Piper Drummond, head a wee bit higher, just a touch - and hold."

I had to give the master tailor his due; he was a brilliant photographer. We stood at attention for our first group photograph. We looked handsome and we were proud of it. We posed for our last group photo with our broadswords held aloft like musketeers, for old time's sake.

"All swords touching, that's good - and hold," said the master tailor. "Oh, that is nice. I like that. See you tomorrow, boys."

The following morning couldn't come quick enough. I hurried around to the master tailor's and got the photos. I sprinted all the way back to our barrack room, and burst through the doors only to be greeted by, grim ashen faces. Bear's eyes were filled with tears. Fadge's bedside locker and the floor were caked in blood. I stared in horror at the blood-ridden bed space. Cassie hesitantly approached me.

"There's been an accident, Hector."

My eyes flashed around the room.

"Where's Fadge? Oh, Christ no!"

"He's alive, but he has lost his bottom two fingers."

I unconsciously mouthed the word, 'How?'.

"He tripped and put his hand down on the bedside locker to stop himself falling. The rings on his fingers caught the edge of the bedside locker, stripping and severing his fingers as he fell. We scooped up the bones, but the finger flesh is all mangled to hell. They're going to call us as soon as they can."

I sat down and tried to collect my thoughts. Fadge's lifelong dream had been acquired by ten years of dedicated endeavour - just to be stolen by a few tragic seconds. If a piper is robbed of his ability to play, during his prime, you might as well tear his heart out, as the loss is inconsolable. Your ability to play is a well-earned treasure and without it – a piper's life becomes meaningless.

The pipe major came into the room.

"He will never play again, so don't give him any false hopes, but if he wants to, he can still pass out as a dummy piper in the band. He also has the choice of leaving the army, but if I know MacFadyen, he's made of stronger steel than that!

I've spoken with the commanding officer, and he's recommended MacFadyen for promotion in a duty company, so he has that option as well. Sergeant Wallace is also willing to give up his own leave to train MacFadyen up for his cadre promotion course, should the boy want it.

MacFadyen's now on medical leave until he's made his decision. Now, I can go and see the boy, but I think he'd probably prefer to be cheered up by seeing one of his friends. Who wants to go and see him?"

I looked at Cassie and Bear, but they both shook their heads.

"I'll go, Sir." I sighed. "Does he need any kit?"

The pipe major handed me a large roll of notes.

"See that he doesn't want for nothing. Let him know his options and tell him to have a good think, there's no rush. If he wants a warrant home, let me know and I'll arrange it. The Land Rover is outside, MacTavish, as soon as you're ready."

The Land Rover sped along. I was oblivious to the driver's blethering or the fact that I was still holding onto our photos. I stepped out of the Land Rover and composed myself as best I could. The desk nurse gave me Fadge's ward number and warned me he might still be woozy from the anaesthetic.

"He's probably still in shock, so just be patient. It might take him awhile to find his feet," said the nurse.

I gave her a hard stare.

"Oh, I'm sorry. I didn't mean it that way!" the nurse apologised.

I entered the ward. There, two beds down on the right, was Fadge.

"I need to learn, I really do," I roared.

Fadge gave me a smiling nod of affection. Before I could say anything else, Fadge announced his intentions.

"I'm stayin in. I'm going to a duty company and I'll be a sergeant major or an SAS commander within eight years."

His determined face was alert and focused. He had barely been operated on and he had already re-planned his entire life. I stared at his bandaged hand and spoke without thinking.

"Two weeks, ya eejit, just two bloody weeks to our passing out parade. Oh Christ! Am sorry, Fadge."

"Thank you, Piper MacTavish, any other words of comfort and wisdom?" Fadge chuckled. "What's that you've got?"

"Oh no," I gasped. "I've got our photos with me!"

Fadge shook with laughter.

"Any other bugger would have brought grapes, a get well card, but no, you bring big photos, just to remind me of what I've just lost, you insensitive bastard!"

I buried my head into his bedclothes, trying to hide my laughter and shame.

"A forgot a had them, Fadge, God am a knob."

Fadge dunked me on the head. The two of us were now in hopeless fits of laughter. I wiped the tears from my eyes and laid the photographs of us out on the bed. Fadge lovingly stroked the photographs.

"Christ! We look good, and if you say anythin about Tipp-Exing my fingers out, I swear to God, I'll kill you!"

That was it; the two of us were off again.

"Where's the other two?" Fadge asked.

"Well, Bear would have hugged the shite out of you, Cassie is trying on your gloves and am here to pawn your rings."

Fadge's, shameless filthy laughter filled my ears. It was good to hear.

I got Fadge some washing and shaving kit, juice, sweets, a paper and some fags, and gave him the money from the pipe major. I began to snigger again. Fadge started as well.

"What is it now, ya daft bastard?"

After a few attempts to quell my laughter I managed to blurt out, "I was goin to get you some porn . . . but a didn't know what hand you used."

The two of us were crying with uncontrolled laughter. Every time I tried to stop, Fadge would fling in a barbed comment and set me off again. I dried my eyes and told Fadge what the pipe major had said.

"He's a good wee man. Thank him for me. I'll give him my final decision when I get out. Should only be a couple of days at most," said Fadge.

After a few days Fadge was allowed out as an outpatient at the camp medical station. Nurse Louise Baxter, alias Nurse Lusty Busty, cleaned and dressed Fadge's hand on a daily basis, which proved to be rather ironic as Fadge was soon undressing her - on a strictly, rampant basis.

We pleaded with Fadge to pass out as a dummy piper in the band, but he would not be swayed.

"I'm no a piper any more boys. I'm missing two fingers. Time to move on - onwards and upwards!"

He was right, and too proud a man to sacrifice his principles. He came up to the piping school to give the pipe major his final decision.

In typical Fadge style he was one step ahead of the game and in resilient form. He stood immaculately to attention with a pace stick under his arm, proudly bearing the rank of Junior Regimental Sergeant Major.

This was the greatest honour any recruit could have bestowed upon them at the training depot. He now held full regimental powers of a Regimental Sergeant Major, with complete control of over 2,500 recruits, until the end of the passing out parade. The responsibilities and pressures were immense, but to old Fadge - they were just a walk in the park.

Fadge had always been the best recruit and had constantly turned down promotion. If anybody deserved this honour and rank, it was Fadge. Every detail of his uniform was perfection; his slashed peak, brasses and treble tapped drill boots radiated polished sunshine. He even exuded that fearful regimental omnipotence, which only true RSMs possess (it just demands respect, and consumes all within its wake).

We sneaked out to the back courtyard of the piping school for a fly farewell fag. We laughed hard as we recalled our exploits as the infamous Four Must-Have-Beers. It was the end of an era and we all knew it. Cassie got up and presented Fadge with a silver cigarette case, which bore the simple inscription, 'All for one, One for all, Always for ever'. Fadge lovingly stroked the inscription. His eyes began to water.

"It's beautiful - a should get a fair bit for it."

Fadge was spared any embarrassing speeches by the sudden return of the pipe major.

"Show time," said Fadge.

Fadge marched briskly around and halted immaculately outside the pipe major's office, with a thunderous halt.

"Pipe Major, have your men fallen out on the road."

"MacFadyen, you're a drill pig," the pipe major roared affectionately.

"I'm not in the habit of repeating myself, Pipe Major!" Fadge growled, with a cheeky wink.

"You heard the man, on the road now!" bellowed the pipe major.

We were formed up on the road ready to go. Fadge rifted the regimental band for being late, much to the pipe band's amusement. Fadge stepped us off at a brisk pace, to the 'Atholl Highlander's' set. The sound of brass and pipes was superb. The pipes provided the strong powerful melody and the brass, the additional flourishes and fanfares. The rhythmic genius of the pipe band, snare drummers' crisp beatings made the tune come alive.

Fadge was magnificent; his forethought and charismatic spell forged the giant parade into a precision military, performance.

"By God, gentlemen," the RSM roared to his company sergeant majors, "there's a Scotsman born tae command!"

We didn't need to have reveille sounded on the morning of our passing out parade. We were all too excited to sleep. Most of us got up at five just to re-check and touch up our dazzling uniforms.

At six a.m. we went for a run. We just sprinted with boundless energy, running harder and harder. It seemed that no distance or speed could take its toll upon us. We stretched off and enjoyed an ice cold shower. The volume and depth of Bear's soapy shower flatulence was deafening.

"Is that it, you neo-vandal ape, is that about the depth of your communication limits?" Cassie screamed.

There was a small pause before a more solid argument hit Cassie's shower cubicle.

"Bear!"

After breakfast we lit our fags up and savoured our tea. I don't know where the army got its tea from or what brand it was, but by God, I loved it. It had a nice, strong refreshing flavour that satisfied and quenched your thirst.

We wandered over to the piping school and played our pipes for an hour.

"I want you all here, dressed and ready to go, with pipes tuned for ten o'clock," the pipe major ordered. "Enjoy your day, boys, you'll no have another like it!"

After a year of hell, this was it - our passing out parade had arrived. Our first hurdle to becoming a piper had finally been cleared. My heart began to pound louder and louder the closer we got to the square.

The main drill square lay open before us. It had been pristinely swept and glossed. Excited parents, families, girlfriends and fiancées filled the seating, which framed the sides of the vast drill square. Old veterans from the regiment were given pride of place at the front. Standard-bearers were stationed at each entrance and corner of the square.

Each platoon was played on with great pageantry by their regimental band, according to their regimental march and custom. After all the platoons had been marched on, only two groups remained off the square. The vast acre of tarmac bristled magnificently with the different uniforms of proud recruits.

The depot commandant waited for a suitable lull and finally announced:

"Ladies and gentlemen! This year's winner of Champion Platoon is from the regiment's annual contingency, Celt Platoon. Sergeant Major!"

Fadge's clear commanding drill voice emitted its superb drill commands, rolling all his Rs like a seasoned pro.

"Celt Platoon, supreme Champion Platoon, will step off to the rrrregiment's pipes and drrrums, in column of rrroute, by the rrrrright! Quick March!"

The crisp sharp roll of the snare drums signalled our step off. The pipes and regimental band struck in with 'Highland Laddie'. Scots or not, the entire audience erupted with ecstatic cheers, foot stamping and clapping.

Above all the din of the crowd, pipes, brass and drums, I could make out the voice of Mum.

"Dad, look! Look! Its oor Hector, look Dad, wave to the boy."

I glanced out of the side of my feather bonnet tails and caught the mortified face of my father trying to hide. Mum was in full flow and nobody was going to stop her, least of all the British Army.

"Is that him, Mary? Look, that's Mary's boy.

"Wave to us, son, would you like a scone or a pancake Betty? They're today's."

All the Scots mums had got to know each other and were probably carrying about two tonne of scones, Scot's pancake and shortbread between them. I suspect my mum would be carrying about half of that. Mum offered Betty a can of coke, which had travelled all the way from Ayrshire. It exploded in a black towering fountain over most folk within Mum's range. This caused an awful commotion, and attracted the attention and barks of the security dogs. The incredulous looks of the snotty officers made the moment even more humorous to me. Mum enveloped most of the crowd in kitchen roll, offering her apologies and more scones as a form of penance and compensation.

Celt Platoon gave the rifle salute on the march and the present arms at the halt for the depot. All the extra hours and higher demanding standards now paid off; they were heads and shoulders above all the rest in sheer regimental magnificence. The pipe band marched around to the rear of the square and halted at the centre of all the other regimental bands and corps of drums.

As we finished playing, the entire parade marched around in review order in slow and quick time. During our small playing break the pipe major broke ranks and marched up to me.

"I'm taking a wee guess that your mum is the one with the carbonated water cannon?"

I nodded with rampant pride.

"She's magnificent, Sir, and she's the Scone Queen of Scotland, Sir."

The pipe major smiled and patted his belly.

"Tell yer mum I'm rather partial to a really good scone, MacTavish, especially a really good treacle scone. Can she make treacle scones?"

"Yes, Sir," I said, nodding with pride, "sweet or tangy!"

"Well, well, you must introduce us."

The prizes were given out with cheers and jeers, as Celt Platoon won every single award. Celt Platoon was the last to leave the square. They marched off with the pipe band leading them off powerfully to 'The Black Bear'.

As soon as I was dismissed I felt my Mum's loving arms immediately envelope me, automatically force-feeding me scones at a machine-gun rate. I diverted Mum's murderous onslaught onto a grateful pipe major. I don't know if it is physically possible to climax because of treacle scones, but our pipe major was in a world of ecstasy.

We ushered our families into the immense

regimental marquee. The bar was in full flow. Bear and Cassie were drinking like drought-ridden camels. Fadge was still on heat and was positively straining at the leash to give Nurse Lusty Busty a thorough ravishing. We were just savouring our moment of glory when our pleb of a platoon commander, Lieutenant Smedly-Snodgrass, came bumbling over. We had seen him a total of six times out of the entire year. He was about as welcome as diarrhoea in a naked game of Twister.

"Well, Mr MacTavish, your son has joined the cweam of the Bwitish Ahh-may."

"Cannie be that good if you take wankers like him," said Dad.

Mum was horrified, but Sergeant Wallace and myself couldn't stop coughing up our lager with laughter. Dad was ex-SAS, and a Para RSM, with 26 years of military campaigning. In Dad's own inimitable words, 'When I joined up, they were needin them, no just feedin them'. Dad eyed Sergeant Wallace's insignia and medals. I don't know what they discussed, but I could tell Dad had been highly impressed by Sergeant Wallace.

When Dad came back I received a rather begrudged, "Apparently, you've done well."

I burst out laughing at Dad's one and only life attempt at giving me a compliment.

"Poof!"

Mum smiled.

"Nice to see you two boys getting on so well. Your dad gave you a compliment Hector!"

"He called me a poof!"

"It's the way he said it," Mum explained.

I got changed, grabbed my cases and we left the barracks. We had a few hours to kill in London before we boarded the sleeper home. I had money to burn and I wanted to really treat Mum.

Mum loved musicals, so I searched around the theatres and ticket booths for a show, but all the top shows were sold out. Eventually we managed to get tickets for a production of Captain Brown, a musical celebration of the World War One ace who supposedly shot down the Red Baron. The tickets were vastly overpriced and the queue consisted of extremely pompous socialites and would-be critics.

We sat down in the theatre and waited for an interminable age. Eventually the stage lights lowered and the great velvet theatre curtain began to rise. It was one of those bloody awful music and mime shows where the meaningless mime is accompanied by bloody awful incidental music.

"Bugger this pish, Mum! I'm no going to watch some arsehole in a black pullover leapin about the stage like some pished up eejit!" Dad roared.

"Sh!"

"Don't tell me to sh, ya prick, or you'll be eatin soup for Christmas!"

Mum's shoulders began to pump up and down as she giggled away with resigned acceptance.

"Come on, Dad, let's go."

Dad was raging, but did as he was told.

"Come on! Get me and Hector to a bar, Dad."

We drank enough to sink a battleship and made our merry way to Euston Station. We were relieved to finally slide onto the sleeper. My head felt like it had barely hit the pillow when the guard knocked on the door.

"Only half an hour to Kilmarnock, Sir."

I thanked the guard and got myself ready.

When we got home I sat down and gave my presents to my parents. Mum hugged the official photograph of the 30-strong platoon.

"Oh, look how handsome they all look, Dad. There's oor Hector and big old Bear as the company's pipers. We'll hang it above the mantlepiece, Dad."

I handed Dad a bottle of his favourite Martell and a brandy glass with the regiment's cap badge engraved upon it. After tea I grabbed my pipes to deliver my last present in style.

I marched up Murdock's drive playing my pipes. The door instantly flew open. I finished playing and we shook hands wildly and laughed.

"Come in, come in, Christ its good to see you, boy," said Murdock

"Wait a minute, I've got a wee pressie for you, it's in the taxi."

I ran back to the taxi and got my platoon photograph for Murdock.

"Champion Platoon eh! This calls for something special," Murdock said, pulling out a bottle of Glenlivet. Murdock stamped on the cork. "Silly things! I don't know why they have them? They're so anti social!"

Murdock and I quickly absorbed the Glenlivet and set off downtown. We staggered into Jekyll's tavern. There were four naked men with hats on, playing dominoes.

"Aye, Thursday night is strip dominoes," said the barman.

"Where else could you receive this Renaissance culture?" I asked Murdock.

"No many places," Murdock agreed.

In the morning I peeled my head off Murdock's couch and rubbed the red coach pattern emblazoned on my face. Murdock was still lying sparko in his chair, with a crafty grin and a sock full of dominoes. I heard the front door open and the warm Irish tones of Meemee entering the house.

"Hector! My wee tortoise," she roared, holding my face. "A wee Ulster fry love and then you can hear all my latest goss."

"Go on," Murdock urged.

Meemee and I were insatiable gossips. Meemee was the eager orator and I the avid listener. Meemee constantly amazed me by always looking so slim and radiant, especially for a woman who lived on fags, gin and anything fried. She slid off her cashmere coat and revealed an exquisite velvet dress, trimmed with fine Irish lace.

"Business lookin up, Meemee?" I asked.

"Hector, sex always makes money even when it's nearly passed its sell by date!"

Meemee winked, patting her arse and pursing her lips. Meemee was a testament to the human spirit, and the cruelty of its race. She had been sexually abused in a so-called, Christian orphanage. Meemee was only 13 when she had run to the North of Ireland to escape her abuse. Alone and penniless, most people would have succumbed to futile defeat, but not Meemee. She started off as a prostitute's runner and a go-between for clients. By the time Meemee was 15 years old, she had beaten off a stabbing and two attempted rapes. Her determination and quick business mind had made her a rapid wee fortune.

At 16 she bought her first dilapidated house, which was quickly renovated by her girls and their clients. Meemee was a madam without equal. She had a simple and well thought out plan to ensure her success.

Meemee made her clients pay for the night and not just a girl. Meemee had figured out that her clients spent a fortune in clubs, hotels and taxis. Meemee's clients booked into her house like a hotel. Her clients enjoyed the pleasure of a girl's company and a room for the night, their clothes pressed and laundered and, in the morning, they breakfasted on a fine Ulster fry.

The advantages were huge; it gave Meemee a vast mark up, really happy girls and regular customers.

Meemee's next stroke of genius was to keep her houses small and inconspicuous, to avoid trouble and attention. This suited Meemee's clientele and her business. Meemee also made a hefty profit with the sale of her properties.

By the time Meemee was 22 she had amassed houses all over Ulster. She was a hell of a businesswoman and her energy was boundless. She cooked, scrubbed, cleaned, managed and doggedly built up her little empire. For seven years she tirelessly worked to give herself wealth and power.

In her quest for fortune, Meemee had forsaken her own personal life and happiness. Her sadness became even more tragic, as she now feared any form of physical tenderness or intimacy. Rather ironic for an outstandingly good-looking woman who ran eight brothels.

Meemee was constantly propositioned, but she always declined. The cruel hand of fate had made intimacy a horrific fear of pain. Women would often throw insults at her back, but Meemee had become hardened to these and had developed rhino skin and a razor sharp tongue.

Her one outlet for her love was benefiting

deprived children. This was something that she did anonymously and generously, as nobody wanted money from a Fenian whore. Meemee despised false charity and the hypocrisy of faith, for these had been the causes of her abuse and the theft of her childhood.

This was how her life was lived until one day she noticed a group of kids playing the pipes in the street. All their eyes were locked onto the fingers of a handsome army piper. He wasn't armed or protected. He was teaching Protestants and Catholic children alike, without a care in the world. They were good, and the music was fine. Meemee made her driver, Mike, wait awhile as she was enjoying the children's performance.

Meemee's driver, Mike, spotted her interest.

"He's called, Murdock, he's mad, they've given up trying to kill him, but he won't stop teaching those kids for anything. God love him, he's as mad as a hatter."

Meemee gave Mike a 100 quid, a hell of a lot of dosh then, and instructed him to give it to Murdock. Mike returned and handed the cash back to Meemee.

"He won't take it and neither will the kids."

Meemee saw her trusty driver look at Murdock with a grin. Murdock nodded determinedly, to urge Mike on. The driver paused and sighed with hesitation.

"He said, 'Why don't you get off your bonny Irish arse, grow some balls and talk to him yourself'."

The words had barely left Mike's mouth before Meemee fired herself out of the Jag. A torrent of abuse streamed out, mercilessly blasting poor Murdock's ears. Murdock waited patiently for Meemee to stop.

"You want to ride me don't you?"

Meemee drew her hand back to punish his rude audacity. Murdock never flinched. He obligingly offered Meemee his jaw. Meemee halted her hand at the last moment.

"You're fuckin mad!"

"And you're fuckin gorgeous, now answer the fuckin question."

"I do not!" shouted Meemee, her face beginning to smile as she walked away.

"I'd love to screw you senseless!" roared Murdock.

"So would the taxman," yelled Meemee, as her Jag pulled way.

"Tell me boys, what's the name of that gorgeous woman who's put a lump in my kilt?"

Meemee did everything to repel her persistent

suitor, but all attempts failed. He did not care what she did for a living, no threat scared him off and he couldn't be bought with money or sex.

Murdock's masterstroke came on Meemee's birthday when he got the kid's band to play, 'The Black Velvet Band' for her. Murdock took Meemee's hand and the two of them waltzed in the street, completely oblivious to the cold Belfast snow. From then on Meemee followed her beloved piper wherever he played.

There was a cruel twist in love, which I could never fathom, until one night I lost my temper with Murdock. He had strayed yet again. Murdock tried to get me to back up his excuse for his eight hours of philandering.

"No! I've had enough, Murdock. You lie to Meemee, keep me out of it! She knows you're with other women! I hate havin to lie to her. Why? Why do you do it? It's obvious you love her, so why do it?" I asked.

"Because she is a beautiful woman and a lady and-"

Tears began to trickle down the great ox's face. I had never seen Murdock cry before - watching him made me feel so shallow for wounding him.

"We can't, Hector, we just can't," said Murdock. "Nothing would make us happier, but we can't. Those bastards! They hurt my Meemee, they hurt her a lot. They raped her virginity and stole her childhood. They crippled her love and all her natural desires, forever! I've never forced it or demanded it - and she really has tried and tried - but apart from kissin, huggin and makin me feel good, that's it. I've been patient for over 30 years, Hector - but she can't.

She's been to the best head doctors, but it just breaks her wee heart, so we have an unspoken arrangement. And I lie because she's too good a woman not to. I know she knows. I love her too much not to lie. But you're right, I shouldn't involve you. It's just you're the closest thing we have to a son."

Murdock's great hands covered his face to hide his shame. I put my hand on his broad shoulder and handed him a handkerchief.

"So I got lost and you found me shitfaced in a hedge."

Murdock smiled and then scowled.

"That's ma hanky, ya thieving wee shite!"

From that day on Murdock never involved me in any of his excuses. To be honest, after that night, I no longer cared.

Meemee asked me about my love life and I told her about Dolly. In return, Meemee furnished me with the latest hot gossip and scandal.

Meemee gave me an envelope.

"A wee present for you, Hector."

There was absolutely nothing wee about the present. There was £1,000 cash in it.

"Before you say anything it's from me and all the girls, so take it," said Meemee. "They wanted to give you something else as well, but I told them if they did, I'd sack them."

"Meemee, I can't!"

"Spend it, enjoy it and don't argue or there will be murders!" scowled Meemee, doing her best Taggart impression. She looked at the platoon photograph and smiled. "Oor wee Hector."

"Its too much, Meemee, it's far too much."

Meemee just smiled.

"How long do you think it will take for you to spend it, Hector?"

"Five minutes tops, Meemee, I'm so deliciously weak," I answered, honestly.

We both laughed and hugged each other. I thanked Meemee and took the envelope with as much hidden relish as I could possibly muster, much to Meemee's amusement.

We finished our Ulster fries to the tunes of Murdock's snoring.

"Why is it that fry-ups taste so bloody good after a night on the razz, Hector?" Meemee asked.

I nodded my agreement and mopped up the last of my egg and bacon fat with some soda bread, just as the taxi driver rang the doorbell.

The doorbell chimes propelled Murdock from his slumber. Murdock sprang from the couch like a kangaroo, with both his feet expertly landing on the windowsill. Meemee and I nearly wet ourselves, as we witnessed Murdock's honed ninja reflexes.

Murdock's instinctive escapology came from years of intimacy with married women. Once Murdock realised he was trying to get out of his own window, he pretended to stretch and take in the morning air, like some dedicated body builder. Meemee and I couldn't stifle our laughter.

"Well, give us a tune before you leave then!" Murdock snarled, as he climbed down from the windowsill.

I struck my pipes up. Murdock reached forward to tune my drones as he had always done. He quickly retracted his hands out of professional courtesy.

"Fuck it, you tune them!" Murdock barked.

I shook my head and nodded to Murdock to tune them. When my pipes were in tune, we both smiled and nodded.

Meemee opened the front door, I gave them a wink and marched out playing 'The Black Velvet Band'. I looked back from the taxi at Meemee and Murdock, their arms still waving frantically as I disappeared from view. I told the driver to drop me off at the bottom of our brae. Our brae veered sharply and steeply off the main road for about an eighth of a mile.

I walked up our brae enjoying the stiff cold breeze against my face. The trees on either side of the brae overlapped at the top, which formed a welcoming wooded arch during the day. At night the brae turned into a terrifying tunnel of terror. The trees would appear to jump out at you, as sudden headlights swept across them. No matter how far away the cars were, their hungry headlights would always lick your heels, as if they were about to devour you.

"How are they?" Mum enquired.

"Both just the same, Mum, just their usual - wonderful selves."

I pleaded with Mum that I had just eaten. Mum just ignored me and gave me a mountainous breakfast. Dad looked over his Scotsman and smiled at my plight. I returned the compliment as Mum repiled Dad's plate with a fresh breakfast that resembled the Grampians.

"Bitch!" Dad snarled. Dad now turned his venom on me. "I suppose you're going to piss off, get drunk and make a complete prick of yourself?"

"Oh, aye Dad, oh aye."

Dad just nodded and resumed his position behind the massive pages of his Scotsman.

"No pipe or bricks this year, son?" Dad sneered.

Mum started to snigger.

"Nice one, Dad."

Dad's brick quip referred to the first time I came home on leave.

I had promised to give Dad the kicking of his life, from the safe confines of my departing train, when I left to join the army. I had been under a slight misapprehension that the army would instantly turn me into Bruce Lee or a Shaolin Monk.

When my first leave came around I made sure I was armed with a half brick in each of my mac pockets, and a length of lead pipe down my No. 2 dress trousers. My game plan was simple; a salvo of bricks and then leather Dad with the lead pipe. If that failed I would alert Norris Macwhirter that a new sub two-minute mile was about to be set.

Mum welcomed me in with a huge boa constrictor hug.

"Oh, Dad, look how handsome he looks in his uniform."

Dad inspected me with his experienced eye, from his recumbent throne position on the couch. He grunted a 'not bad' and nodded down to the coffee table. There was a bottle of Glenlivet, a water jug, a glass and 40 Embassy Regal on the coffee table.

Dad knew I smoked and drank whisky, but I would never dare to do either in front of him. This was either Dad's way of letting me know I was old enough to make my own mistakes, or a cleverly baited trap to taunt me before he gave me the kicking from hell. Before I could make my mind up to fight or thank Dad, Mum offered to take my coat.

"God, it's an awfy heavy coat, Hector," Mum

exclaimed, holding the coat and demonstrating the weight to Dad.

I prayed to God she would just hang the coat up, but no . . .

"What are you doin with half bricks in your pockets, Hector?" asked Mum.

It was insane, but it was the first thing that came to me.

"It makes the coat hang better, Mum."

Dad's eyes began to narrow as he weighed up the absurdity of my statement.

"Sit down, Hector, and have a dram and fag while I get the dinner on," Mum urged.

I winced and tried to make the excuse that I wanted to get changed first.

"Nonsense," Mum cried, "we want to see you in your uniform, don't we, Dad?"

I tried my best to sit down with the two foot of lead pipe down my left leg. I kept my left leg straight and lunged sideways into the chair.

"What's that down your leg, Hector?" Mum asked, unwittingly digging my grave.

Dad now began to sit upright on the couch,

rolling up his sleeves and raising his eyebrows in mock enlightenment. There was no use in prolonging the inevitable, so I stood up straight, whipped the pipe out and placed it on the table.

Mum went to speak, but Dad halted her with a gesture of his hand.

"Tell me, does the length of pipe down your trousers make you look well hung too?" asked Dad.

I sat down, sparked a fag up, gulped down some Glenlivet and began my excuse.

"I thought I was going to get mugged."

"What, walking up our brae?" Dad snarled.

It was a good point. Dad's face was inches from mine "That was for me, admit it!"

"Aye! And so were the bricks!" I roared.

We both sat down. Dad gulped his brandy and I swallowed my Glenlivet.

"It's an awfy nice pipe, Dad," Mum said, appreciating its suitability for the task.

Dad and I both nodded our assassin smiles at each other. We sat in silence and drank our bottles dry. Each of us doing our level best not to smile or laugh at Mum's repeated efforts to spark up an amicable conversation.

This was the incident that Mum and Dad were ribbing me over. I nodded in exaggerated glee, acknowledging their less than welcome pun.

Mum handed me a load of paper with scribbled drunken messages, phone numbers and addresses. I inevitably met up with all my friends in the Heilanman's Umbrella. I managed to blow my leave money and £400 from Meemee's grand, on whisky and fun.

I eventually said my goodbyes to Mum and Dad. I still had ten days' leave left. I was looking forward to a rather physical week, at a wee B. & B. in Aprington.

.

CHAPTER 10

I decided to use the last two days of my leave to batter my blue book tunes. I kicked the barrack room door open and stumbled through the door with my suitcases. I jettisoned my cases onto my bed, and walked to the end of the room.

Ronnie and Cassie were sprawled on the couches watching some bestial porn. I thought I would kick the usual form of introductions off.

"Ah see your mum's made another film with that donkey again, Drummond."

"MacTavish! You lowland whore!" bawled Cassie.

"Douglas," I bellowed, "you toucan billed fucker!"

"MacTavish! Ya wee Arab's dagger!" Ronnie roared, shaking my hand.

It always made me smile when army friends met. They would always address each other by their surnames, and immediately enter into a vile exchange of playful obscenities. The viler the torrent, the greater the friendship. You could always tell if someone was really hated, as they were always addressed in the most civilised of terms.

I was just about to ask where Bear was when the room door slammed open. Bear came charging towards me in his flip flops and bath towel. I was determined to avoid a death-crushing hug, so I jumped over the couch, narrowly missing Cassie.

"Maclean, you freak, how's it hingin?" I howled.

"I-I've got a n-national t-treasure," Bear shouted, casually whipping off his bath towel and slapping the monument off Cassie's face.

"Bear! Every day I get this, every fucking day!" said Cassie, with fatigued disgust.

We quickly caught up with each other's gossip. Bear's Cora was now in Edinburgh. Ronnie's dad had been refused parole. Cassie had been re-ostracised by his family for advertising the family's, prestigious, Lord Drummond's Annual Highland Ball to 'Gaylord's's Anal Highland Ball'.

"One had absolutely no idea that so much leather and PVC existed in Scotland!" said Cassie.

Over the next few days we practised like hell, making sure our blue book tunes were perfect. We had been warned in no uncertain terms by the pipe major that we would be vigorously tested, and woe betide any transgressors of perfection.

The more experienced pipers drifted in the night before muster parade. They made sure all their kit was immaculate before they left, enjoying the late night sleeper home. They also played all their blue book tunes, first thing every morning, as part of their daily hangover cure. This was a practice that I later favoured.

After muster parade every piper played their blue book tunes to the pipe major. This gruelling process took a week to complete, but it quickly returned us all to top playing form.

After our second week back, we were ordered to parade in the main practice room. The pipe major came in with a large, thick brown envelope.

"Pipers! Listen in for your names," the pipe major ordered. Only 12 of us had our names read out.

"These names will represent the regiment at the Edinburgh Tattoo. Maclean, wait for me in my office. Sergeant McBain, issue the tattoo tunes out. The rest of you will receive your posting orders."

Cassie, Ronnie and I had been selected, but poor Bear hadn't. Ronnie and I were wondering why Bear hadn't been picked.

"Maclean, close the door, son," the pipe major ordered.

You only ever closed the pipe major's door when you played for him, or for something very serious. Bear walked out of the pipe major's office with a blank face of bemusement. The pipe major had a broad grin on his face and a chest full of pride.

"Maclean will be this year's Lone Piper at the tattoo! He will be leaving us to go on his Senior Pipers' Course."

Cheers rang out from the piping school and only a few envious pipers refrained from congratulating Bear.

To go on a Senior Pipers' Course was an incredible honour. Senior Pipers' Courses were usually given to the best battalion pipers and it was also the first rung on the promotion ladder. To be awarded a Senior Pipers' Course during training was an amazing reflection of the regiment's confidence in Bear's ability and promise.

Bear had also been given the prestigious post of Lone Piper at the Edinburgh Tattoo. I struggled for words to express my happiness and pride for him, but

Ronnie summed it up admirably.

"You big, fuckin, jammie, arse kissin, big cocked, son of a brown nosing bitch!"

Bear smiled awkwardly, and foolishly looked up at me for some comfort and defence. I turned to the pipe major.

"You know, Sir, I would try and kiss your arse, but I don't think I would be able to get past Maclean's brogues."

Bear administered one of his so-called play punches, which sent me reeling over the practice table.

"Maclean, stop that! Look after your fingers, they're piping gold," said the pipe major. "And next time, MacTavish, try greasing Maclean's brogues."

I helped Bear pack. He was more excited about seeing Cora, and was completely oblivious to the honours that had been bestowed upon him. We all waved goodbye to him at the station. I was worried about Bear, as the letters from Cora had become less and less. I only hoped I was wrong.

The next three weeks were spent feverishly learning and practising the tunes for the tattoo. Exact chalk line representations of the castle's courtyard were drawn out, for us to practise and hone our performances on.

Formation after formation and all playing scenarios were stringently drilled and rehearsed, until they were inch and step perfect. We resented a lot of the pipe major's incessant drilling, as we all knew we would be drilled for a further three weeks rehearsal at the castle.

We embarked by train for Edinburgh. I had an uncontrollable sense of excitement and pride about playing at the tattoo. Damascus was calling her wellied disciple.

Pipe Major Macmillan issued his warning and embarkation speech.

"You! Are ambassadors for Scotland, the British Army and the regiment! I will! Personally! Disembowel any bastard with my brogues and use their intestines for drone cords, if anybody brings us dishonour! Is that clear, gentlemen?"

"Yes, Sir!"

"Now, if you feel the need to be refreshed during the journey, and I'm sure you will, make sure it's a Scottish native variety. I am a keen ornithologist myself, and have delighted in the amber plumage of the low flying bird, and can highly recommend its intent study!"

We nodded dutifully in tones of sublime reverence, and passed the time by playing whisky draughts with Cassie's beautifully crafted drinking set. The set was a true drinker's thing of beauty. The board's squares were made from polished onyx and silver, the white piece glasses from frosted Edinburgh crystal and the black pieces from polished tortoiseshell. The tall king pieces were devilishly constructed with high pointed flutes, which meant you had to throw the drink back to avoid unforgivable spillage.

It had been a hard fought tournament, but I had managed to drink my way to the semis. My last victory against the formidable Cameron Younger had been a bruising affair. I now faced Cassie in the finals. Cassie possessed the better draught skills, but I possessed the greater whisky capacity. We eventually ended up having four kings apiece.

"Can we not just get inebbbi, inebrrrrriii . . .pished?" Cassie gurgled.

"I am," I slurred confidently.

The pipe major popped his head round his chair.

"I will not stand for defeatism, play on!" he commanded, gulping down the last remnants of his second bottle of Grouse. "Extraordinary plumage this one, Sergeant McBain."

"I can't see," Sergeant McBain reported, with a victorious scrunched face. "Damned clever camouflage, Sir."

While Sergeant McBain discussed his eyesight with the pipe major, I tried to focus my own mind on the game. Whisky draughts get harder and harder, as every time you take an opponent's glass, you drink it. Kings become doubles and one game usually sees the winner victoriously merry. By the end of two games all intelligence and rationality have gone out of the window. By three games, even moving your glass becomes a major ordeal; never mind making an intellectually inspired move.

I was now reduced to a gibbering wreck, but luck was on my side. I accidentally moved my king the wrong way and succeeded in making a surprisingly good winning move. I celebrated my stupendous victory by conking out for eight hours.

"Reveille! Edinburgh in an hour," roared the guard.

We quickly got washed and shaved, and removed all traces of our partying, to leave the carriage sparkling. All the top windows were pulled fully open to allow the cold refreshing air to remove the stench of booze, fart and smoke.

Sergeant McBain thanked God for the return

of his eyesight, but reported to the pipe major that the use of his legs had been stolen. The pipe major acknowledged the theft and hoped that Sergeant McBain would catch the culprit before Edinburgh, as it had been some time since he had used his broadsword for surgery.

I wandered through to the buffet car and enjoyed a nice strong cup of tea with my usual, restrained four sugars. I lit my fag up and admired the orange cracked dawn that spanned the bonny Tweed. Its wonderful rays bathed me and the buffet car in a warm, soft orange glow.

The train galloped along the spectacular east coast into Edinburgh. It felt good to step on to Waverly's busy platform. I couldn't hide my excitement as I smiled at the beckoning castle.

We started off marching fairly casually, but the nearer we got to the castle, the more disciplined our drill became. We collected our uniforms and cases from the four–tonner, and quickly set about preparing our uniforms for our first morning rehearsal.

In the morning we assembled on the castle courtyard. There were pipe bands from just about every regiment you could think of: Royal Scots; Scots Guards; Black Watch; Scots Dragoon Guards; Kings Own Scottish

Borderers; Argyles; Gordons; Queens Own and the Royal Highland Fusiliers. The various bands tuned their pipes after the Tattoo RSM had called the roll.

The noise was a magnificent swirl of pipes, brass and snare drums mixed into a wild cauldron of music. The Tattoo Sergeant Major, RSM Macmillan, ordered silence and turned to his little brother.

"Pipe Major Macmillan! Put your boys on first, and let's see what they can do!"

Our crafty pipe major nodded dutifully and turned to face us.

"You heard the man, lads, form up, we're first on. Concentrate and get it right - first time."

All our endless hours of drilling paid off; our performance was absolute perfection. All the other bands still had to learn their paces, turns, halts, positions and routes.

"Pipe Major, march your men off! I'll no need your boys for awhile," the RSM commanded.

"Right you are, Sir," chirped the pipe major. "Right boys - you have a cushy three weeks, as long as none of you get into any drama. Keep your bed spaces immaculate and we'll only have an hour's rehearsal in the afternoon. Then the rest of the day is yours – if that's okay, boys?"

His shrewd mind and detailed preparation had effectively bought us three weeks leave in Edinburgh.

"Any, any drama at all, and it will end," warned the pipe major. "Any failure to attend muster parades or keep your rooms immaculate, it will end. Woe betide the bastard who buggers this up! I will make their life a living hell! Got me? I'll see you all tomorrow afternoon, gentlemen, fall out."

The pipe major called me over.

"A big pal of yours is top of the Senior Pipers' Course, but he is in serious danger of being thrown off." The Pipe Major nodded, cocking his hand in a mimed drinking motion. "He should be in the Naafi now, do your best, MacTavish."

I packed my pipes away and made my way to the Naafi. I spotted old Bear on his own, vacantly staring at his badly bulled brogues. He looked terrible and as miserable as sin.

"Hoy, freak boy! Show us your beef bayonet!" I roared.

Bear turned his head away in shame. I popped a fag into his vague hand, which he took without a word.

"You stink like a distillery, your kit's in shit state, you have eyes like whippet bollocks, but apart from that you look just peachy, Bear."

I nodded, moving my face into his line of vision as I lit his fag. I watched a little grin quickly flick across his troubled brow.

"Bear, did you smile, did you actually smile, you miserable son of a bitch?"

Again a little smile came.

"G-good to see you, H-Hector." Bear finally stammered, giving me a desperate hug. "I-I'm in the shit, H-Hec!"

"You certainly smell like it! What you supposed to be doin right now?"

"G-got tt-two days to c-compose a w-wee 2/4 hornpipe."

"Done it already?" I asked.

Bear gave me an au naturel nod.

"Good! First things first. Hit the showers, get into civvies and then we'll sort your kit out!"

"W-what about your r-rehearsals?" Bear asked.

"It's okay, I've not got any until tomorrow. Come on, let's go."

I listened to Bear's tale of woe as he scrubbed himself clean in the shower. It turned out that Cora had rejected Bear's proposal of marriage.

"You're still shaggin her though?" I reasoned.

"Y-yesss, but it's n-no the s-same," said Bear

"You're too young to get married, Bear, besides, I need you a lot more than Cora does, you selfish bastard."

"Think so?"

"Look, Bear, we're both fucked up! When we're on our own we get in the shit – we need each other, just to stay out of the crap! You know that!"

Bear nodded.

"Y-y-you're r-right I-I know y-you're right! C-Christ we make a hell of a team, Hec."

I tried not to smile.

"If you carry on drinkin they'll throw you out. You'll be in Civvy Street and I'll be in the army! I need you flying straight, and fit for duty!"

Bear came to attention in the shower and gave me a salute.

"P-Piper Maclean, S-sir, what are your orders?"

"Well, first of all, stick some pants on, Bear. It's hard to feel superior when I'm lookin down the barrel of that thing!"

Bear and I got stuck into his kit and laundry, and after two or three hours we soon had things shipshape. Bear handed me his hornpipe composition.

"I–I think it's the b-best I-I've ever written."

Bear's compositions were always those of a genius, but this hornpipe was like no other.

"Wow, Bear . . . play it!"

Bear struck his pipes up and played. I couldn't have stopped my foot tapping even if I wanted to.

"Nobody, and I mean nobody is going to stand a chance against that."

"Y-you really like it? What's it like c-compared to my usual s-stuff - better or w-worse?"

"Bear, it is your best! I love it. Did you write this after Cora turned your proposal down?"

"H-how did y-you know?"

"Oh, the title of 'Hoor Bitch' sort of gave it away."

"A-a could rename it. W-what do you s-suggest?"

"How about 'Free and Easy'?"

Bear eyes hardened.

"A-a still love her, H-Hector!"

"No you don't! You love shagging her, you love a woman who lives for drink. If you try and pressurise her with marriage she'll bolt, and quite right too! Just have some fun! If it lasts longer than three years, then take it seriously."

Bear was sulking and I could tell he was mad, but eventually he smiled and penned the title, 'Free and Easy', with a wink.

"Right, I want your word, Bear! No daytime drinkin, finish the course and no more talk of marriage crap!"

Bear gave me his hand and shook.

"Y-you have my w-word a-and I-I will k-keep it!"

"Och, a know you will! Let's get changed and we'll go on the town with the others."

Cassie, Ronnie, Bear, Cora and I all went out on the town together. Bear drank about a bottle just to be sociable. Cora selflessly promised to shag the booze out of Bear, morning noon and night. I thanked Cora for her philanthropic charity, as this course of action clearly went against the grain.

It was a great night. Ronnie was busily engaged in trying to transplant his tongue to the bottom of a wee blonde's ankles. The wee blonde was one of the Highland dancers from the tattoo. Unfortunately for Ronnie, his progress was somewhat thwarted by the presence of her three Amazon colleagues.

"Lord – MacTavish, what would you call those three female Titans?" Cassie whispered.

"A know you wouldn't think it from their size, Cassie, but they are the most graceful and nimble footed Highland dancers . . . I've ever seen."

"But what would you call them, MacTavish?"

"Six foot three, and anything they asked me to," I answered honestly.

The three sisters were good looking, but their powerful, male-threatening physiques scared the bejesus out of me.

"Would you shag them, MacTavish?" Cassie whispered, out of the corner of his glass.

"I'd be too frightened not to, but it would have to be safe sex. I'd insist on crampons and a gumshield."

Full of Dutch courage, Cassie and I chatted and danced with the three sisters - to give Ronnie a sporting chance with the wee blonde.

I spied Ronnie creeping into our barrack room about four in the morning.

"Slut!"

"If you've got it, flaunt it, big boy," Ronnie chuckled in a loud whisper.

Ronnie was filling us in about his sexual exploits with the wee blonde at dinner. Ronnie was on a high.

"She says a really satisfied her."

"Why, did she shag your nose?" I asked.

Poor old Ronnie was just about recovering from my jibe when the wee blonde walked in with her hand down the back of an Argyll Drummer's kilt. Ronnie made an excellent recovery.

"It's no the fact she's a slag, but wi a drummer – a fuckin drummer!"

We all fell about, as pipers and drummers always regarded each other with such comical contempt. Drummers called pipers, Octopus Shaggers, and if the pipe band drummers got to play with the regimental band they would announce:

"It's so good to actually play with real musicians for a change."

Pipers would call drummers, The Windbreak, as the pipe major would always position the drummers to form an effective buffer against the wind and rain.

Poor old Ronnie had a lucky escape and the last laugh. The wee blonde's promiscuity was brought to a rapid halt when she was sent home in disgrace after spreading a horrific dose of gonorrhoea. The dancers were now referred to as 'Goldie Pox and the Three Bears'.

I felt very sorry for the three sisters who were left. They were practically ostracised through association with the wee blonde. Ronnie actually had a thing for really big women, but he was too petrified to go near the three sisters because of his past endeavours. We invited the three sisters out with us whenever we went out. Ronnie gradually began to make some headway with the tallest sister. Her name was Rhoda - so Ronnie did.

Our first actual performance in the daytime went well.

We were all straining at the leash for the night-time performance. Eventually the castle gates opened on the night. I was on fire with excitement.

"Massed Pipes and Drums by the centre, quick march!"

The crowds went wild with cheers and applause. They clapped their hands raw until we finally marched off.

"Fuck the majorettes, we want more pipes!" Granny MacTavish roared.

When we finished playing the reels at the grand finale I thought the crowds would never stop, then, from the castle ramparts, came the sound of the Lone Piper. Bear played 'El Alamein'. His music bounced off the castle walls and lingered sweetly on the night air. I had always wanted to play the pipes as the Lone Piper, and hearing Bear just rekindled the dream. When Bear finished we re-ignited the crowd as we marched off with 'The Black Bear'.

After the performance we all met up in the Esplanade Bar and began to celebrate in style. The place was alive with pipes and laughter.

Ronnie was quizzing Bear on how much whisky he could drink in a day. Bear had never ever really thought about it or measured it.

Bear deliberated awhile and casually said, "S-six, ag-good s-six bottles."

Ronnie looked at me with genuine shock.

"Yer arse," came the scornful reply from a Black Watch Piper.

"This man has gills, and will out drink anyone, anywhere, anytime!" I roared.

"Yer arse," came the baited reply.

"Game for Games!"

Cheers and chants rang out across the bar.

"Aye but no here," the Black Watch Piper replied.

Everyone grabbed their booze and props for the Games. Games were a highly lucrative and fun way of making money during training. They basically consisted of a sweepstake for bizarre party pieces. They were hilarious to watch and a great way of letting off steam during training.

It was decided that the practice hall would be the ideal venue for the Games. The Games were limited to cover the three disciplines of cockatoo, drinking and entertaining. Cameron Younger, Bear and

I were chosen for our team. Money changed hands and a book was set up for the sweepstake.

It was decided to use the method of Mothers to decide who would control each event's format. Deciding the format of each event was the key to winning, and Mothers was a quick and fun way to decide who would gain the golden advantage.

Mothers was an insult competition. Each team selected a man to trade insults about their opponent's mother. The man who got the greatest laughter from his insult, won the round. After some brilliant and cutting one-liners, the finals were now down to myself and a wee Ian from the Royal Highland Fusiliers. It was even-stevens and nobody could decide between us, so we were allowed one more insult apiece, as a tiebreaker.

The referee called for hush.

"Whenever you're ready, gentlemen!"

Wee Ian kicked the festivities off with a short, but clever, insult.

"Your Mum swims after troop ships!"

The laughs rang out. I had trouble keeping a straight face as my mother really was an Olympic class swimmer. Wee Ian tilted his jaw as he waited for my final retort.

I waited for the laughter to subside and

delivered my last salvo.

"They call your mother, Polo, because she makes a mint out of her hole!"

The hall erupted with hysterical laughter and cheering. Wee Ian shook my hand as the tears streamed down his scarlet face.

"You win, you call the tune."

I opted to go for the best piece in the Cockatoo event, rather than overall team length. One by one, some spectacular exhibitions of Scottish manhood were revealed. There were some arguments over the final measurements, then it was our turn. I cleared my throat and announced:

"Ladies and gentlemen! I give you, the Wallace Monument!"

Bear proudly lifted his kilt and beamed.

"I-is that n-no a cracker?"

"F-F-fuck aye!" came the crowd's cry.

"My God! Is that a third arm?"

"Jesus, if that thing gets hard, we'll have to evacuate the hall."

Thanks to Bear, the tape measures were dispensed with. We only needed one more win to secure the tournament dosh.

The drinking event was next. This had to be handled carefully as bravado would often overtake common sense. We decided to limit the event to one bottle of whisky, and make it a simple speed event. It didn't matter how the team drank the whisky; the winner would be the first team to drink their bottle dry.

The umpire raised his hands.

"Gentlemen, stand by your bottles . . . go!"

Bear expertly broke the seal and span the cork off with a single flick of his hand. The whisky went straight down his throat as fast as it came out of the bottle. He wasn't even swallowing, he just poured it down his throat. I was sure Bear would win, but it was declared a dead heat with MacGuinchy, the Black Watch Piper. Bear wanted another bottle to settle it, but I opted for a larger boat race. The relayed boat race was declared a dead heat as well, so after much heated debate, we settled for an event draw.

It was now down to the final event of entertaining.

First up was a Black Watch Piper with an amazing flatulent rendition of 'Highland Laddie'. I managed to just pip him by drinking a bottle of Dettol whilst gargling the signature tune of Doctor Finlay. There was a steward's inquiry whether it had actually been Dettol in the bottle, but thanks to my sterilised breath and garish white tongue, I was victoriously vindicated. We were close.

The Black Watch's next contestant was a wee piper known as Dead Eye Dick. His party piece was being able to knock a paper cup off a rifle rack from six paces, by ejaculation. It was greeted with gasps of astonishment. It was a brave attempt and a direct hit, but not hard enough to knock the paper cup off the rifle rack. Nobody was in a real hurry to shake Dead Eye Dick's hand. But his friends stalwartly reaffirmed their belief that he was still a first class wanker in their eyes.

It was all down to Cameron Younger to win the day for us. Cameron tossed his kilt over his head. He had a large face painted on his lower back with an enormous pair of red lips painted over his bum. Cameron produced a bag of Golden Wonder crisps and calmly began to feed his red lipped bottom, crisps. Somehow Cameron managed to contort his bum cheeks to chew and swallow the crisps. It was priceless and his finishing burp had everyone in kinks. There wasn't a single crumb anywhere. Cameron's expressive derriere crisp meal munched us to victory.

Nobody contested our victory. We revelled in our cheers and laughter. Cassie came around with our winnings - we had about £160 each. This was why Games were so popular during training.

We all wandered off to bed, but Bear stayed up with MacGuinchy, to continue their epic drinking duel.

"Hector, Hector wake up!"

I looked up and saw the bleary-eyed figure of MacGuinchy.

"Bear's missin! Cora and me cannie find him."

"He's not on parade until six tonight," I said, yawning.

"He's missing in uniform!" whispered MacGuinchy.

"Shite, when did he leave?"

"I don't know. I conked out after the third bottle."

We all quickly scrambled and grabbed some of Bear's civvies. Being caught drunk in uniform out of barracks was something the army punished without mercy. It was half seven in the morning, so that helped us narrow the search down. Bear had been seen in Princess Street Gardens about five minutes before we had arrived, so he couldn't be too far.

One of the uniformed park guides called me over.

"You lookin for a pissed up piping giant?"

I nodded.

"He's fast asleep in the flower clock and he's stopping the hands from going around. Am not sure, but I think somebody's called the police or an ambulance."

I thanked the guide and slipped him £20 to give the police a false description of a four-foot, piping midget with an Afro. We cut across the park and charged towards the flower clock.

The large flower clock in Princess Street Gardens was made up of flowers in the city's colours of maroon and white. There in the centre of the giant floral timepiece lay Bear. He was sprawled on his back, with his pipes in one hand and an empty whisky bottle in the other. A little crowd had gathered around him trying to wake him before the police came. An American couple called the Flooglemires were rather gingerly pulling on Bear's great tartan plaid, trying to reason with him.

"Are you the Lone Piper, honey? How come you drink so much?"

"C-Cause I'm lonely," said Bear.

We threaded a pair of trousers over Bear's legs and pulled his kilt up, briefly exposing the Wallace

Monument.

"Move along, folks! Nothin to see," the park guide urged.

"Oh, I don't know," blushed Edjeana Flooglemire.

Her husband Frank tried to pull Edjeana away, but Edjeana was having none of it.

"Gee, honey, those guys said they wore nothing under their kilts. Hell! Those guys sure are modest."

We stripped and dressed Bear like a gang of crazed funeral directors. We had just got him to the corner of the park gates when we saw the police running towards the flower clock. I smiled as I watched the wee park guide using his hands to describe a four-foot midget with an Afro.

Bear was giggling to himself, like a dog dreaming in its sleep. He weighed a tonne and we had one hell of a time carrying him up the castle hill.

I put Bear to bed. We polished and pressed Bear's full dress uniform. At three o'clock I went to wake him up, but he was still paralytic with another empty bottle at his feet. By six o'clock he was vaguely conscious, but still as drunk as a lord. It was useless, there was no way he was going to make it. I thought about saying he was ill, but they would only come round and check on him.

"Desperate times call for desperate measures." I sighed. "I'm going to do it! I've always wanted to do it and if I get caught, I've lost nothing. I'll say I hid his gear because I wanted to play the pipes as the Lone Piper. That way, at the very worst, Bear is safe and I get a few days in the pokey."

Cassie thought carefully and nodded.

"See the pipe major first and report sick, that'll stop you being marked absent or AWOL."

The pipe major gave me permission to retire from the parade and ordered me straight to bed. I double-checked on Bear - he was still out of it. I waited nervously until I heard the finale tunes. I double-checked my tuning. I was ready.

I marched smartly by the castle guide and climbed onto the great castle stone ramparts. The castle guide nodded to me and I gave him the thumbs up.

"Roger, Control, Lone Piper tuned and in position, over."

I waited till the end of the finale. The powerful searchlights suddenly glared onto me. I gulped hard and struck my pipes up. I couldn't believe it. I was going to do it, I was actually doing it. I gave it everything I had, and tried to focus on giving the performance of my life.

The powerful wind swirled hard onto me, so I braced myself hard against the battlement. I was loving every second and just wanted the moment to go on forever. The acoustics were fantastic and my old pipes sounded powerful and sweet. I finished with a smart salute and the spotlights were cut. It took a couple of minutes to sink in. I had done it. I had always dreamt of being the Lone Piper at the tattoo, but I had also wanted people to know that I was the Lone Piper at the tattoo. Still, a wee piece of a dream is better than no dream at all.

I walked tentatively down from the ramparts. A match suddenly lit up the grinning face of Bear. He was in full uniform and looking remarkably sober. He handed me the lighted fag. I took a large steadying drag. Bear smiled.

"Y-you okay? S-sounded really good, Hec."

I nodded.

"You did this on purpose, a could be in the pokey!"

Bear shook his head.

"I-I'm here, s-so who would they blame? I-I c-could have played, but when I heard y-you suggesting you should play I-I thought it was a g-great idea!"

"Were you play-acting all the time?" I asked.

"N-no, th-that MacGuinchy can drink! That was f-five bottles I sh-shifted last night."

"Yeh, five bottles will tend to do it."

"Y-You've always w-wanted to do it, s-so a let you. We're pals a-aren't we? All f-for one, always f-forever?"

We finished our fags and sauntered down to meet our fate. The coast was clear, so we crept into our barrack room. I was given a rousing cheer and a severe slagging from my pals.

"I'll do it! I'll do it!"

"Honest, Pipe Major, that doesn't hurt at all."

"Hi Edjeana, I'm the Lone Piper!"

"Mum, look, an Action Man in a kilt!"

I didn't offer any reply, as a single bite from me would have led to a fresh onslaught of abuse. I pretended to deafly polish my kit and keep a deadpan poker face. I finished my kit, casually walked to the door and gave my best Terry Thomas response.

"You really are a shower, an absolute shower!"

We had a whale of a time at the tattoo, but like all good things it had to come to an end. The last night was sublime. After our last performance we all charged into the Esplanade Bar. Everybody was partying as if the world was going to end tomorrow.

We were waiting to get served when the pipe major called us over to a castle sentry guard.

"Tell them what you told me!" said the pipe major.

"Well," the sentry began, "there's a guy outside, pissed as a parrot. He keeps asking to see yous three. Every time I ask him why, or who he is, he keeps saying: 'Who's hung like a bear? Who shags like a train? Who speaks French? Moi!'"

We all shouted at the same time:

"Fadge!"

The pipe major nodded.

"Bring him in, son, he's one of us."

Fadge sauntered into the room. He was well on, but still in good form. He had come top of both his cadre and parachute courses. In only seven months he had achieved rank and completed two of the toughest courses in the British Army. Even the most determined professional would have taken at least two years. If it hadn't been Fadge, you would have said it was physically impossible.

He was 17 and the youngest lance corporal in the regiment. His nearest contemporary was considered a wonder kid at nineteen. It was impossible to book on to these courses never mind complete them in such a short space of time. Fadge smiled his wide, fox-like grin. He could tell we wanted to know his secret.

"She's got really, really big tits, she works in the records office, she's as ugly as sin, but she'll have me a general within the year."

Fadge was in mid-sentence when Bear wrenched Fadge's head under his kilt - face to face with the Wallace Monument.

Fadge calmly announced, "I'm no that desperate for promotion. Oh Christ, he's just been using it! Bear!"

Fadge had taken absolutely no leave and didn't intend to. Tomorrow was the start of his eight-week Long Range Snipers' Course. This was to be followed by his Section Commanders', with only three weeks between each course. He then had his Senior Brecon Beacons two months after that. I wanted to congratulate Fadge, but I gave him the standard.

"You lazy bastard!"

This was a superhuman and punishing feat of dedication. Fadge was effectively going to achieve all the hardest and necessary promotion courses for his career in under a year.

"Barring injury, nothing is going to stop me. These courses and physical endurance will toughen me up for my last and final test," said Fadge.

It was a bold and ingenious training scheme using each course to build up his skills, knowledge, physical and mental endurance. He was steeling himself for SAS selection as well as pole vaulting his career. But I was worried he would burn himself out with all his superhuman efforts. He was buzzing with enthusiasm, and I felt happy for him.

Fadge's graphic description of his sexual exploits with the ugly girl in records had us all in fits. The ugly girl in records was under no illusions. It really was a case of quid pro quo, as each course was bought by relentless sex from Fadge. Fadge's only real worry was that his career Klondike would become impregnated or discovered by a career rival.

Fadge paused awhile.

"You just looked fantastic, you've no idea how good you all looked; the power of all the pipes, the crowd goin mental. It was so good, I would have given anything to have been out there with you, boys."

It went quiet as we all looked into Fadge's watering eyes. I struggled to give him some form of consolation.

"W-what, as a s-six fingered drummer?" asked Bear.

We all spat and choked on our drinks. Fadge managed a token rebuff.

"You forgot, c-c-corporal, you big cocked f-f-fucker!"

We reluctantly escorted Fadge to Waverly Station in the morning and said our goodbyes.

"Still got these babies to insult you with." Fadge cheered, giving us the Vs with his bad hand.

We gave Fadge the Scouts' three-fingered salute back. Fadge cracked up and gave us his two-fingered one thumb salute back as the train pulled away.

We walked back to the castle. We had the rest of the day to pack our kit up and one more night's drinking before we got the train back. As we entered the practice hall all hell broke loose.

The pipe major was trying to separate Sergeant McBain and Piper Manly.

"Right! If either of you speak or move I'll have you court-martialled!" the pipe major roared. "I mean it! One more peep or move, and I'll guarantee you'll forget what daylight looks like!"

After some rather astute questioning, the pipe major had ascertained that Sergeant McBain was slightly miffed at Piper Manly for sleeping with his girl and broadcasting the fact around the band. Sergeant McBain had taken a little personal revenge to even the score up, and that's when the fight had broken out.

The pipe major was now passing judgement over the matter.

"Look, Piper Manly, you know as well as I do that putting a hair under a drone reed tongue is a quick recognised cure to make a drone reed work."

"But, Sir, that bastard-"

"Sergeant McBain, Piper Manly!" the pipe major intervened.

"Aye, Sir, Sergeant McBain, the bastard, didnae pluck the hairs from his head, he ripped them oot o his arse! That bastard-"

"Sergeant McBain!"

"That dirty bastard stuck his arse hairs in my reed and asked me to blow it!"

"Did the drone work, Piper Manly?"

"Am no going to blow the reed, Sir, that's hellish!"

"Now listen here, Piper Manly!" the pipe major roared. "You were keen enough to munch Sergeant McBain's girl's hair, so it's seems only fitting that you sample Sergeant McBain's. Now blow the reed - and that's an order! If it doesn't work, I'll get Sergeant McBain to blow and sort the reed out for you."

Piper Manly blew the drone. The drone worked well and sounded remarkably sweet.

The pipe major smiled.

"Now, Piper Manly, go and have a good gargle with some Grouse, and if you're any type of piper at all, you'll buy Sergeant McBain a few for sortin your drone out. And if Sergeant McBain is any friend of mine, he will return the favour. Let's celebrate our last evening in style."

We drank through the night and staggered onto the dawn London train. We looked like drunken vampires returning to their satanic crypts. The carriage blinds were pulled down to protect its sleeping corpses from desecration, until we reached the dark cloak of Euston Station.

.

CHAPTER 11

Bear and I spent our leave together at the barracks. Bear had been given early posting orders to join the regiment in Hong Kong. He had come top of the Senior Pipers' Course, and the regiment were desperate to show off their new, piping jewel.

Bear had been allocated three, large wooden MFO boxes for his personal belongings. This seemed a trifle indulgent as his only possessions consisted of a Harris Tweed suit, his pipes and a porn projector he had won in one of Fadge's dodgy raffles.

We placed the bulk of Bear's military kit into one of the boxes and screwed it down tight. I felt a bit like a distraught mother saying farewell to her only son. I thought of all the times that I had cursed him, and I knew I was about to say farewell to the most loyal and truest of friends.

We waited for the taxi together as I reeled off my endless checklists.

"Got your tickets, your passport? Have you got

your posting orders?"

Bear nodded dutifully.

"Money, have you got enough money?"

Bear smiled and nodded again. The taxi pulled up and we headed for the train station.

"Right, no excessive drinking, no a mean it, and no whipping the Wallace Monument out when they ask you, 'have you anything to declare, Sir?'."

Bear rocked his hand back and forth in a so-so motion.

"Serious, Bear, be careful. A lot of them will find you a threat, so keep shtum, and try to blend in," I said, talking to the six foot seven inched giant with the strength of Hercules.

Bear nodded again.

"I-I know, Hector, I-I know."

"I know you know, but don't, Bear! Please, don't - especially the drink. That's what they'll use to trip you up with."

The train pulled in and Bear loaded his pipe case and luggage.

"Tr-try and n-no become i-immune to p-penicillin, Hector, it will ruin your s-social life!" said

Bear.

"You know a condom could stop that green shit leaking out the front of your trousers," I shouted back.

I watched the train pull away into the distance with Bear's mammoth arm waving for all it was worth. My farewell warning to Bear became sublimely ironic, as drunkenness and trouble became my unshakeable companions.

The army administered its justice and punishments in a rather one-sided ceremony called Orders. Orders were supposed to be a fair trial, but they were more akin to the Spanish Inquisition.

Orders started off with the RSM standing you at ease outside the prosecuting officer's door. The RSM would then scream, 'Open the door!'. The officer's door (although inanimate) would obey the order and fly open. The RSM would bring you up to attention and then march you through the doorway at the speed of light.

The format for Orders would generally go like this.

"Orders! O ... des ... s, shun! Open the door! When I say B, your left foot will strike the ground.

When I say R, your right foot will strike the ground. Quick march! Brrrrrrrrrrrrrrrrrrrr! Mark time! Orde . . . s halt!"

The purpose of this first ingenious phase was to completely disorientate you and let you know that you were unconditionally at the mercy of the prosecuting officer's, omnipotent power. The prosecuting officer would then identify you and read out the charge in an unintelligible, Lord Charles accent. Even if you could understand the officer there was absolutely no way you would decipher the army's legal jargon. This was deliberate, as you could quash the whole prosecution by simply refuting a keyword from the charge.

Once the charge had been stated, the sergeant major would then adopt the role of Torquemada, and read out the circumstances of the crime. This always started with the war cry of, 'Inasmuch as . . .'.

The chief prosecution witness would then read out a statement, or the RSM would read out documentary evidence on their behalf. Documentary evidence was the usual format, as not many people would argue with the RSM. The prosecuting officer would then ask you if you had anything to say. This was your chance to present your case for the defence. This was usually hampered by the RSM punctuating your every spoken word with:

"Shut up!"

Once you had surrendered to the futility of your defence, the prosecuting officer would utter the charming phrase:

"Do you accept my ward?"

You were obliged to say 'yes' without knowing his verdict or punishment. The prosecuting officer would then find you guilty and state the punishment, which would be carried out immediately.

After gaining many striped suntans in the guardroom, I quickly began to understand the ingenious concept of army law. In army law, innocence had absolutely no bearing on the case whatsoever. The army was never wrong. If they said you had buggered the queen's corgies on a unicycle, while getting a clear round at the Badminton Horse Trials, then you bloody well had!

It was the legal process that mattered to the army - not your innocence or punishment. This was their Achilles heel, and I fully intended to blow their feet off with a belt-fed bazooka.

I quickly purchased a copy of The Queen's and King's Regulations of Army Law from Peebody's second-hand bookstore in Aldershot. It proved to be the most judicious of investments. The Queen's Regulations gave me the charges, keywords, punishments and, most importantly, the means of my admonishment.

I became wholly addicted to King's Regulations, as they actually gave you live examples of army law. My favourite example was when a bandmaster of the Royal Anglicans was charged with 'rape by fraud', as he had been fondling a band member of the Woman's Royal Army Corps breasts under the pretext it would vastly improve her bugle playing.

I studied the army law tirelessly and formulated the MacTavish Defence Stratagem. The MacTavish Defence Stratagem had three easy tactics that could be applied to any case, regardless of innocence or evidence.

My first tactic consisted of learning and refuting the keywords of the charge at the start of the trial. By proving the vocabulary of the charge incorrect, you were automatically admonished. This was a very quick and powerful method, particularly if you were innocent. The only real drawback with this method was trying to maintain amateur status.

The second tactic was to learn the admonishing circumstances, and make them the basis of your evidence. It was vital never to be drawn into arguing your innocence (a condition I rarely suffered from). This tactic allowed the army an honourable surrender under determined fire. It was by far and away my most successful tactic.

When faced with overwhelming and damning evidence your only other tactic was to lie like Baron Munchausen - the more unbelievable, the better. If you could make them drop their monocle or split their jodhpurs, admonishment was the prize. The army didn't mind outrageous lying, in fact they positively encouraged it.

My father's explosive temper and veracity of wrath had ably equipped me with this noble facet. I was so terrified of my dad I would instinctively lie about the most trivial of matters. The madder Dad got, the more I lied.

The most ridiculous lie I ever told my dad happened when I used his exploration camera. Dad had specifically banned me from going anywhere near his treasured camera so when Dad saw the photos of me photographing myself in the mirror with his beloved camera: he went mental. Dad's anger seemed to increase somewhat when I denied it was actually me in the photographs.

"It's you! It's fucking you," Dad screamed, "with my exploration camera! It's you taking pictures of yourself in the mirror with my camera."

"I admit he's wearing my clothes, Dad, but how the hell did he get into our house?" I asked.

"It's fucking you!"

"The similarities are quite uncanny, Dad, but-"

"It's fucking you! It's fucking you, just admit it, it's fucking you!"

"You would think so wouldn't you, Dad?"

Dad had unwittingly given me the tenacity and necessary legal skills that became the envy of the entire depot. All recruits hailed the Admonishment King.

However, if the army really wanted you, they would get you one way or another. The army phrase of, 'Your arse is grass, laddie, welcome to Mower Land!' explained the army's ability to punish you no matter how innocent you were. If the army really wanted to, they could prove you invented cholera. Anyway, the army didn't need a reason to punish you; it was part of their job.

Most soldiers appeared on Orders about once every three months. My batting average was now five times a week. My incredible story telling and legal skills had turned me into the number one, box office draw on Orders. Even the RSM admired my unblemished admonishment record.

My high admonishment rate wasn't solely due to my honed legal skills, for, as I have already mentioned before, if the army really wanted to get you they would, one way or another. My real luck lay in the fact that both the adjutant and the depot commandant were charismatic Irishmen. They lived life to the full, and at a damned sight faster pace than I did. They admired bold wildness and character in a piper. They could have punished me any time they liked, but they much preferred to listen to my own entertaining version of events and admonish me.

The commandant's name was Colonel Pat Fansy. His adjutant was Captain John O'Connell. Together they were known as the Blarney Twins. They were notorious womanisers and they lived life to a sinful extreme. My daily visits to them on Orders broke the monotony of their desk jobs, which they so hated.

Colonel Fansy was a great comedian and knew that Captain O'Connell and myself were totally unable to hold our laughter. He would remorselessly try and get us to corpse with laughter during Orders, with relentless double entendres and spoonerisms such as:

"I'll have your guts for garters or my name's not Fat Pansy!"

Sometimes Colonel Fansy would hide behind his office curtains and roar at bemused recruits through his loudhailer:

"Warning! Warning! This is not a drill, this is a megaphone."

The only penance Colonel Fansy placed upon me was that I was obliged to play his comedic version of Mastermind. Colonel Fansy's jovial version required great skill in composing the questions. As I had the most to gain, I was usually given the role of quizmaster. If I lost, I was generally made to carry out some moronic task or forfeit. If I won, I was usually guaranteed admonishment from my next charge.

We would normally play during our dinner break or immediately after Orders. The rules were simple; as the quizmaster you had to remain totally straight-faced and devise your own jovial questions and answers. Each session took great preparation, as each question and answer had to be totally original. The contestant was allowed no passes and had to provide constant quick-fire quips, with a totally straight face, for the full two minutes. This kept the pace fast and furious, making it immensely challenging and enjoyable. Any delays or use of recognised jokes meant immediate defeat.

Poor Captain O'Connell was our adjudicator and audience. His infectious, high whooping laughter made keeping a straight face practically impossible. In some ways the humour was a bit like a 'Carry On' film, as it was the set up question that was really funny as you could almost guess the punchline from the question.

Our sessions would usually go like this.

"Name and occupation?"

"Pat Fansy, Colonel."

"Correct! What is the correct term for a dehydrated lesbian smoking cannabis?"

"A dry stoned dyke."

"Correct! Complete the following phrase, 'The boy stood on the burning deck . . .'"

"It's a silly game of cards anyway."

"I'll accept the answer, but I was really looking for, 'pass me the oven gloves, big boy, it's my deal'. Define a hormone?"

"Syphilis and the exchange rate."

"Correct! My dog has no nose, how does he smell?"

"Through a system of bi-optic valves."

"Correct! What game do they play at the blind school?"

"Blind man in the buff."

"Incorrect! I hear with my Big Ear. What did the rain in Spain do?"

"It ended under the fascist dictatorship of General

Franco."

"Correct! Why do birds sing when you are near?"

"I have a bad case of worms."

"Correct, please sit still! Give a valid argument for euthanasia and necrophilia."

"Barbara Cartland."

"Correct, but personally I think they're just a wonderful social icebreaker."

The main reasons for my high charge rate and troubled times, came from the new teaching staff at the piping school. The new Pipe Major McMuchie was twisted with hate. The two new pipe sergeants who accompanied him were his sadistic sycophants. They were all due to be thrown out of the army, but they were determined to poison the waterhole before they left.

We had been thoroughly warned about Pipe Major McMuchie and his staff by Pipe Major Macmillan.

"They are pure shite! Get posted, boys, as quick as you can," warned Pipe Major Macmillan. "They can only do you harm, so keep a low profile, and get posted as quick as you can. I'll do my best to speed your posting orders, but they have friends in high places."

From the moment Pipe Major Macmillan left the piping school, our happy world vanished. Nobody was exempt from McMuchie's bullying reign of evil.

They made poor Ronnie's life a living hell. He could hardly play through nerves. Pipe Major MacMuchie's sergeants, McMainge and Maclumpher, didn't only confine their bullying to the piping school. They would ransack our rooms at all hours of the night pretending to be searching for drugs, then give us room inspections in the morning.

Sergeant Maclumpher was about six four with a fat pockmarked face. His matted ginger hair and thick specs gave him a Mr Potato Head look. Sergeant McMainge had a droopy bandito moustache, with sallow skin and jaundiced eyes.

You could tell the contempt in which Pipe Major McMuchie and his sergeants were held, as nobody ever referred to them by their rank. We were constantly reminded to use their rank titles, with beatings and penile punishment.

To forget Pipe Major McMuchie and his crew altogether, we used to shoot off downtown to get absolutely hammered. Unfortunately for us our money didn't stretch far, so we would busk on the weekends or carry out bizarre bar bets, to boost up our money.

By far and away our best cash generator in bars was my ability to drink the weird and wonderful. For some reason, Brasso drinking used to get us tons of cash. My baby face combined with the vileness of the task seemed to appeal to the pub-betting crowd. People would clamber to take up the bet, even if they'd seen me do it before.

I used to pour the can of Brasso straight down my throat and not stop until the last drop was gone. I would always ham it up and take the little residue out of the Brasso top, as if I was desperate for the stuff.

Occasionally someone would accuse me of substituting the Brasso or watering it down. Cassie would capitalise on this and make even more money by betting the accuser. It also added to the whole theatre of the spectacle.

After my Brasso session, I would leave a suitable pause for the excitement to die down. I would then find some godforsaken spot and force myself to retch. It didn't matter how intently I tried, there would always be some painful residue left in my stomach. The acid residue stung like hell and the oils made me queasy. I tried all kinds of remedies from olive oil, chalk, milk and gallons of water, but none of them really worked, so I would usually just get pissed as a parrot and enjoy the rest of the evening.

It was Ronnie's birthday and we were partying our tartan socks off. The whisky flowed at a dam busting rate. I was so drunk I'd forgotten to empty my stomach of Brasso. When last orders were called, Cassie whipped out his not so flexible friend.

"Gentlemen! As a birthday present to Ronnie two beaks, I insist we all go down to the Islamic Leap. My treat!"

The Islamic Leap was our affectionate name for the Dewdrop Indian Restaurant. The Dewdrop's cuisine was excellent and the staff were brilliant hosts. In the restaurant the staff were courteous, professional and dressed handsomely in Bengal uniforms. But we much preferred to go upstairs to the more relaxed atmosphere of the staff's café. It was far more entertaining and a lot more akin to our means.

We would regularly party with the staff until dawn. We were always royally entertained with the staff's bill of fare and their love of music. You would imagine with all the rich and diverse cultures of music from India and Asia to draw upon, the staff would be spoilt for choice, but no, they only favoured one type of music and that was country and western. They were cowboy daft and loved to wear silk fringed shirts with

Stetsons. The pride and passion that went into their versions of these songs and dances was enthusiastically infectious.

Raj, the owner, who preferred to be called Roy, did a superb John Wayne accent that had us in tears.

"Well, pilgrims, tonight's the night where the Indians take the reservations. We got Apache Rogan Gosh, comes in longhorn and rooster. A'd steer clear of the Chicken Phall, or you really will have some blazing saddles. Now, you enjoy your meal, ya hear!"

Roy and the boys did us proud. We finished the night off by singing the Dewdrop's farewell anthem of, 'Ring of Fire'. We thanked Raj and the boys, and staggered back to barracks.

I'm a deep sleeper at the best of times, but with a good drink in me I become an unwakable zombie. I began to cough hard in my sleep. A wash of blood and Brasso acid formed a large choking bubble in my throat, which forced me awake. I couldn't breathe in or out. My eyes streamed with water and my lungs began to burn with desperation. I bounced off lockers and fell onto the floor flailing wildly for help, but it was like trying to wake the dead. I floundered onto the floor, bucking and fighting for breath.

Ronnie slammed the lights on and saw my grimaced choking face. I began to wildly point to my neck and desperately slap my throat.

"Hold him down," screamed Ronnie.

Cassie and Cameron grabbed my arms and pinned me to the floor. Ronnie grabbed his dirk, fished the long pronged fork from its side sheath and plunged it down my throat. The pressure from my lungs exploded blood all over Ronnie and splattered it onto the high white ceiling. I began to cough and throw up blood and acid onto the floor. Ronnie slapped my back as I gasped and spluttered for air. My throat pulsed with pain where Ronnie had harpooned the fork into my throat.

Cassie wiped my eyes, and the blood off my face and neck. As my breathing steadied I began to hear the shouting of my friends.

"No need to ask what caused that to happen," Cassie said, nodding and looking at the puddles of oil-ridden blood on the floor. "No more Brasso, Hector, no more. It's too fucking dangerous-"

"That's right, Hector, no more Brasso - no more fucking anything! Get to the guardroom, move!" Sergeant Maclumpher snarled.

I could hardly stand, but he force-marched me to the guardroom. He was drunk and filled with hateful glee.

Sergeant Maclumpher had tried many times to cause my downfall, and now he had the evidence and the means for my demise. He charged me with drunkenness, conduct unbecoming and self-inflicted wounds. I was remanded in the guardroom cells, awaiting commandant's Orders.

The first two charges weren't really a problem, but the self-inflicted wounds could be used to get me kicked out. The trouble was I didn't know how long Maclumpher had been there, how much he saw or how much he would concoct.

I was still in a lot of pain, but I was clever enough to appear sober and unscathed to the RP and guard sergeant.

"You sure you want to do this? He looks okay to me," the guard sergeant asked Maclumpher.

"Oh yeh!" Maclumpher smirked. "Bang him up good and proper, and I want him examined."

"We'll have to take him to the med centre," the guard sergeant answered, trying to avoid the paperwork.

"Good!" Maclumpher sneered.

"You'll have to make a statement," said the guard sergeant wearily.

"Not a problem!" slurred Maclumpher, falling

against the wall.

"Go and have some coffee and come back in half an hour, unless you want to go in the book yourself!" said the guard sergeant in disgust.

Maclumpher gave the guard sergeant a hard drunken glare.

"Okey-dokey, see you in a mo," Maclumpher said, holding up his hands in submission. "I just want a word with him before I go."

Maclumpher couldn't resist baiting me through the cell hatch

"You're out now! All that work and you're out, and there's nothin you can do," Maclumpher said, tittering. "The duty medic's goin to take some samples, so you're fucked! No commandant, no smart arsed bullshit is going to save you now!"

"That's the last time I'm warning you," said the guardroom sergeant. "Fuck off now, or you're goin in the book."

"All right! Keep your shirt on. I'm goin, okay!"

"I'll take MacTavish over to the med centre," said the RP corporal. "That Nurse Baxter's on tonight, and she's fuckin gorgeous!"

The RP corporal straightened his beret before

ringing the med centre bell. Nurse Louise Baxter answered the door looking more bustier than ever. She completely ignored me as if we had never met.

"I've got everything ready for him. I'm glad it's you, Steve," she cooed.

The RP corporal almost forgot why he was there. My escort gave a hard cough just to remind him.

"Well, bring him in then!" the RP corporal ordered. "Where do you want him, Nurse Baxter?"

"Just sit him there, Steve, and call me Louise, all my friends do," she said, taking his arm. "What's his name and number?" she asked.

The RP corporal got his notebook and gave it to her.

"I'll just get his notes and I'll give you your notebook back in a minute. There's some brew kit over there, make us a nice cup of tea, Steve," she said, pouting her lips.

Nurse Baxter returned with my medical notes and a kidney tray.

"Roll up your sleeve," she ordered.

I went to speak, but she quickly dug her nails into my arm. She took two samples of my blood and put them into her smock pocket then calmly pulled out two fresh samples from her plastic apron and placed them into the kidney tray.

"Steve, get those lads to watch him pee in these," she pleaded.

"You heard her," the RP corporal shouted.

The barrack guard gave her my samples and she wrote my details on the specimen bottles.

"I'll do a preliminary check here and send the others off for a cross-check," she said. "Only takes a few minutes to check for booze or drugs. Back in a minute."

The RP corporal nodded and sipped on his tea. Nurse Baxter returned 15 minutes later looking perplexed.

"He's as clean as a whistle, Steve. I'll send his other samples off for analysis, but I'm sure he's clean. Is some bugger playing games?"

"Probably that Sergeant Maclumpher. He's as pissed as a newt himself," said the RP corporal.

"Well, I'll give him a good examination just to be sure. Right, strip!"

I did as I was told.

"You can see for yourself, Steve, not a mark on

him apart from a couple of old bruises on the shins. Right, get dressed. You make a lovely cup of tea, Steve," she said, winking. Nurse Baxter signed her examination report. "I'll need your witness signature, Steve, and then you can have a copy for evidence. Save you writing anything out."

"Cheers, Louise."

I was escorted straight back to the guardroom.

"He's as clean as a whistle," the RP corporal complained to the guard sergeant.

"Nothing at all?" the guardroom sergeant asked angrily.

"No, just a couple of old bruises on the shins. Here's the medical report."

"That wanker Maclumpher's not come back or made a statement! Go find him, Steve. I want him here now! He's married. Try his quarters first and get the pissed up prick here. Tell him he's got 30 minutes to get here or he's going in the book!" said the guard sergeant.

The RP corporal locked me back in my cell.

"Staff, what about my kit for Orders?" I asked.

"I'll radio the barrack guard to get it. If I was you, I'd stay up all night and make sure it's immaculate," said the RP corporal.

About three in the morning my cell door swung open. Cassie and Ronnie handed me my No. 2 dress, my cleaning kit and my washing and shaving kit. I nodded gratefully at the immaculate brogues and kit. Cassie winked.

"Nil desperandum!"

"You there! No talking to the prisoner," bawled the RP corporal. The RP corporal slammed my cell door shut and escorted Cassie and Ronnie away.

My stomach felt fine, but my throat was nipping a bit. My kit was already done to a gleaming standard, but I thought I'd better just check it to make sure. As I checked my kit over I noticed a tiny note pinned to the inside of my No. 2 dress jacket.

Gargle with the bottle of warm salt water. There's also ether spray, Goldspot and mouthwash in your wash kit. We are all denying you were drunk or drinking Brasso! And that Maclumpher was just picking on you because he was so drunk. The room's been bleached and cleaned. Good luck, old thing.

The inside of my throat was still sore, but I swallowed

the note straightaway. I carefully gargled with the salt water and spat my swill through the bars of the window. My spit was a dirty blood red. Lumps of hardened blood began to dislodge and dissolve. I repeated this throughout the night. As the night wore on, my swirl became clearer.

My throat was still a wee bit rough, but the ether soon cured that. All in all I was in pretty good shape.

There was no physical evidence against me - it was my word against Maclumpher's. I went through the possible scenarios in my head and rehearsed my answers. I had to be careful because the one thing I couldn't afford was a court martial. If I was placed on a court martial they would examine me properly and that would be it for me, and Louise Baxter. She had risked her career for a piper she hardly knew. She was some girl, in physique and spirit. I eventually closed my eyes and got an hour's sleep.

"Breakfast, you toatie, tartan pie-eyed Piper of Hamilton!"

I would have recognised the voice anywhere. It was Sergeant Wallace.

"Ten minutes to slop out, wash and shave, or, if you're intelligent, drink your slop and flush the breakfast. You aw right, son?"

I smiled back and quickly got myself ready. Sergeant Wallace marched me to breakfast. I swallowed down the breakfast, it stung a little but my throat felt a lot better.

"I was Sergeant in Waiting last night," said Sergeant Wallace. "Maclumpher was in the mess. Pissed up and bragging he was going to have you thrown out. He was out of his box. We poured him into a bunk and I've only just woken him." Sergeant Wallace opened his Orders folder. "He's not even submitted the charge to me. So he needs to get that typed up and get his kit ready for Orders. He's failed to give the guardroom sergeant or me a statement, so he'll have to give evidence himself!" Sergeant Wallace laughed. "When we get back, there'll be a copy of Queen's Regs under your bed pack. That gives you half an hour to prepare, so make the most of it, son. Ready to move, MacTavish?"

I stood outside the commandant's office shining like a new pin. There were six others on Orders. All the prosecution witnesses were present except for Maclumpher. Sergeant Wallace chalked up the names along with their charges on the Orders board. The last charge of bigamy got a resounding cheer.

Out of the corner of my eye I spotted the dishevelled figure of Maclumpher running along the road. Maclumpher looked terrible; his face and neck were caked in blood from hurried shaving. He was still drunk, and desperately trying to hide the fact.

Colonel Fansy and Captain O'Connell briskly marched past us. Sergeant Wallace brought us up to attention and saluted.

"Work the door, Sergeant Wallace, the sergeant major's on course," the commandant ordered.

"Yes, Sir," replied Sergeant Wallace.

After a quick glance at the charges, Colonel Fansy signalled that he was ready to start.

"Open the door!"

"Okay, MacTavish, get ready," whispered Sergeant Wallace. "Orders! O . . . dess shun! Quick march! Lef righ, lef righ, lef righ, lef righ, mark time! Orde . . . s halt! Right turn!"

"You are Piper MacTavish 2-2-4-6-8-9-3?" asked the commandant.

I took a pace forward and saluted.

"Yes, Sir."

"Piper MacTavish, you are charged contrary to the Army Act with drunkenness, conduct unbecoming and self-inflicted wounds. Type of evidence, duty sergeant?" Colonel Fansy enquired.

"Evidence from Sergeant Maclumpher, Sir," Sergeant Wallace replied.

There was a pause as the sweating Sergeant Maclumpher tried to pull himself together.

"Proceed, Sergeant Maclumpher," roared Colonel Fansy.

"Eh, eh, eh on the night, Sir, on the ehhhh."

The colonel lifted his steely blue eyes and fixed them on Maclumpher. This just made Maclumpher worse.

"What in God's name did you fucking shave with, man? A fucking broken vodka bottle, or did you drink that before you came through the door? You're in shit state! That's not a shave, that's a fucking skin transplant! You're lucky I don't charge you with self-inflicted wounds, in fact, you're on a charge. Fall in behind Orders once we're finished. Do you understand? Do you understand!"

"Ye-s, S-sir," Maclumpher stammered.

"Now recite your evidence!" Colonel Fansy snarled.

"Well, S-sir, on the night of eh, eh," Sergeant Maclumpher havered.

Colonel Fansy stood up to reveal his immense height and frame.

"If you don't want me to add drunkenness and conduct unbecoming to your charge sheet, I would strongly suggest you withdraw the charge!"

"Y-yes-ss, Sir," whimpered Maclumpher.

"Any more of your drunken night visits to the pipers' block and I'll post you to Siberia to test fucking PT shorts! Give him four extra duty sergeants, adjutant, and think yourself lucky you're still a sergeant! Get out of my sight!"

Maclumpher scuttled out of the door. Colonel Fansy's face suddenly transformed into a picture of saintly serenity.

"And, now for you, my wee Trojan hero. The charges have been withdrawn, so there are no charges to answer. Will you accept my ward?"

I held my head high and braced myself up.

"I accept your ward, Sir!"

"Nothing will appear on your records, MacTavish. I doubt they could fit anything else on them anyway. But I am going to send you on recruitment tour. It'll keep you away from Pipe Major McMuchie and his spawn"

"Sir, if I could speak, Sir-"

"It's usually stopping you I find such a chore," the commandant said, smiling. "Go on, MacTavish, say your piece."

"Well, Sir, Piper Douglas is the one in need of the greatest protection. I would prefer him to go, Sir."

"Would you now? Anybody else?"

"Pipers Drummond and Younger, Sir."

"Can Younger actually play, MacTavish?"

"No, Sir, and that's because McMuchie's lot aren't teaching him. He'd actually learn off us, and he would be safe, Sir."

"He may learn from you, MacTavish, but I would doubt if the man would ever be safe. Very well, mark it down, adjutant, Pipers Douglas, Drummond, MacTavish and Younger to go on the recruitment tour. You leave tomorrow. Come down in an hour and pick up your orders, and the adjutant will brief you all up. Anything else, adjutant?"

"Yes, Sir, our supplies!" the adjutant urged.

"Ah yes! As your mother has now got us wholly addicted to her scones and shortbread, we would be most grateful if you would kindly furnish us with some more of those culinary masterpieces. A fair exchange

MacTavish?" Colonel Fansy asked, preening his moustache.

"Sir, I've got some in the room, but if you were to thank her personally by letter, I guarantee you'll never want again!"

"Capital, MacTavish, capital! Now, be a good chap and get ready to open the door for Sergeant Wallace's next onslaught."

I saluted Colonel Fansy and gripped the door handle.

Colonel Fansy took a deep breath and bellowed: "Open the door!" I whipped the door open. Sergeant Wallace marched the next poor devil through the door at warp factor four. I slipped out of the room and closed the door silently behind me.

CHAPTER 12

The RSM marched Cameron, Cassie, Ronnie and I into Colonel Fansy's office. Colonel Fansy poured himself a bracing Glenlivet as he realised the full implications of his otherwise glittering career.

"You have your warrants, uniforms, pipes and luggage?"

"Yes Sir!"

Colonel Fansy took a deep gulp of his whisky with the look of a doomed man.

"I realise that it is completely futile to ask you to stay out of trouble during your eight-week recruitment tour. So I'm asking for something, which is realistic! I want quality recruits and I want plenty of them! Don't give me anybody - you wouldn't want fighting at your shoulder. Is that clear?"

"Yes Sir!"

"No I really mean it," Colonel Fansy growled.

Ronnie cleared his throat.

"Sir, I know you think we are going to treat this as an eight week bender to rape anything in Scotland-"

"Preferably something with a pulse, Douglas."

"Cannie afford to be too choosy," Ronnie argued.

Colonel Fansy gulped down the last of his Glenlivet at the chilling sincerity of Ronnie's answer.

I tried to give Colonel Fansy a ray of hope.

"Sir, you've stuck your neck out for us and we intend to give you the finest fighting men Scotland has to offer. You have our word on that sir!"

Colonel Fansy raised his glass to us with an affectionate smile.

"I don't doubt your sincerity MacTavish, but if you could refrain from knocking the shite out of somebody before the train departs from Kings Cross I would consider it a miracle of piping decorum," Colonel Fansy sighed, recharging his glass with a mischievous grin. "Make sure you are sober when you report to Sergeant Major Grey. He was my old RSM. He's been up and down the ranks like a yo-yo. So don't try it on with him, cause he'll eat you for breakfast! If you get in the shit! Tell him straight away, is that clear?"

"Yes Sir!"

"Pipers are the ambassadors and cream of our regiment. Act like it. I warn you now! If anybody gets into drama wearing uniform or while on duty, my full fury will be at their service. Good luck lads . . . and good hunting."

We were all in a buoyant mood when we set off on the train to Newcastle. Our tour was to start there and then gradually work its way up through Scotland.

I loved Newcastle and its nightlife. My first introduction to Newcastle happened when I had been thrown off the train, when I had foolishly gambled my warrant to regain my wages in a vicious game of shoot pontoon. I was left in Newcastle feeling sorry for myself with no money and no ticket home, when the station guard took pity on me.

"If you can play 'Blaydon Races', you'll make an absolute fortune. They're at home today, you know?" he said, nodding towards St James's Park.

After about ten minutes on my practice chanter, I produced a lively version of 'Blaydon Races' with a few extra flourishes to wow the crowd. I straightened my kilt and fired my pipes up with 'Blaydon Races'. The station went mental. The guard twisted his black and white scarf around my pipe cords.

"Go get em, son."

There were huge crowds of excited fans at each of the stadium's gateways and all of them were champing at the bit to get in. I positioned myself near one of the gateways and fired my pipes up. Cheers rang out (with various unclean versions of 'Blaydon Races'). My pipe case was filled within minutes.

The Newcastle fans took me into the game and around their various CIU clubs. I had an absolute ball on the town with the Toon Army. At the end of the night they poured me onto the Edinburgh mail train. My only problem now was trying to explain to my mum and dad why the army had decided to pay me in a pipe case full of coins.

I always think you can really judge a city by how they welcome and help strangers. I love Newcastle for these very reasons. The Geordie's frank sense of humour gives them an innate ability to ignore hardship, and makes them and their city world class.

Newcastle was Cameron Younger's hometown. Cameron was one of those people who never tried to be funny, but his every thought and action was naturally comical. Cameron had blond hair with a natural front flick. He was the spitting image of Herge's, Tin Tin. His clueless dress sense somehow suited him. Cameron's tasteful ensemble usually consisted of red Ryder boots, loud checked trousers and a vile Hawaiian shirt. Cameron Younger was five foot ten of pure, fighting psychotic vim. He may have looked like Tin Tin, but he had the fighting prowess of Astrix the Gaul.

As far as I'm aware, Cameron was the only boxer to ever be banned from army boxing, due to overuse of his head and feet. He could never ever get your name right first time either.

"Wha Bill, Pete, Bob, Hector?"

"It's Hector! It's always been Hector, you senile Geordie bastard!"

"Wha am sorry, a don't dae it on purpose Bob, Hector, ya kna."

Even after 35 years he still can't get my name right. God knows how long it took him to complete his wedding vows. All I know is the girl must have loved him.

Many great pipers had come from Newcastle and joined the regiment's pipe band. Unfortunately, Cameron wasn't one of them. He didn't care or mind. He just liked the idea of being a piper. He never, ever, practised to improve or develop his playing. Cameron spent nearly all his time memorising fire brigade manuals and textbooks.

Cameron had tragically lost his father at the age of fourteen. He admired and loved his father so much he had decided to completely emulate his life. His father had been a soldier in the regiment and a fire chief for Tyne and Wear. Cameron was determined to do a few years in the regiment and then become the greatest fireman that Newcastle had ever seen.

Pipe Major Macmillan had generously indulged Cameron, as Cameron's father had been a good friend of his in Malaya, but Pipe Major MacMuchie was determined to end Cameron's idyllic lifestyle.

Cameron's greatest and most priceless flaw was his raw and brutal honesty. His blunt frankness could cripple the most resilient of Spartans. It was always completely unintentional, but it was remorselessly unforgiving to its victims. One of Cameron's more tactful moments happened shortly after his father's funeral.

Cameron's mum was still in mourning for her late husband, but she had decided to go to her niece's wedding. She had bought a new hat to lift her spirits. She tilted her hat to a favourable angle in the mirror.

"Well, how do you think I look, son?"

"I think you look a complete twat, Mam."

Cameron's mother nodded serenely and wondered why her son had never considered a career as an ambassador or in politics.

Cameron's frankness would usually bludgeon its victims to a speechless apoplexy. He would often re-ignite his victims' agony by genuinely agreeing with any insult they could throw at him. The man was an impregnable tank, which regularly tracked over Pipe Major McMuchie with unintentional ease.

Cameron guided us to the Newcastle TA Centre to meet up with the recruitment team. There were two sergeants and an old sergeant major. The sergeant major explained we were to play our pipes and help with the testing of candidates.

"Now for the good bit," said the sergeant major. "Each of us will receive a £5 bounty for every successful recruit. The army needs men and we all love cash, so work your nuts off! The trailers are all loaded, so have a night on the tiles. If you're ever late or absent, I'll jail you and you're off, so use the heed and have a good tour lads."

Cameron decided to take us on the town, via some CIU clubs, to meet his brothers. Cameron had six brothers who were all renowned bare-knuckle and unlicensed boxing champions.

Cameron's local CIU club was a huge affair. There were some good acts on and the beer was the way pipers like it; free-flowing, strong and cheap. The club steward came over.

"If you fancy free drink all night, give us a few tunes on your pipes, bonny lad."

My pipe case sprang open on the closing syllables of 'free drink'. The steward smiled.

"You're on after the stripper, son. You've got five minutes."

I gave my pipes a quick tune and gaped in awe at the stripper. Sexy Sadie was 70 if she was a day. Her vital statistics consisted of a six-foot circumference. Her blue-veined, wrinkled, stark white body was a challenge for even the strongest of stomachs.

Sadie was now down to her purple crimplene knickers and bra. She undid her bra with a whip-cracking sonic boom. The sudden weight of Sadie's breasts on her navel, instantly took years off her face. She didn't give a jot about the barrage of rude abuse. If anything, she seemed to thrive on it, as she gyrated away to the club's Hammond organ.

Sadie began to home in on a young lad whose friends had obviously set him up for his birthday. Sadie winked provocatively at him, as she flicked her false teeth in and out to the quickening beat of 'Devil Woman'. Sadie whipped her knickers down and fired the young lad's face into her crotch. The boy's petrified shrieks for mercy were muffled by Sadie's vice-like grip on his ears. Grown men wept in tears of sympathy for the boy's head, which was lost in the explosion of grey wire wool.

Eventually Sadie released the poor shell-shocked boy who seemed less than grateful at his friends' thoughtful present. Sadie is the only stripper I've ever seen getting cheered putting her clothes back on.

"You're on now, piper!"

I got the crowd going with 'Scotland the Brave' and some toe tapping jigs. I finished off by playing 'Happy Birthday' as I marched up to the shell-shocked birthday boy. He ran away from me screaming, petrified I was going to give him a male introduction like Sadie's. This brought the house down, along with our beer.

Newcastle is filled with cracking nightclubs and bars, but those weren't the sort of places that required the pugilistic talents of the Younger brothers. In the first bar run by Cameron's brother, a giant of a man ran into the bar every 20 minutes, ripped a pint out of someone's hand, punched them out cold and downed their pint.

The barmaid calmly announced:

"He's a regular, ya kna? Doesn't buy fuck all, but he's regular."

Cameron's brother allowed this to happen on Fridays, as it was classed as pub entertainment.

In the next bar run by Cameron's brother, the bouncer was whipping a thief with a car battery. The thief obviously wasn't the most intelligent of criminals, as he had just broken into the bouncer's car and tried to steal his car radio in front of him. The bouncer looked up.

"I'll be there in a minute, our kid."

Cameron smiled.

"That's, our Davie, he's the quiet one of the family."

I could just picture the headlines in The Newcastle Echo, 'Thief Charged with Assault from Battery'!

It was late when Cameron took us to the Riverside Nightclub to meet his remaining brothers. All of Cameron's promises about the club being a real classy joint, sort of, faded when I saw the club's disco.

The DJ was inside a steel turret with a slit, which was screwed into an armour plated sound system. Glasses were bouncing of his turret, as he casually introduced the next song. When the DJ needed a pee. He shuffled off inside the turret and peed from a screw lidded porthole into the Tyne. He did his best to avoid the swimmers that Cameron's brothers had thrown from the third storey loading hatch (euphemistically called, The Departure Lounge).

The club did have one superb overriding factor; the place was packed with gorgeous talent. I always liked Geordie girls; they weren't shy and they were always up for a laugh. We ended up with some student nurses at the owner of the club's palatial home. With absolutely no sleep, we staggered back just before reveille. Our convoy set off for two weeks in the, thankfully near, Scottish borders.

We worked hard in the borders. By the time we had finished there we had already met our tour quota. The sergeant major was ecstatic, and generously gave us a quarter of our bounties in advance. We had never been so rich. Our next stop was in bonny Ayrshire, the land of Robert Burns and the home of my childhood.

We set our recruitment stand up right in Ayr town centre, opposite the Parachute Regiment's recruitment stand. I made some phone calls and got my friends to choke and harry the Para's recruitment drive. At the end of the two weeks we had 22 confirmed signings and the Paras had only four (and two of those were on day release). The embittered Paras knew we were at the back of their sudden recruitment slump and they wanted revenge.

Ayr's Royal British Legion had laid on a cracking farewell bash for the two recruitment teams. It was a great night; the beer was free and we had been granted a late start. A few scuffles had broken out in the legion between the Paras and us, but these had been quickly quelled by the sergeant major. The legion rang last orders at half ten. We were all absolutely howling, but we wanted more, and the night was still young.

You never go out on the town in uniform because you're easily identified, you bugger your kit up and if you get into trouble the punishments are a lot stiffer. But we were too drunk to care. We staggered around Ayr in our uniforms, boldly endeavouring to push back the alcoholic barriers that had so constrained medical science.

We finally managed to find a new nightclub that would let us all in. We grabbed a table and I stumbled to the bar to get the round in. As the strobe light flashed, I saw a terrible sight - every flash seemed to illuminate a maroon sweatshirt.

I tried to focus on the two maroon blurs either side of me at the bar. I squinted and moved my head back and forth to gain some focus. I managed to pick out desert boots, jeans and maroon sweatshirts with a blue Pegasus. Yep – it was the standard drinking kit of the Parachute Regiment. I began to snigger as I remembered how my friends had buggered them about for the week. God, I wish I hadn't!

The tall cockney lifted the hem of my kilt.

"I thought only women wore skirts."

Before I could stop myself, I started to poke the wings on his sweatshirt.

"I thought only fairies had wings!"

The Para looked down in horror, as he noticed me urinating on his jeans. I followed up with a swift Highland brogue to his crotch. His friend greeted me with a barstool, which fired me across the dance floor.

Ronnie was chasing a Para with a chair leg shouting:

"You had to hit my nose! A tellt you no to hit ma nose."

Cassie punched the lad who had panned me with the chair, and slid him in a red smear next to me on the floor. I drew back my fist, but the Para lad just held his jaw and offered me a fag. I accepted his chivalrous offer and gave him a light. We both sat back and admired the ensuing brawl. It was a cracker.

The club was now a melange of maroon sweatshirts and kilts, spewing battered casualties onto the floor. In the end it was just down to Cassie, Cameron and three Para lads. They fought like possessed men. All of a sudden the military police came bombing up the stairs.

We all sprang to our feet and observed the first, universal law of army drinking - always beat the crap out of the military police first. As the MPs came up the stairs we threw them out of the fire escapes, but the steady tide of MPs began to overwhelm us.

"Remember Bannock Burn!" came the valiant cry.

The MPs smashed mirrors and tables with their wild baton flaying, in their clumsy attempts to subdue us.

As soon as we saw the Ayr Police, the Paras and us stopped fighting immediately. The MPs still laid into us smashing skulls, flesh and bone with sadistic glee.

"Remember Culloden, you bastards!"

The Ayr Police tried to stop the MP overkill and were mistakenly attacked by the MPs' frenzied aggression. Ayr Police were no mugs and they quickly overcame the military police, giving them a sharp taste of their own medicine.

Ayr Police Station was chock-a-block, so we

were all flung into a large detention cell together. The desk sergeant casually sighed.

"Ayr's toon where none surpasses, full o' pissed up squaddies and broken glasses."

Ronnie and two Para lads were taken to Seafield Hospital for stitching and X-rays. We gave the Ayr Police our name, rank and number - nothing else. Most of Ayr Police were ex-servicemen and you could tell they knew the score. The Ayr Police very kindly let us keep our fags and gave us water and cotton wool to clean ourselves up.

About three in the morning, Ronnie, two Paras and an old gent were locked into our cell. Poor Ronnie's nose was bigger than ever. It had been broken and was swollen up like a hornbill.

"Why do they always hit my fuckin nose?" Ronnie seethed.

"Because it's hard to hit anything else on your face," Cameron answered.

Cameron's blunt honesty had the whole cell in fits.

The old gent was in a blue, well-tailored pinstriped suit. He was as drunk as a lord, but he managed a graceful, controlled slide down the wall. Cassie and I helped him on to one of the cell beds. He rolled onto his side and began to shiver with the cold. I took my great plaid off and laid it over him, and prayed to God that he wouldn't pee it.

Big Tam, the arresting police sergeant, opened the cell hatch.

"I hope you've got big pockets, boys. They're after £10,000 for damages. You're up in front of the sheriff first thing. Look after the old fella, boys, he's knockin on a bit and he's had a skin full."

I pointed to my plaid wrapped around the old boy. Big Tam winked his thanks.

As soon as the cell hatch closed we began to make our plans. We needed to work together. It was now us versus the MPs. We needed to know the exact charges and the police's official position.

Our only real hope of salvation lay in getting Big Tam to help us. When Big Tam checked on us again, I offered him a fag and asked him honestly for help.

"Look, there's no way we did £10,000 worth of damage, but we are guilty of hitting each other and a few over-enthusiastic MPs," I reasoned.

Big Tam paused and rubbed his chin.

"You're being charged as a joint group for criminal damages of £10,000 and seriously assaulting two of our police officers."

"We punched the crap out of the MPs, but we didn't touch any of your boys and we only broke a few stools and that's all. It was the MPs who done your boys, and them that wrecked the joint! Your lads must know who hit them, so surely they can help?"

"Don't fret yourself too much, boys. Hope springs up in the strangest of places." Tam nodded, with a reassuring smile. "I'll bring you some breakfast and then you'll be up in front of the sheriff."

Breakfast consisted of large, bacon doorstop sandwiches and huge mugs of tea. I gave the old fella a gentle shake. His eyes blinked open and he frantically began to search his pockets.

"We're no thieves," I assured him. "The police have probably got what you want."

"No, they always let me keep my cigarettes and my lighter," the old man said, forlornly.

I handed him a cigarette.

"You're a regular then?"

"You could say that," said the old man as he continued to search his pockets.

I gave him a light.

"Thank you," said the old man, "you're very kind."

A look of disappointment washed over his troubled brow as he gave up his search. Cassie's keen eyes spotted the source of the old man's trouble. He reached under the cell bed and pulled out a solid silver lighter, which bore the cap badge of the Cameron Highlanders.

"This what you're looking for?" Cassie asked.

The old man's face lit up with delight. He triumphantly shook the lighter in his hand.

"Thank you." The old man beamed. "It's a sort of a good luck charm. I had it all through the war."

"I think it's the most beautiful and finest of Scots cap badges," said Cassie.

The old gent lovingly traced his finger over the Cameron cap badge.

"The finest - and the bravest of the brave," chirped the old man.

This was greeted with incredulous jeers. The old man laughed and straightened his hair. You could tell he'd been a soldier by the way he savoured his tea and his fag. We offered the old man a sarnie, but he declined.

"I'm going to be late if they don't let me out soon," the old man sighed, as he banged on the cell door.

Big Tam looked at the old man.

"Right, you can go, but behave yourself you old bugger!"

The old man saluted and winked at Big Tam as he marched out of the cell.

All the bravado and comical remarks faded into desperate silence as the time of reckoning approached. We nervously waited, wondering if we would be sentenced under civilian law, remanded for military law or receive the dreaded double jeopardy.

The jingle of the keys and the lock slamming open rang out across the silent cell. We were marched briskly along the long stone corridor and escorted to the bottom of the dock steps.

The leading policemen whispered, "Remain silent until spoken to. Always call the sheriff, Sir, and stand to attention when addressing him. It all helps. Good luck."

The dock doors were noisily unbolted. We all quietly filed into the large wooden dock. The court clerk checked our names, ranks, numbers, regiments and posting addresses.

"Court is in session, all rise!"

We all stood up and the sheriff briskly walked in and sat down.

"Oh God!" gasped Ronnie.

"No, but I have omnipotent powers in here, young man, so remain quiet or I'll have you in contempt. Do you understand me?"

"Yes Sir," Ronnie answered, and the rest of us nodded in silent awe.

We were screwed. The sheriff was the old man who had been in the cell with us. He had probably overheard everything. He wheeled towards the owner of the nightclub with a cold piercing glare.

"I wish an independent assessment of the damage and the cost of repairs to be carried out under military police supervision. As I feel you are more than a little generous with the costs, Mr Crosby, and we don't want a repeat performance of the last time do we?"

"No, Sir," said Mr Crosby, realising he had just been out manoeuvred.

"You can await the military police assessment today, Mr Crosby, good day."

The sheriff turned to the military police officer.

"I suggest you conclude this matter and settle the damages, yourselves today!"

The infuriated MP officer went to object, but the wily old sheriff cut him short.

"If you do not settle this matter in full, I will conduct a full investigation into why the MPs' incompetent handling of the situation resulted in excessive damages, and the unnecessary injuring of two of Her Majesty's Ayrshire Constabulary. Do you understand me?"

The officer nodded reluctantly and left the courtroom.

The sheriff looked over his bifocals and squinted at us.

"Are you all Church of Scotland?"

The cockney Paras and us all chorused back:

"Yes Sir!"

"God bless you all, case dismissed!"

We were led away and reissued our ID cards and personal effects. The cockney Para pointed at Ronnie.

"Fancy being in front of the beak twice in the

same day."

We all tried not to acknowledge the joke, but the anger on Ronnie's face made it impossible.

"What is it wi ma nose, why does everybody pick on my nose?" Ronnie grumbled.

"It would take an entire shift of miners to pick that thing properly," I said, gently patting poor Ronnie's swollen nose.

We had our knuckles rapped when we got back, and Sergeant Major Grey pocketed our bounty money for Ayr, which seemed only fair.

CHAPTER 13

Eventually we made it up to the beautiful land, north of the Spey. Cassie's family country estate was only 20 miles away, encased by the obligatory, high stone wall.

"Lord, how I love this place Hector. It's the people that make this place, so special." Cassie smiled as he skimmed pebbles into the loch. "The only blot on this land are the so-called gentry. I hate to be associated with them, I really do."

I could see the pain in Cassie's face. He was the noblest of human beings who was an outcast of his own society and class. I tried to get Cassie, on to a more cheerful subject.

"So what's the chances of a young piper being overcome by nymphomania in this fair land?"

"I'm glad to say," said Cassie, with a stifled grin, "that it's never been fully eradicated, and there are some quite dynamic strains within the vicinity."

"And where would one find a plague strength epidemic?"

"Well, if I were you I'd start looking for a girl with a ring of midgy bites below her derriere."

"Then let's find some lumpy-arsed girls," I urged.

"I know a great place where the booze is cheap and the odd lumpy-arsed girl can be found, but we'll need to . . . walk, just a wee bit!"

Cassie could spot my immediate reluctance at the mention of the 'W' word. We were forced to march and run long distances all day long, so we naturally avoided any form of walking during our own time off. We would wait hours for a taxi rather than walk a few hundred yards. This was the phobia that Cassie was trying to overcome.

"Hector! I promise you the finest pub in the world and company that would grace the gods. We'll get the okay from the sergeant major, and Ronnie can drive us up in the Land Rover. I swear to God you will thank me."

I could see the excitement in Cassie's face, and I wasn't going to waste the chance to cheer him up.

"Lead on, MacDuff," I roared.

We approached Sergeant Major Grey for a 48-hour pass with the Rover.

"You might as well, as we'll be bloody busy in Inverness," said the sergeant major, "but I'll need one piper to remain here?"

"I'll stay," said Cameron. "I've just got a fantastic book on reverse osmosis that I'm dying to get stuck into."

"You're no quite the full shillin are you, Piper Younger?" asked Sergeant Major Grey.

"No Sir!" Cameron answered categorically.

"I want the Rover back without a scratch, fuelled and with the paperwork, and a don't mean traffic tickets!" Sergeant Major Grey warned, with oracle foreboding.

We drove for about 30 miles into some spectacular scenery.

"Stop! Stop Ronnie. Take a left down this track," Cassie ordered.

We carefully edged the Rover along the precarious track that followed the rugged contour of the mountain. The track ended abruptly at the base of a steep glen.

"We're here," said Cassie.

"There's fuck all here!" bawled Ronnie. "Look, am from Glasgow. We don't class sheep as a leisure centre!"

"A little patience my proboscised friend, just a wee stroll and you will enter heaven," said Cassie.

"That's what am worried about!" said Ronnie.

Cassie looked at his watch, the light and then the mountain mist.

"We'll have to stretch our legs, boys, bad light and mist can kill around here."

"Great, fuckin marvellous, he's not only going to get us to leave the Rover in the land that time forgot, he's goin to force-march us into the valley of death," Ronnie moaned, nodding with meerkat ferocity.

We set off at a blistering pace. Cassie was so desperate to take us to the inn, he had quite forgotten that Ronnie and I were mere mortals. His great wide strides just ate up the ground in single effortless bounds. Poor Ronnie and I were at full stretch running just to keep up with Cassie.

As we crossed a burn Ronnie pleaded for a rest. We stopped briefly, just enough to catch our breath. Dusk was turning to darkness and we could see the mountain mist rapidly descending towards us. Cassie began to scan the base of the hooked summit.

"It's here, I know it is."

"Oh, marvellous, Captain Scott!" Ronnie sneered.

Cassie held up his hand as the dusk began to darken. A small yellow light winked briefly and then vanished into the darkness.

"Gentlemen, I give you El Dorado," said Cassie, pointing his hand to where the light had flickered.

The building could have won a combat stealth award. It was only 50 yards in front of us and we still couldn't see it. As we drew nearer, we could just make out the sound of fiddles, whistles and small pipes. Cassie halted us and put his finger to his mouth.

"Keep quiet and let me go in first. They won't be expecting visitors at this time of night," Cassie warned.

"Who won't?" whispered Ronnie.

"Sh!" Cassie ordered, angrily.

Cassie heaved the stout door, which grated open. Cassie was immediately consumed by a pair of huge arms encased in a Fair Isle jumper. Cassie head butted the giant bearded monster repeatedly and kneed him in the family jewels.

"Ma boy! Ma wee boy's come home. Ma plums are achin, buy me a pint of Dalwhinnie," the monster groaned.

Cassie hugged the bearded giant who looked like the love child from a grizzly bear and a Highland cow.

"MacTavish and Douglas, this shy, wee retiring violet is Big Donald - a legend in his own lunch-time session. The greatest warrior, piper, poet, hunter, teacher and friend," said Cassie.

"You forgot love machine," said Big Donald.

"And lover of livestock," agreed Cassie.

Big Donald had virtually brought Cassie up. He was the family's head gamekeeper. Cassie's family despised Big Donald for the same reasons that Cassie loved him. He had taught Cassie how to fight, pipe, hunt and live life to the full. Big Donald looked over and nodded a warm welcome to us.

"Big Donald, let me introduce you to Hector of the Glens and Ronnie Fucking Big Nose, who is in the process of changing his name to Really-Fucking Big Nose. The hyphen shows breeding, don't you think?"

Cassie smiled, pulling two bottles of Dalwhinnie malt from the shelf. He placed them on our table and wrote our names on a strange looking blackboard.

Big Donald had a handshake like a gin trap and his arms were like the legs of a Clydesdale horse. He radiated confidence and you could tell he wasn't used to being questioned.

The inn was an old smugglers' haunt. Its superb geography and remoteness had ensured its survival. Illicit whisky and beer barrels were sledded up to the inn by horse, where it was quickly consumed at the inn or sledded down the mountain by kamikaze Highlanders. The suicidal sleigh ride was known as Satan's Sleigh.

"Banzai," Big Donald said, nodding towards our names on the blackboard, "and welcome to the Brotherhood of Satan's Sleigh. Don't worry, boys, you're allowed to drink as much as you want before you ride to hell."

I don't know if it was shock or the whisky, but Ronnie was remarkably calm.

"Call me Rudolph-Fucking Big Nose," Ronnie cheered.

"You're a bugger for changing your Christian name, Mr Fucking Big Nose, but I like the cut of your jib," Big Donald said, clinking Ronnie's glass.

"Don't forget the hyphen," Ronnie slurred, "shows breeding."

You could tell when Ronnie was happy, as he relaxed and lost a lot of his startled meerkat qualities. It was good to see him happy and relaxed again. Life had dealt Ronnie some hard cards, but he still remained a warm decent man and true-blue friend. He was a nervous wreck and a pessimistic optimist, but Ronnie Douglas's heart was as kind as an angel and as brave as a lion when in defence of his friends.

Cassie had not exaggerated about how amazing the place was. The standard of musicianship was staggeringly sublime. The company was warm and welcoming. There were no pumps for the beer. Large earthenware jugs brought the beer to us, while the whisky was almost intravenous.

Time and the night just flew by. The shutters were drawn back and the sharp sting of daylight told us that day had come. It was like a scene from a Hammer House of Horror, watching all the ardent drinkers recoil from the dawn's morning rays.

During the course of the night, Big Donald had got us invites to the day's ceilidh. We all helped clean and wash the bar out. By the time we had finished laying out the tables in the barn, we were called back into the bar for breakfast. There was a large cast iron cauldron of hot thick porridge. Next to the cauldron was a large plate of freshly home-baked bread and some bottles of that Highland fruit juice called Glenlivet.

"Jesus, when do you shut?" Ronnie asked the landlord.

"December and January," the landlord apologised. "We have to the weather's too bad."

Ronnie instantly collapsed into helpless laughter. The landlord's puzzled face, why we found his answer so funny, just made Ronnie's laughter even more uncontrollable.

After our Highland breakfast, it was full speed ahead back on the liquid front. Woman of all ages seemed to appear from nowhere, carrying food or table linen. They decked the barn out beautifully. By midday more and more people began to fill the barn. I had nothing but admiration for the ceilidh band's fortitude as they came into view with their amps and microphones strapped to their backs.

We went outside into the warm sunshine and looked at the ingenious design of the inn. It had been hewn out of an outcrop, making it blend perfectly into the mountain. The external stone walls had been vitrified black, and the green moss expertly broke up its shape. This drinking stronghold was aptly named the Fortress. It was one of those closely guarded secrets that everybody knew about, but of which nobody spoke of.

At about eleven in the morning we were beginning to drink ourselves sober. The air was filled with the lovely smell of roasted venison. In front of the Fortress was a large trench full of peat bricks, which gave off a spectacular heat. Above the trench were huge carcasses of venison on spits.

Cassie smiled at Big Donald.

"They can be such a nasty pest to a family estate, don't you think?"

"Not at the rate they're eaten here, my lord," Big Donald reasoned, with a wide grin.

The venison was served with lovely fluffy roasted potatoes, peas and a large dollop of wild, redcurrant jelly. It was a fabulous feast. The breathtaking scenery and the fantastic company made it easy to understand why Cassie loved the place so much. I had only been there a night and I was already smitten.

I really wanted a large cup of tea to finish off the meal, but I knew it would be considered sacrilegious in this testosterone charged male environment, so I just accepted a huge glass of Highland Park, with a willing smile of sweet surrender.

The ceilidh began with each person introducing themselves and asking a question. It was a beautiful and original way of breaking the social ice. A tall attractive girl welcomed everybody and started the introductions off.

"My name is Fiona, I've tried everything to rid my garden of moles, I've even had a man in."

This was greeted with wild cheers.

"I've tried traps and poison, but nothing seems to work."

"Could you not just try a dating agency?" Big Donald roared.

After a few more comical answers, it was agreed that four men would visit Fiona's garden, rake the mounds clear and kill the moles with sledgehammers. I'm reliably informed that, although it sounds brutal, it is a quick death and a permanent remedy.

As the questions worked their way around the room you felt part of a strong welcoming community. I felt as if I'd known these people all of my life.

Ronnie got the shortest answer and the best laugh when he said:

"Ma name's Ronnie. Does anybody think ma nose is really that big?"

Gradually it dawned on me that it was soon going to be my turn, so I thought of a genuine question that had bothered me for some time. I stood up and introduced myself as Hector of the Glens. All the men laughed, mimicking my action of listening to their whisky bottles. I smiled and began to set the scene for my quandary.

"We travelled to South Uist on the small ferry from Ullapool. Now, I admit we had had a few drinks, but we still managed to climb down the narrow, steep winding stairway to the belly of the boat, into the ferry's bar."

You could see the folk smiling as they visualised the same experience. I took a sip of whisky and carried on with my tale.

"The weather was bad and the crossing was made extremely memorable by a prize winning Highland cow standing at the small bar. The farmer hugged his arms around the great beast's neck and kissed its Best in Show rosette. The noble piece of beef received hearty cheers and roars of laughter from the bar every time it gave a powerful blast of bestial relief.

Now, the only way in and out of the bar is up and down that tight winding stairway. You couldn't lead the cow, winch it or lower it in there. I suppose they could have brought the beast on board when it was a calf, or built the boat around the animal. But that doesn't explain how they keep getting the hairy bugger in and out of the bar, and on and off the ferry, so how in God's name do they do it?"

To my great surprise my question received a reverent silence and a great deal of sincere consideration.

"The cow's name is Rainech Mor," said old Angus, "and your question is a riddle that has perplexed the finest of Highland minds, Hector. Nobody has seen it board or embark. Maybe it's just a wee enigma that would be spoiled by resolving it," suggested old Angus.

I smiled and nodded.

The questions continued until everybody had taken their turn. Wonderful poetical recitations and story telling followed. I loved every moment, but we hadn't slept in 28 hours of hard drinking, so Cassie, Ronnie and I went for a wee sleep in the stables. We clearly lacked the stamina and drinking prowess of these seasoned ceilidh athletes.

Big Donald's fine piping woke us up, after a good seven hours of deep sleep. We quickly washed in the ice cold mountain water and had a shave with Donald's, murderous cut-throat razor. We donned our tunics and freshened our breaths with a fine Scots mouthwash called Glen Ord. This form of Highland dental hygiene was very fastidious, as it required us to finish the entire bottle before entering the ceilidh.

As soon as we entered the ceilidh, Ronnie was immediately grabbed by a rather big lusty girl called Shonna. Ronnie hooked arms with Shonna and spun her around and around. The faster they spun the more Shonna's kilt rose. Cassie smiled and nodded to the line of midge bites that underlined Shonna's derriere.

Ronnie had a slender and graceful physique, but he had an obsession for big women, and I mean big women. Somehow big women seemed to sense this; and they'd pounce on him, like a hound on a fox. Ronnie would always try and claim that he had been brutally overpowered; but it was more a case of the lady, protesting too much. Ronnie was a fantastic dancer, and amazingly agile and nimble on his feet. He needed every ounce of grace and skill to cope with the ferocity of Shonna's lustful exuberance.

Cassie and I were soon up dancing. We danced eightsome reels and jigs without a break. It was exhausting, but enjoyable. I could feel the whisky vaporising out of every pore. I was grateful for the rest when the band hushed for some beautiful Hebridean song.

Cassie and I wandered out of the barn into the cold pleasing air and listened to the rhythmic genius of women walking the cloth. The last song was a musically emotive song called 'O Mhairi'. The girl, Fiona, put so much emotion and music into her love song it transcended my ignorance of the Gaelic language. Her plaintive song of the heart still haunts my mind today.

The band was just about to play when Cassie and I heard the distant euphoric pleading of Shonna.

"Oh God, Ronnie! Again, again! Go on, Ronnie! Now! Ronnie, oh, God now! O . . . oh Ro . . . nnie!"

"Well, she's obviously not heard him play," said Cassie, "but she seems more than happy with the encore."

Ronnie and Shonna received rousing cheers as they gingerly appeared from the heather. Shonna scuttled off into the fortress with embarrassment while Ronnie sported a scarlet blush of welcomed recognition. We staggered into the bar to toast Ronnie and Shonna's union. Glass followed glass, bottle followed bottle, and the night marched boldly on.

The slim fingers of dawn began to claw back the day. The morning mountain mist was too cold and pure to remain asleep. I looked around at the mass of bodies. It looked like the aftermath of Flodden. Bodies lay strewn across the heather. I reached forwards and warmed my hands from the peat embers of the trench. My tunic and plaid held the heavy scent of peat and whisky. Ronnie looked snug as a bug within Shonna's mighty and encompassing embrace. This tartan Kong knew how to keep her man safe.

Cassie tossed a lighted fag over to me, which I gratefully smoked. I nodded my thanks as I breathed the smoke through my nose.

"See, she's got a couple of new notches on her gun handle," I said, pointing my fag at the new, red swollen bites on the back of Shonna's thighs.

I tried to get to my feet, but my legs were still asleep and I fell on my back, with my legs and kilt flopping over my head.

"This year's Turner Prize goes to Hector MacTavish, with his poignant work entitled, Welcome to the Church of Scotland," said Cassie.

I lay on my back and watched Big Donald and the landlord strip tarpaulin off a rather inconspicuous mound at the side of the stables. I couldn't help but admire the sledge as it was unveiled.

"Jesus, she looks like a real goer!"

Shonna's head flipped around and gave me a livid scowl, which amused Cassie no end.

The sledge was an awe-inspiring, piece of Scots engineering. It was six feet wide and seven feet long. The crates of whisky were secured by bridging straps through an ingenious floating cradle system, which acted as a superb suspension unit. There were two sets of steering pedals at the front and hand lashings for two people at the rear of the sledge. The runners were clad in sealskin, and cleverly scalloped to give a wide surface area. It had a simple robust, but well constructed, design.

Cassie mounted the sledge and took up his driving position.

"No crash helmets?" I asked.

"No need to tempt providence," Cassie replied.

Donald smiled and looked over to Ronnie.

"Ach, he's a natural nose for the Gaelic," said Big Donald.

This was met with infectious cheers and laughter. I was just about to enquire what was so funny, when Ronnie sleepily turned around to face me - Ronnie's poor old nose had received yet another drubbing.

"Blame them buggers and that old Bruce Lee bitch in black!" Ronnie scowled.

This received roars of laughter. Ronnie explained that he'd asked Big Donald whom to thank for the ceilidh. Big Donald pointed to the old, staunch Presbyterian Church woman in black, and taught Ronnie how to thank her correctly in Gaelic.

"You'll need to really shout, Ronnie. She's knocking on a bit and she's as deaf as a doorpost," Big Donald advised.

Ronnie practised his Gaelic phrase a few times to get the pronunciation just right. He lent over close to the old woman's ear and shouted:

"Tha uisge-beatha math airson a choileach!"

The old woman smashed Ronnie in the nose with a haymaker from hell.

"Maybe it is, young man, but I have no wish to know!" the old woman stormed.

After the laughter had died down, Big Donald explained that, 'S'sheairde coileach drama', meant, 'whisky is good for the cock'.

I smiled at poor Ronnie's nose - it was just a magnet for trouble. Ronnie read my mind and just nodded with a sigh of resignation. He was still half-asleep from his nocturnal labours with Shonna and hadn't really taken in the full implications of his impending sleigh ride.

Big Donald slapped our half-conscious Ronnie onto the back of the sledge.

"Remember, Ronnie, when I shout port, port, dig your boots in like hell until I shout port up, port up! Okay? The same for you, Hector, when I shout starboard, starboard!" Big Donald shouted.

It was only when the crowd began to cheer and push the great sledge forwards that Ronnie began to fully realise, his wakening fate.

"Oh no, no, Jesus no . . . o!"

Satan's sleigh began to pick up breakneck speed at an alarming rate. Cassie and Big Donald were lashed into the front and were expertly piloting the sledge as it raced towards Mach 1 and eternal glory.

"Stop! Stop, am goin to be seeck. I'm goin to be seeck," Ronnie begged, but the sledge thundered on with bullet increasing speed.

Ronnie and I lay at the rear sides of the sledge with our legs bent up to avoid them scraping the ground. We held on for all we were worth as the sledge thundered on down the mountain. Occasionally, as we went airborne, we would get the command:

"Hold on! Hold on!"

The sledge would then land with a resounding thud, knocking the wind out of us.

"I'm gonna be seeck, stop! Stop! Am gonna be seeck!" Ronnie pleaded again.

Ronnie's prayers were eventually answered when the sleigh began to scythe its way through uphill bracken. The sleigh gracefully came to a welcomed halt.

"Seeck! Am gonna be Seeck!" Ronnie wailed.

Cassie smiled at poor Ronnie.

"You wish enlightenment from the Sheikh faith, Ronnie? How inspiring."

"After his last clash with the Presbyterian Church of Scotland it's only understandable," said Big Donald.

Ronnie's eyes were still tightly screwed shut and his face was drained of all colour. We managed to prise poor Ronnie's hands free from the sledge before he kept his promise. Once Ronnie had finished retching, he announced that he would be permanently retiring from the Brotherhood of Satan's Sleigh.

My stomach and ribs were sore from the bruise cruise, but I was grateful to be alive. We pulled a camouflaged tarpaulin over the sledge and kicked the tall bracken back to hide the sleigh and her entry tracks. The sledge and her cargo were now completely hidden. We strode down the last few hundred yards towards our Land Rover.

Big Donald walked over to a large boulder and heaved it around until the sharp shard of rock was pointing directly at the sledge's position. It wasn't James Bond, but had kept the excise men at bay for over two centuries. I looked up and scanned the mountain. There was no sign of the Fortress, nothing - nothing at all.

We retired to Big Donald's cosy lodge on Cassie's family estate. We got cleaned up and changed into our civvies. It felt funny wearing jeans again. Our uniforms were taken away to be cleaned.

"All part of the service," Big Donald said, smiling. "Don't worry, they'll be immaculate. It's not exactly the first uniform they've cleaned."

Big Donald pulled out four large legs of lamb from his great oven. "Someone has to get rid of the vermin," he said, grinning as he served the meal.

Cassie nodded approvingly as we tucked into our

meals. We washed the meal down with ice-cold flagons of redcurrant juice. It was just so nice to refresh and rehydrate our bodies with something non-alcoholic. It felt good to be on speaking terms with my liver again.

About a couple of hours later there were giggles and playful screams as the maid squeezed passed Big Donald. The maid handed us back our pristine uniforms.

"Please, Sir, your mother and father are in residence. Do you want them to know you're here and will be joining them later?" the wee maid asked, with sincere empathy and tact.

Cassie shook his head.

"No, Moira, that won't be necessary, but thank you for making such a splendid job of the uniforms."

"It may not be pleasant, but it would be the right and constitutional thing to do," Big Donald nodded, aiming his pipe smoke at Drummond's, heraldic pipe banner.

The pipe banner bore the family motto, 'For Right and Constitution'.

Cassie sighed, "Tell them I will be up presently, thank you, Moira."

Cassie got dressed in his pristine uniform and set out for the great hall. We had barely got back into our own uniforms when the door swung open to reveal Cassie's dejected face. Cassie nodded to the heraldic pipe banner.

"It should read, for shite and prostitution!"

Cassie's parents had dismissed him from the hall because they couldn't risk making their dinner party a thirteen. Without a by your leave they handed Cassie a large roll of notes and wished him a safe journey.

Cassie attempted to fling the large bundle of notes into the fire, but Ronnie nimbly caught the notes.

"Fuck all wrong with havin a shite or a prostitute," Ronnie reasoned.

Cassie could no longer bear to be on the estate. We could tell that he was hurt and desperate to leave. Before we left, Cassie gave Big Donald an exquisite silver and ivory powder horn. Big Donald instinctively shook it to hear the gentle slurp of whisky inside.

"Thanks, boy, it's a real beauty. My favourite type of charge I trust?" Big Donald enquired, cocking his head to one side.

"Reindeer milk - apparently it's awfully good for you," Cassie reassured Big Donald.

"Naw, it's just bloody awful!" Big Donald insisted.

We left Cassie to say his goodbyes to Big Donald. Cassie jumped into the back of the Rover and we quickly sped out of the estate with a farewell toot to Big Donald.

We spent two weeks in Inverness frantically recruiting. Inverness had always supplied the regiment with fine soldiers and pipers, so we were working at full tilt. Inverness was a great, traditional Highland garrison, so we were banned from going out on the town.

Sergeant Major Grey was determined to prevent any incidents from souring our successful tour. I liked Sergeant Major Grey; he was gruff and as rough as whinstone, but he was as straight as a die.

We were split into two groups. Ronnie, Sergeant McBride and myself were to cover the Islands of Harris, Mull, Lewis, Barra and Uist, whilst Cassie and the others covered the remaining Highland towns. We had to adhere to a strict and punishing timetable. We were only allowed one night on each island because of the small populations.

After a fruitless morning on South Uist we headed for North Uist. Bear had given us the address of his real mother, so Ronnie and I were itching to meet her. We had a bundle of cash to give her, as we hadn't used any of our expense money throughout our island tours, thanks to the outstanding generosity and kindness from all the islanders.

CHAPTER 14

Bear's cousin, Ian Maclean, warmly greeted us as we drove into North Uist. Ian was a leaner six foot four version of Bear, but the likeness was uncanny.

Ian was the only recruitment candidate from the small island. He effortlessly sailed through all his basic entry tests and he was a fine piper. Ian was champing at the bit to get in, so we agreed to take him to Glasgow for his medical and audition. Ian said farewell to his parents and jumped in the Rover.

We bought Bear's mum a surprise bumper of shopping from Mrs MacPhee's Highland Emporium. Sergeant McBride carefully threaded the Rover's lights through the treacherous darkness. The lonely mountain track weaved its way up the wild glen to Bear's mum's, remote Highland croft. There were no lights on.

"There's no electricity," Ian explained. "Auntie Biddy is probably in bed. Head for the corners of the room and you'll find oil lamps and matches. Then we'll get the shopping in."

Ronnie and I pulled the latch up and pushed the door open. We peered into the black abyss of the pitch-black room. We gingerly inched our way in.

"Hello, Mrs Maclean, Mrs Maclean are you-"

We were abruptly halted by a living moving wall. No matter how or where we moved, the quivering force field barred our path.

"What in God's name is it?" Ronnie whispered.

"I don't know! You fuckin ask it?"

All of a sudden the force field relented. Ronnie and I stumbled forward into the corner of the room. We fumbled for the matches and lit the lamp. I turned the wick of the lamp up to reveal the powerful physique of a rather sombre looking carthorse. Ronnie stared at the huge beast.

"Mrs Maclean?"

"Oh shut up, Ronnie!"

Ian came in with the shopping.

"Auntie Biddy, there's a horse in the living room!"

"Ach, it's not feeling too well, Ian. Light the fire, I'll be down in a minute. His name's Noah. He's a nice old boy," Auntie Biddy replied, blandly.

There are many different types of Scottish humour, which I adore, but the Highland humour of accepting the incredible as normal is one of the funniest and most endearing of them all. Here's a wee example.

"You know - I came home last night and caught my wife making mad, passionate love to an elephant."

"Was it an African or Indian elephant?"

"Well, according to David Attenborough, it would have been an African elephant, as it's the one with the really large ears."

"Ach, he's a great man that David Attenborough, a great man."

"He is indeed. That's enough water, Angus, no need to drown it!"

This type of humour exemplifies the easy-going Highland nature of making extraordinary feats seem normal. Highland folk often carry out feats of genius with sickening ease and humility, which is tragically overlooked by those who despairingly refer to them as teuchters.

Ian and Sergeant McBride ferried the groceries by the now rather inquisitive horse. Noah hadn't lived on the planet this long without being able to sniff out a few calories.

"Well, his nose isn't blocked," chirped Sergeant McBride.

Thankfully for Ian and Sergeant McBride, Noah was far too big to follow them through to the kitchen. Eventually Ronnie and I got the great peat fire going. Far from being scared, old Noah edged his way round, so he could warm his great head by the fire.

Old Noah had a lovely, wise old Eeyore quality about him. His large old head was stooped close to the hearth, so he got the main benefit of the fire's heat. He stubbornly subdivided the small room into two, for the sake of his own comfort.

You could tell Mrs Maclean was Bear's mum right from the off. She greeted us with welcoming hugs, despite the jealous obstacle of old Noah. Mrs Maclean politely asked Noah to go out. Noah's ears went back as he looked out at the rain lashed window, and then his eyes mooned over to Mrs Maclean.

"Okay you can stay, but only till the hard weather lifts," Mrs Maclean relented.

I swear to God that old horse smiled before it dipped its head in thankful courtesy.

"You probably think I'm daft," said Mrs Maclean, "but he's been a faithful servant and friend to me and the croft. Besides - he likes my singing."

Mrs Maclean gave us a huge bowl of stovies with some lovely rough bread. I told Mrs Maclean about Bear coming top of his Senior Pipers' Course and how wonderful he sounded as the Lone Piper.

Mrs Maclean looked a little puzzled.

"But Roddy said that you were the Lone Piper, Hector?"

"Not officially, Mrs Maclean." I smiled. "Not officially, no that honour went to your son, Mrs Maclean, and he was magnificent."

I looked at her proud doting face. Mrs Maclean or Auntie Biddy, as we now called her, was a tall, strong noble woman. Her eyes were expressive and thoughtful, like Bear's.

"I have much to be proud of," she said, sighing.

Noah let out a terrific blast. His ears shot back and his head dipped in instant remorse.

"Och, don't worry, Noah, we all do it, you're just a lot more honest than we humans are," said Auntie Biddy, as she patted old Noah's repentant head.

The rain had stopped beating and the slamming gates had hushed.

"Hector, the door please," said Auntie Biddy, pulling Noah's blanket over him.

I opened the door and stood back. Noah nuzzled his great head against Auntie Biddy for a last reprieve.

"I love you too, but we have guests, Noah."

Noah glared at us with silent disdain, but dutifully edged his way round to the door. Noah eyed the clear sky and gently eased himself through the doorway.

"Isn't it amazing how much love and respect you get from an animal, just from a little kindness? And yet humans abuse it so much ... with such thoughtless cruelty," Auntie Biddy said, with a sigh. "You boys must be tired? There's bedding in the settle and a bottle in the press."

We were woken in the morning by Auntie Biddy in the kitchen. We breakfasted on thick creamy porridge, strong Scots cheddar and oatcakes washed down with ice-cold milk.

"Auntie Biddy, Roddy gave us this money to give to you. He wanted you to get yourself something nice," I said, handing her our expense money.

"That's four times his wage packet," Auntie

Biddy scoffed.

"He must have had a bit of luck on the horses or the cards, Auntie Biddy," Ronnie chipped in.

"Did he fill the larder and shelves with food as well?" Auntie Biddy asked.

"It would have went to waste in the back of our Land Rover," I reasoned.

Auntie Biddy thanked us with a farewell hug as we said our goodbyes.

We met up with the rest of the recruitment team in Inverness, and headed for Glasgow. Glasgow was the end of the tour and Mr MacFadyen was in town. Sergeant Major Grey very kindly let us stay with our friends and family while the paperwork and recruiting bonuses were processed.

I stowed my gear into the taxi and gave the taxi driver Fadge's address. I had never been to Fadge's home before, as we nearly always met up at the Heilanman's Umbrella and slept there. The taxi turned into a stunning Georgian square and pulled up outside the most palatial of Glasgow townhouses. I stared hard at the driver.

"Are you sure you have the right address?"

"Arglin Square number 12, it's the only one in Glasgow," the taxi driver assured me.

I paid the driver and stepped from the taxi. There was no way this was Fadge's home. I climbed up the beautiful, white stone steps and rapped the huge brass door knocker. To my surprise, Fadge actually answered the door.

"Just so I know, Fadge, are we talkin burglary or embezzlement?"

"It's mine, well, ma maws." Fadge laughed. "Come on in."

Fadge led me into the breathtaking hall and up the impressive stairway to my panoramic bedroom.

"Did your folks win the pools?" I asked.

"I didn't get on with ma dad, Hector, but he knew how to turn a buck."

"Did he work in the city?"

"Sort of, he was a clippie on the buses."

"Your dad bought this by being a clippie on the buses?"

"Oh aye, he was a man of the strictest principles, Hector. He believed the company should have at least half."

I smiled. It wasn't hard to see where Fadge had acquired his shrewd acumen from.

Mrs MacFadyen came in and gave me a big hug.

"Nice to finally meet you, Hector. You're stayin here?" she asked, patting a set of pyjamas.

Fadge and his Mum roared with unrestrained laughter.

I tried to suppress my growing blushes.

"Aye, it's a great country that China. I'll make every effort to thoroughly map it for you. It's so nice to have friends who can really keep secrets," I said, nodding with an embarrassed smile.

We had a lovely meal together. I recited all our recruitment adventures and told Fadge and his mum about my favourite candidate, Shug McPeenie. Shug had appeared on the last day as we were closing the recruitment doors in Glasgow. He was four foot four, pigeon–chested, with Guinness bottom specs and acne like a spot welder's bench. We did everything to get rid of him as there was no way he would have had the physical capacity to withstand the regiment's, brutal training regime. But what Shug lacked in physical attributes he more than made up with in mind numbing stubbornness.

"You are physically too weak and too small to join the regiment!" I bawled in exasperation.

"I can train and grow, it's no a problem!" Shug countered.

"You've failed ever basic army entry and IQ test. Christ, you're thick!"

"I can learn, it's no a problem."

"Could you kill a man?"

"No intentionally."

"Shug, come back next year when you're sure you could tear a man's beating heart out with your bare hands." I said, clenching my hands theatrically.

"What time?"

"Half five in the morning, Shug, don't be late."

Fadge and I retired to the living room for a few nippy sweeties. He looked terrific. I had never seen him so happy.

"How did you get on with your Senior Brecon Course?" I asked.

"Came top o that and ma Section Commanders," Fadge replied.

"That's some list you've got now, Fadge; Para, Sniper, Senior Brecon and Section Commanders. You want to be careful you don't burn yourself out. You've done about six years' worth of courses in a year and a half. That only leaves the SAS, Fadge."

Fadge gave me a cunning grin. I decided to be tactful.

"Or have you done all the courses you need to?"

"Am happy Hector, am really happy."

Fadge's sister, Carrie, drove us to Queen's Street recruitment office. We were desperate to get our recruitment bonuses and find out how Ian had got on.

We were a wee bit early, so Fadge and I waited outside for Ronnie. There was an old boy outside the entrance selling copies of The Big Issue. I whispered into the old boy's ear and offered him a tenner and my handkerchief. The old boy laughed and agreed to take part. Fadge and I hid in the recruiting doorway. We spied Ronnie across the road. I tapped the old fella on the arm.

"That's him."

The old fella waited until Ronnie approached the recruitment entrance. He held up my hanky and roared:

"Big Tissue, Sir! Big Tissue, Sir!"

Our laughter erupted from the doorway and gave our position away. Ronnie peered into the doorway.

"Thank you, my man, but I prefer to blow my nose on my friends' bed sheets."

Fadge and Ronnie hugged each other as they exchanged their abusive introductions. We grabbed our bonuses and met up with Ian. Ian had passed his medical and had been accepted by the regiment as a piper. We watched Ian give his oath of allegiance and take the Queen's Shilling. That was it - Ian was in.

"We'll wet your head in the Heilanman's Umbrella, and meet up with Cass," said Fadge.

"Is he banging that bitch?" Ronnie asked, nodding with glee.

"If you mean is Lord Drummond negotiating a carnal relationship with Lady Fiona of Dalhinsey," I said, adopting Cassie's high tone, "the answer is yes."

"She was in Penthouse. She's got the most amazing tits!" Ronnie said, nodding filthily.

As we entered the Heilanman's Umbrella, Minna pointed to the corner. Cassie had already got the round in. Before Cassie could offer a suitable abusive welcome, Fadge laid five tickets on the table. Old Fadge had triumphed again.

The tickets were for the annual Donald MacLeod and Duncan Johnstone Piping Recital. These were two of the world's greatest piping legends, and the tickets were like gold dust. The man was a magician.

We all got suitably refreshed and made our way to the recital.

We sat back and listened to a night of enthralling piping genius. These were two master pipers who were kings in the world of piping. I didn't know Duncan Johnstone, but I knew Donald Macleod. Wee Donald was the front man for the pipe makers, Grainger and Campbell.

My dad would collect our band's pipes from Grainger and Campbell. I would always try and accompany him on these outings, just to meet the great man. I would ask wee Donald for endless tips and advice. He always had time for absolutely anybody, even a rather talkative wee boy from Ayrshire. Nothing was ever too much trouble for him. His genius of playing and his genuine humility let even the most stupid know that they were in the presence of true greatness.

In the morning we awoke in a jumbled mass on Fadge's living room floor. Ian was missing and his train was due in half an hour. I wandered about the house searching for him, just in time to catch him creeping out of Carrie's room. He had that unmistakable look of, 'I've just been shagging for the first time', written all over his face. I could see the panic in his face, so I gave him an understanding wink.

"I wouldn't let Fadge know. It's a sort of unwritten law, we don't shag each other's family," I whispered. "I need to get you to the station, no time for breakfast I'm afraid."

I don't think the words even registered in young Ian's ears. Carrie drove Ian to the station.

It was late October when we finished our recruitment tour. None of us was looking forward to returning to Pipe Major McMuchie's fiefdom of the piping school. I was 17, with two years of useful boy service behind me. I was desperate to join the regiment and get the hell away from McMuchie and his scum.

Sergeant Major Grey had lied through his teeth and had given us all glowing reports and recommendations without incident. Pipe Major McMuchie eyed the reports with sneering scorn and flung them into his filing tray. He smiled as he held our posting orders.

"Such great assets like yourselves can't be rushed to the regiment, so I've had your posting orders delayed until the end of June."

Ronnie's face could not hide the disappointment or fear from the continued dread of his torment. Poor Ronnie couldn't take much more.

To counteract McMuchie's excesses and cheer himself up, Ronnie began to play the most awful practical jokes on us.

The piping school used to be the old guardroom. McMuchie made us learn our tunes in the solitary cells. We weren't allowed to smoke or talk whilst in the cells.

McMuchie would patrol the cell corridors trying to catch us out. But we could always detect his approach from the sound of his triple-soled brogues, which made his footsteps distinctively loud and heavy.

Ronnie was really enjoying himself by impersonating the pipe major's imminent approach, by really stamping his brogues along the cell's corridor. Every time I heard the heavy echoing footsteps, I'd throw my fag out of the cell window and immediately start practising on my practice chanter. Ronnie would prolong the agony by halting outside my cell door. He'd peer through the eyehole of my cell door and pretend to be the pipe major studying my playing. After a couple of minutes, Ronny would pee himself laughing and shout:

"Captain Beaky and his band! The bravest piper in all the land!"

I had already wasted four fags and the novelty was beginning to wear thin. I heard the stamp, stamp of the distinctive heavy brogue impression. This time I decided to pay Ronnie back.

I tiptoed to the side of the cell door so I could just see the eyehole. I adopted my practice chanter into a cueing action grip and waited for my quarry like an Eskimo by a seal hole. I could hear Ronnie giggling at the far end of the corridor. Sure enough the loud brogues stopped outside my cell door. As soon as I saw the eye come up to the eyehole, I shot the tip of my chanter through the eyehole. I heard a terrific scream and a clump as the body crumpled to the floor.

I took a double drag of my fag, whipped the door open, blew a huge cloud of smoke and shouted:

"Have some smoke, fucking Captain Beaky!"

I cannot tell you the horror I felt when the smoke cleared to reveal the pained figure of Pipe Major McMuchie writhing on the floor, holding his eye. I tried to run by him, but he clutched my leg.

"Stay where you are, assassin! You won't go on

Orders, but I swear to God! I'll make your life hell, you little Ayrshire bastard!"

"I honestly thought you were someone else, Sir, I really did!" I pleaded.

McMuchie came back from the medical centre sporting an absurd eye patch. I was released from my cell and fitted with leg manacles and a 26-pound iron ball.

"You will no longer be allowed Naafi or dinner breaks," the pipe major sneered. "The manacles will be fitted first thing in the morning and taken off last thing at night. You will stay chained to my desk and only be released to make tea." McMuchie beamed with sadistic triumph. "Let's see how smart you are with some iron on your legs."

McMuchie, Maclumpher and McMainge adopted the role of the three ugly sisters. I was forced to listen to their sycophantic praise of each other as they engineered a new humiliation for me. How they loved watching me struggle to bring their tea in as I dragged my manacles and iron ball.

It was virtually impossible to bring a cup in without spilling any tea, so they had a further laugh by making me mop the floor with my shirt.

I decided to quickly put a stop to my situation with some active counter-terrorism. I began by putting bagpipe seasoning and horse laxatives in their teas. After their sudden bouts of diarrhoea and stomach-ache they scrutinised my every action when making their tea. This did not deter me in the slightest, as I simply carried on their demise by rinsing their cups out with Flash (a product that really lived up to its name). In the interest of holding their food down and keeping their pants dry, I was released from the manacles and banned from making tea.

We decided to divert our practical jokes onto the poor, depot barrack guard. Apart from the pipe band, only a few special operation teams ever used our part of the depot. The barrack guard consisted of two young recruits armed with pickaxe shafts. They would often rest and have a fly fag by the bins near our block.

Ronnie had done a cracker on the barrack guard by dressing up as an iridescent zombie. Ronnie had hidden in one of the large bins and waited until the guard crouched down for a fly fag. Ronnie sprang out of the bin and flopped his hands onto the barrack guard's shoulders with an eerie moan. The poor barrack guard nearly had kittens, and took to their heels. In their panic the guard had left their radio. Ronnie grabbed the radio and tried to give it back to the retreating guard. Ronnie chased after them shouting:

"Your radio! You need your radio!"

"Fuck it! Keep it!" they screamed, as they carried on running for their lives.

Cassie eventually caught up with the petrified pair, and led them back to our block for a calming fag and a cup of tea.

It was my turn to scare the barrack guard. I would have to pull all the stops out if I was going to beat Ronnie's last effort. Before dismissing us from parade, Pipe Major McMuchie issued us with a stiff warning.

"Keep away from barrack room C on the far side of the block. There is a troop of SAS in there, and they are not to be disturbed or bothered in any way. Do I make myself clear?"

"Yes Sir!" we all chorused back.

Far from deterring me, I counted the SAS on the far side of the block as a bonus as no one would dare enter our block with them there. I decided to go for a demonic ghoul look with a burning cross. I got a sheet and turned it into a white poncho. I pushed a cardboard head cone into a pillowcase and cut out two diamond eyeholes. I made my cross by tying a rolled up newspaper to a broom pole, with hemp, and soaked the top of the broom pole in white spirits.

The plan was to slide along the cat boards of the roof. This would prevent me from going through the fragile asbestos roof panels, and scare the bijesus out of the barrack guard. For a grand finale I would jump into the centre quadrangle, which would make me disappear like a ghost. I tried a couple of dry runs in the dark to test my plan. It worked brilliantly, so I got changed into my ghoulish costume.

We waited until we spotted two of the barrack guard coming our way. Ronnie and Cassie punted me up onto the roof. I lit my cross, which whooshed into a spectacular cross of fire. I proceeded to slide down the cat boards like a gliding spectre of horror, towards the barrack guard.

"What the fuck's that?" the barrack guard screamed to his mate.

"Fuck knows, Tam, shoot it!"

I hadn't quite expected this response, so I ran for my life. During the ensuing commotion, the flames from my oil soaked cross burned through the securing hemp. The flaming crossbar landed on the hem of my poncho, which ignited at an alarming rate of combustion. I frantically tried to beat the flames out as I ran along the roof like a demented Roman candle. I was so busy beating the flames out, I had quite forgotten to stick to the cat boards on the roof. All of a sudden I fell helplessly through the air into black unconsciousness.

The pitch-blackness of my unconsciousness began to soften into blurred shapes and distorted voices. A voice slowly began to get louder and louder.

"Hector! Hector MacTavish! Open your eyes, you mental bastard!"

My eyes opened. My eyes tried to focus on the voice.

"Stay still, you mad fuck, stay still!"

I naturally tried to do the opposite, but was skilfully restrained. As I stared at the shouting face, my focus and wits suddenly kicked in.

"Is that you, Fadge?"

"It's me, MacTavish!" Fadge grinned. "Nice of you to drop in, but we don't do auditions. You have to do the course like any other bugger, all right?"

The rest of the SAS boys chorused with laughter and jeers.

"As soon as I saw the flaming ghoul bouncing off the ceiling joists, I knew, I just fuckin knew it was you!" said Fadge.

A large, grinning black face suddenly came into my circle of vision.

"First words he said was, 'fucking MacTavish! I fucking know it!' He whipped your hood off and cried 'it is, it fucking well is!'" said Bill.

"I hope you were not making a political call on Bill, Hector, he gets awfully sensitive about these things," Fadge said, nodding to the black medic.

"I'll eat your southern balls, white boy!" Bill snarled.

"I'm from Ayrshire!" I protested nervously.

This was met with further hoots of laughter. Bill gave me a sympathetic wink and carried on checking me over. I had cracked a few ribs and driven a long slither of asbestos deep into my arm. Bill skilfully opened up the cut and expertly removed the asbestos with a swift tug of his tweezers.

"The wound's clean, but I'll fling in some iodine, cause I'm a sick fuck," said Bill.

Bill sealed the wound with butterfly stitches and gave me some painkillers.

"Thanks, Bill, I'm such a dick."

"What the fuck were you doing up there?" Bill asked.

I relayed my story back to Bill and watched the room fall about as I described my woeful demise.

"Don't worry about the roof, Hector. I'll fix it, they'll never know," said Fadge, grinning at the hole in the roof.

A tall intelligent man, who was oiling an Ingram, spoke up.

"You'll need to go Hector. We need secrecy! We're not going to say anything, and you definitely can't say anything to anyone - even your friends - understood?"

"Yes, Sir!"

I wished Fadge and the room luck as I limped off nursing my cracked ribs. I got the usual amount of sympathy once everyone knew I was safe. Ronnie nearly peed his kilt with laughter, as he described my ghoul a la flambé across the rooftops.

"Jesus, look at your arm!" shouted Ronnie.

"Watch what you're doing with that nose. I don't want it opened up again." I snapped.

Ronnie cocked his head from side to side, giving me his inquisitive hen impression.

In the morning we marched over for muster parade. There was something up - you could feel it. We were ordered to remain at attention. We were left standing there for an hour. Eventually McMuchie staggered out. He was half pissed. He glowered at us through his half shut eyes.

"Listen in, MacTavish, Drummond, Douglas, Younger! Report to records and receive your posting orders to join the regiment in Hong Kong."

McMuchie glared at us through his spiteful, bloodshot eyes. Waiting for the slightest excuse to unleash his final venom. We remained stalwartly to attention with expressionless faces.

We fell out and marched around to the privacy of the block. We laughed, screamed, hugged and danced for joy. This was it - we were on our way!

We were given two weeks' embarkation leave to say farewell to our folks, as we would be away for two and a half years. Mum was happy for me, but wept. Dad took the news very badly:

"Yes! Oh - God yes! Thank you. Yes! Yes!"

After eight years of civilian tuition and two years of military selection - I had made it! My dream had come true. I was now officially on the battalion roll as a Piper – destined for a life full of tartan adventure and unswerving friendship.

Dear Reader

Thank you for reading *Hector of the Glens*. If you enjoyed the book, please consider leaving your kind review on the Amazon purchase page.

If you would like to join our readers club, know more about the author, characters, insights, exclusive material, events, blogs and backstories go on to our website hectoroftheglens.co

Thank you and Slainte!

Printed in Great Britain
by Amazon